HOARD
it all
BEFORE

A Circus of Unusual
Creatures Mystery

Book One

Hoard it All Before
A Circus of Unusual Creatures Mystery
Book One
ISBN: 979 875 257 346 0
First Edition, January 2022
also available as an ebook

You may contact the author by email at
Tammie@tammiepainter.com
Mailing Address:
Daisy Dog Media
P.O. Box 165
Netarts, Oregon 97143, USA

To anyone who ever believed dragons, satyrs, centaurs, and unicorns were real...especially if you imagined them as attention-seeking performers of silly stunts.

THE TROUPE MEMBERS YOU'LL MEET...

Benny - A behemoth who enjoys a good scrub

Boris - A brownie who does things by the book

Charlie - A chimera you won't see much of

Conrad - A centaur who likes to gossip, husband of Flora

Cordelia Quinn - A human who likes to curse

Duncan (aka *"Brutus Fangwrath, Deadliest Dragon in the West"*) - A dragon who loves omelets and buckets of wine

Ely Zinzendorf (aka *"Zin"*) - A satyr who owns the Circus of Unusual Creatures

Fergus - A chain-smoking unicorn just looking for a good lap

Flora - A centaur who mixes herbal remedies, wife of Conrad

Gladys - A human who gets around, wife of Porter

Gregg - A gremlin who wants a kitten

Helga - A brownie who has a crush

Humphrey - A bogart who makes a mess

Molly - A miniature centaur who's a real ham

Pepper - A cyclops with a penchant for gourmet cooking

Porter Kohl - A human who handles dragons, husband of Gladys

Reinhart - A number-crunching dwarf who talks to himself

HOARD
it all
BEFORE

Prologue

It was a dark and stormy night.

CORDELIA: Wait, no. You can't start a book like that.
DUNCAN: Why not?
CORDELIA: Because it's just not done.
DUNCAN: Even if it was dark and stormy?
CORDELIA: Especially if it was dark and stormy. Besides, you told me you were starting this book on that one morning. It wasn't dark and stormy then. It was bright and sunny.
DUNCAN: True, but that's not very dramatic, is it?
CORDELIA: Look, dramatic or not, I think you should jump right into the story. People aren't going to want to read our banter.
DUNCAN: But that's what we do. We banter.
CORDELIA: Well, we didn't use to. And readers won't understand that if you don't get this story started.
DUNCAN: Oh, yes, right. Okay, here we go…

It was a bright and sunny morning. But there would eventually be a night when it was dark and stormy—
Cordelia? Cordelia, why are you walking away?

CHAPTER 1
SCALY FISHES

I love it when humans curse. There's just something terribly charming about how they seem to imagine themselves spewing fire with their words. They remind me of baby dragons whose fireboxes haven't developed yet. And, as I dotted a napkin over my chin to clean up a few misplaced bits of my morning omelet, Cordelia Quinn was doing a spot-on baby dragon impersonation.

"Duncan, you're wanted in the Tent—" Following my gaze, the smoldering cigarette nearly fell from Fergus's lips. "Well, hello. Who's the new meat?"

I didn't reply, and for a moment we both watched Cordelia do her new job.

Or, try to.

Wielding a push broom nearly as tall as herself, she stabbed it into the mop bucket beside her. She then jerked it out, the bristles flinging soapy water everywhere as she hurriedly scrubbed away at Benny's flank. The instant she finished that spot, the beast rolled over, coating his sparkling clean hind end in a fresh layer of mud.

I grinned as foul words I'd never known existed

erupted from Cordelia's mouth.

"Zin seriously assigned her to Benny? She's too small," said Fergus as he spit out his cigarette butt and crushed it under his hoof. "Then again, if Benny rolls over on her, I could come to her rescue. Bet a firecracker like that would be pretty darn enthusiastic with her appreciation, if you know what I mean."

"Fergus, please. That is entirely disrespectful."

"I'm just saying I wouldn't mind resting my head in that lap for a spell."

"Do you have to be such a horny rogue?"

"Well, I am a unicorn." He shifted his eyes up and center as if I might have missed the silvery twist of horn in the middle of his head. "So what did she do to get stuck on behemoth duty?"

"Showed up on the wrong day."

"Man, every day's the wrong day for behemoth duty. The stink of them."

Says the animal whose chain smoking has left him perpetually smelling like an overflowing ashtray. But he's right. Behemoths reek. They can't help it.

The thing with behemoths is that they're really big. Yes, I know, genius statement, but we're talking about *big* in a way that would make a walrus look like a half-starved kitten.

That said, for their size, behemoths are one of the sweetest-tempered beasts in any troupe. They cause no trouble and are perfectly content to hang out in their wallow and, well, wallow.

Problem is, their size also means behemoths have

trouble executing the twists and turns to clean themselves properly. Take this lack of flexibility, mix in Benny spending his days and nights sprawled out in a mud pit, combined with his steady diet of this strange, green goop Flora brews up for him, and you've got a recipe for a beast with smelly, mucky sludge flowing around, in, and out of him on a regular basis.

To prevent the paying customers from gagging on their popcorn, a behemoth handler's main, okay, *only* job is to scrub clean every last bit of their charges and keep them smelling fresh.

Work as a behemoth handler — or "Mop" as some people call them — is a never-ending chore that requires a strong stomach and quick work with the push broom-slash-scrub brush. For being the lowest of the low positions in a circus, it's not a job for the faint of heart.

And Cordelia was proving not to be faint of heart.

"Turn over," she grunted as she made the hand motion that should have told Benny to shift his weight to the left, which would then allow gravity to do the work of tipping him onto his side.

She was doing all the right things. The trouble was, Benny and I had had more than a few buckets of merlot the night before, so on this particular morning he likely would have preferred a lie-in and a few aspirin to a bath.

"Hey man, gimme a light." Displaying a trick that never failed to impress, Fergus flicked his head. The cigarette that had been lodged behind his ear flipped up and he caught it in his teeth.

"You know I can't," I muttered.

Fergus made a scoffing sound. "We all know it's more *won't* than *can't*. C'mon, just a little cough, just a tiny flame for your old pal." I gave a firm shake of my head and refused to meet his eye. "Fine. I hope you know this isn't easy without hands. Where's a centaur when you need one?"

I ignored him, and soon there came a scratch and a hiss. From the corner of my eye, I caught the flare of a burning match. I cringed at the sight of it, and my nostrils trembled at the scent of sulfur. But just then, Cordelia swore again and a snorting laugh burst from my snout. Her head whipped around and I hastily diverted my attention to folding my napkin and placing it tidily on my empty plate. She turned her back to me and set to scrubbing again, cursing with every stroke of the brush.

The cloying stink of tobacco smoke filled the air around me. Before I could tell Fergus where he could stick his nickel-a-pack cigarettes and his comments, Ely Zinzendorf, known to most everyone as *Zin*, emerged from the Tent — what you'd probably call the Big Top.

His gaze went straight to the table I always ate at. At the sight of me, his face tightened like it did whenever I was late for practice, and he began marching straight across the expanse of dusty ground from the Tent to the Cantina.

Between which stood Benny's enclosure.

Zin should have hustled his cloven-hoofed feet a bit faster. If he had, Cordelia might have been too engrossed in trying to get Benny to turn over to bother him. But Zin marched by just as she was taking a breather after having managed to wedge the massive beast into a new position.

Cordelia threw down her push broom and rushed over to Zin, blocking his path. He rolled his orange-brown eyes and even his horns seemed to give a weary sigh.

"Mr. Zinzendorf, come on, you can't really mean to stick me on this job. It was just a test, right? To see if I was serious about working here?"

Even by human measurements, Cordelia Quinn was small. She wore a pale blue, button-down shirt and men's trousers, both of which were two sizes too big for her. Standing next to Zin, she barely came to his chest. Although satyrs from Zin's line do tend to run tall.

"I didn't *stick* you on this job, Ms. Quinn. You could have left and sought employment elsewhere. But you chose to remain. Tending to Benny is the only job open, so if you're going to complain about it—"

"Look," she said firmly, her elbows jutting out as she slapped her hands onto her hips, "I travelled a long way to meet up with this circus and I'm more than qualified. You'd be crazy not to take me on as Brutus's handler."

"Ooh, she wants you," Fergus said, nudging me. "Can I have her when you're done? I'm not picky."

"So I've heard. Unfortunately."

By the way, *Brutus* is only my stage name. Brutus Fangwrath, Deadliest Dragon in the West, to be exact. Much more dramatic than *Duncan*, don't you think?

Zin mocked Cordelia by standing with his goatish feet determinedly wide and his hands resting on his furry hips.

"Like I told you yesterday: He's got a handler and since Porter's one of the best in the region, I've got no plans to fire him. So if you really want to work for me, you'll have to take what you can get."

"But I—"

"No." Zin tick-tocked his index finger at her admonishingly. "I wasn't the one who told you to show up at my gates the very minute we got those gates set up. I wasn't the one who told you to strut right past the no-entry signs. I wasn't the one who demanded I give you a job." Zin paused, knitting his heavy brow over this strange turn of phrase. "Anyway, you did all that on your own. You wanted a job. I gave you one. And you're already making me regret that decision. You even got references? Experience?"

"Weren't you listening yesterday? I've got plenty of dragon experience. I spent the past three years handling over at Costello's show."

At this, Zin stared down at her with new appreciation. His pointed ears twitched forward with interest. "Costello's, you say? And before that?"

Cordelia let out an exasperated sigh. "I've been working shows more than half my life. I'm an experienced handler. You can't waste me on this." She gestured toward Benny, who drooped his head at her dismissive tone.

Cordelia caught the behemoth's pitiful expression. In complete contrast to her fiery attitude toward Zin, she squatted down next to Benny, putting her at eye level with his sprawling bulk. She then patted him and whispered something to him. When she stood back up, Benny had on the broad smile he wore at the end of a day when visitors had been especially generous with the marshmallows.

It's a big thrill for guests to feed Benny those puffy sweet treats. Trouble is, Benny has a sensitivity to them that only makes his digestive issues worse. But with visitors paying three cents a bag for a penny's worth of marshmallows, it's hard for Zin to resist an easy profit like that.

Especially since he's not the one stuck doing the clean up.

"Let me handle Brutus," Cordelia pleaded. "Just for one performance. Just to show you what I can do. Or, I don't know, let me assist this Porter person."

Zin sneered. "You call yourself an experienced handler? If you knew anything about dragons, as you claim you do, you'd know they only respond to one handler. Unlike certain people, dragons are loyal," he said meaningfully. "They don't go flitting off to new prospects on a whim." That's mostly because circus owners clip our wings. Not that we can't walk, but it's not the most efficient mode of escape. "So, unless Porter retires, quits, or his wife finally kills him, there's no handling jobs available here except for Benny."

"But a Mop? Really? That's rookie stuff."

"If you want to work here, it's either being a Mop or putting on a skimpy costume and joining an act." Cordelia wrinkled her sharply pointed nose at this. Zin leaned in close, a challenging glint in his eyes. "If neither of those options appeals to you, why not go back to Costello's? You claim you were a handler there. If that's the job you want so badly, then why did you leave?"

Cordelia bit her lower lip and looked away from Zin's

gaze. "Because I want to handle Brutus," she finally said in a quiet voice. "It's what I've been working toward with all these other circuses."

She said this with such sincerity that even Zin's normally gruff demeanor softened. His face wore an expression of such admiration that, for a moment, I thought he might indeed fire Porter in exchange for this feisty, passionate little human. Then Zin raised his shaggy eyebrows, and a smirk crept across his lips.

"Well, my dear, if wishes were fishes we'd all be scaly."

Confusion dug a furrow between Cordelia's auburn eyebrows.

"What does that even mean?" she asked at the exact moment I whispered the same question under my own breath.

"It means you asked for a handling job and now you have a handling job." Zin tilted his chin in the direction of Benny's wallow to drive home his point.

"You're telling me that my experience counts for nothing?"

"No, it most certainly does." Zin gave her a taunting grin. "After all, behemoths require a special touch. Now, back to it, this circus opens tomorrow and we can't have the paying public put off by a stinking behemoth."

Cordelia looked about to argue. Instead, she turned on her heel, snatched up her broom again, and Benny purred under the force of her scrubbing.

Zin, smugly pleased at having won an argument at such an early hour of the day, resumed his march toward me and Fergus.

Still five paces from us, Zin's broad nose crinkled with disgust.

"Fergus, put out that damn coffin nail. You know no one likes a stinking unicorn. You're supposed to be magically pure, not a chain-smoking Lothario."

"Zin, I ain't been pure since I was a foal. Why do you think I work for you?" Fergus sucked harder on his cigarette, trying to get as much out of it as possible before Zin snatched it from his lips and crushed it into the ground. "I was just admiring your new hire. Nice choice. Very nice."

"Fergus," Zin snapped. "Cold shower with plenty of fruity soaps. Duncan, you're late for practice, and it better not be because of another hangover."

"No," I said, pointing to my empty plate, "because of an omelet."

"The Tent," Zin seethed. "Now."

I shifted my folded napkin so it was squarely centered on my plate, then stood. It was time to start another day at Zinzendorf's Circus of Unusual Creatures.

Chapter 2
The Layout

Okay, I'll admit, I was indeed hungover. Benny and I had consumed more than our fair share of wine the previous night, as was our tradition whenever we pulled into a new town. But I hadn't lied to Zin since the hangover wasn't the reason for me being late.

After all, even if you do manage to pull your scaly eyelids open on time, you just can't rush a good omelet. Especially not when Pepper gets her hands on fresh quail eggs.

Honestly, given Zin's frugal budget and slim margins, I don't know how Pepper obtains the delicacies she serves us. And I don't dare ask what underworld connections she might have. You learn early on in this trade that you don't go digging into a cyclops's business.

Still, the hangover and the omelet had left me parched, so before making my way to the Tent, I stopped by the water trough at the edge of the Cantina and did my best to undo the damage caused by the drinking game Benny and I had invented. You don't want to know the details, but suffice it to say, the game involved throwing back a bucket of wine every time Benny's digestive system made a noise. And Benny's inner workings are very talkative.

From where I stood gulping up as much water as is reptilian-ly (*shut up, Cordelia, it is too a word*) possible, I faced the circus's main tent with its frayed green flags emblazoned with big gold Zs flapping in the breeze.

For this run, we'd set up on the outskirts of Sherwood and were scheduled to be there for six days. A short stay for us, since runs normally last a full week to ten days, but sometimes that's just how the calendar crumbles.

Still, the set up for Zin's circus was nearly the same whether we were in Portland, Sherwood, Salem, or Scappoose. Beyond the Tent, and mostly out of public view, are the crew's sleeping and living quarters. These are caravans that range from large to small, depending on the size of the creatures within.

Caravans can be tidy and spare like Reinhart's, or a ramshackle disaster zone like Zin's. They can be as homey as Flora and Conrad's humble abode; as fanciful as Molly's gaudy space that was mostly taken up with cosmetic cases, feather headdresses, and glittery doodads; or as cramped as Boris's, which he shares with seven or eight other brownies — by their own choice, mind you, if they could squeeze themselves into an apple box, they'd be perfectly content.

CORDELIA: Duncan, the readers haven't met any of these people except for Zin. You're going to confuse them.

DUNCAN: They'll meet them soon enough. Besides,

20

you're the one who told me I should explain the layout of the place.
CORDELIA: Since when do you listen to me?
DUNCAN: You just want me to jump to your heroic part in the bogart-brownie battle.
CORDELIA: Well, maybe.
DUNCAN: I knew it.

Beyond the caravans, which were arranged in a series of semi-circles, were the trailers that held all the equipment that goes into a circus, as well as our refuse station, and the Cells — a single dilapidated caravan where Zin could toss any miscreants.

As for the main grounds of the circus, the open area in front of the Tent features displays such as the history of Zin's circus and Benny's wallow. Extending in a line to the left are a few smaller tents that house attractions such as the pixies' magic act and Gladys's fortune telling booth. To the opposite side you'll find Eisenberg's Entertainment Alley with its games of chance, some stands selling trinkets, and a few other amusements, including a circular corral with Shetland centaurs (or mini-taurs, as they're more commonly known) for the kiddies to ride.

When the circus grounds are open for business, the Cantina — located not far from the entrance gates — serves as the concession stand. This is where Pepper, much to the chagrin of her gourmand instincts, offers up what the people desire: cheese-coated chips, fried things on sticks, and fizzy drinks with enough sugar to make your dentist shudder.

Surrounding all this is a barrier that, thanks to him having inherited a little magic from a distant elvish ancestor, Zin charms to keep the non-paying customers out and the animal acts in. The only access point is the front gate where Reinhart — a dwarf who manages the day-to-day operations of the circus — mans the ticket booth with an eagle eye.

Having emptied the entire trough, I set a hose inside to refill it, then turned toward the Tent where my handler, Porter Kohl, made a scooping wave with his arm, signaling me to get a move on. I nodded, switched off the hose, and followed his beckoning gesture toward the Tent's striped canvas for my morning practice session.

Now, I can guess what you're thinking: *Duncan, you seem pretty tame. I mean, you're writing a book, after all. Why in the world do you need a handler?*

And if you weren't thinking that, well, um, sorry for being presumptuous. But I bet you're thinking it now.

See, while some dragons can be raging monsters who most definitely do need a firm hand to keep them in line, the majority of dragons can be as lazy as Benny if we're left to our own devices. We don't want to perform tricks, steal maidens, or battle knights who have a weird need to prove themselves by murdering a clumsy reptile.

This doesn't mean we're not active. We spend our youth dashing to and fro, accumulating our treasure hoard, and chasing after any lead that might help us add to our stash. But once we reach an age of about sixty, our main reason for being is to lounge around guarding our goodies. By then, we're ready to enjoy the easy life. A good lie-down on our piles of precious metals and sparkly things is all we really crave. Well, that and, in my case, a good omelet.

Basically, we need a handler to motivate us to get us off our lethargic hindquarters. Because get the right handler on a dragon's side, and we are the biggest showoffs you've ever seen. Just as we yearned for that treasure in our youth, we become addicts for an audience's applause and cheers as we preen, pose, perform stunts, and do all manner of silly things that would make my ancestors wish they'd never laid eggs.

And if we get the wrong handler? Well, I've had my share of them. And the scars to prove it.

With a bad handler, your life is full of abuse, shouting, and then more shouting when you give a bad performance because you want nothing more than to eat the bastard who's swinging a dragon hook at you. Thanks to the treatment of some nasty handlers, my stage name isn't just a bunch of marketing fluff. I really am the deadliest dragon in the West, if not the world.

But let's leave that for another tale.

Porter, thankfully, was the right kind of handler.

In addition to the whole "deadliest" thing, I'm also one of the largest dragons in captivity. When I want to be. I'm normally about the size of a Clydesdale horse, but I'm from a species of dragon who can increase their size. For my act, I make myself as tall as a giraffe with the bulk of a gorilla and (supposedly) the ferocity of a grumpy lion.

Even if I did nothing, some people might come to Zin's merely to witness my combination of size and potential danger. But what was keeping Zin's circus on its feet, what made his one of the most popular shows in the region, was me and Porter putting on a show like no other.

Of course, to make sure that show ran smoothly when the gates opened the next day, I needed to get my scaly butt inside the Tent's flaps and get to some training.

CHAPTER 3
AND IN THIS RING...

Once my eyes adjusted to the low-lit interior, I saw Porter chatting with a centaur named Flora. As I headed toward them, she was handing my handler a jar filled with a paste that didn't seem sure if it wanted to be green or brown.

"You need to apply it every morning and evening," Flora told him. "I should also mix up some lavender and rosemary oils to cleanse your caravan. You could be harboring bad spirits in there."

"That would explain Gladys's frequent desire to kill me," Porter said with a cheeky wink.

"She wants to kill everyone who crosses her," said Flora. "The negativity in her aura is a shame. Has she been taking the chamomile?"

By then, I had joined them.

"Ready, Duncan? Well, come on." He held up the jar as if toasting with it. "My knees thank you for this, Flora."

"Remind Gladys about the chamomile. Her aura will appreciate it."

With barely a tap of the hook on my flank, I followed

after Porter to the center ring of the Tent like a loyal puppy.

The hook is a horrible tool. It's a length of iron rod about a meter long with a sharpened, sometimes barbed, hook at the end. Held with the hooked end flat, it can used for beating a dragon. Held with the business end in the hooky position, it's used to snap a dragon to attention by raking it across or digging it into our hides.

The idea is to use pain to get a dragon to behave as the handler wishes. Which does work in some cases. I've seen once-bold dragons tremble in fear of the hook. In other cases, the pain only makes the dragon more ornery and tougher to control. That's what most handlers think this game is about: control. But some handlers, the good ones, know the best way to get us to do what they want is to be our friend and cajole us with kindness to do what we love best: showing off.

Of course, bribing us with wine and beer and our favorite snacks doesn't hurt either.

Porter used his hook more as a guide, correcting my stance by touching it to a limb that was a little off its mark, or by giving me a gentle tap to tell me to get a move on.

I didn't need Porter to tap me. I could hear his commands well enough, but because we dragons refuse to speak to them, most humans think we can't understand their words.

But we do understand. Obviously, otherwise how would I be writing this to you?

Still, I didn't mind Porter using the hook. A tap from

him was more like a friend clapping you encouragingly on the shoulder, and unlike any handler I've ever worked with, Porter wrapped thick woolen cloth around the nasty end of his hook, making it look more like an oversized cotton swab than a fear-inducing weapon.

The center ring provided an excellent view of the Tent — acts, workers, the audience, everything except what was behind me. As was always the case when we'd just shown up to a new spot, the crew of gremlins were still making adjustments to some of the equipment.

On this day, they were working on the rigging for the seating. And they were having to do so under the watchful eye of Boris, who — having likely just gone over the area — looked ready to scold any gremlin who dared to drop even the tiniest mote of dust on his freshly polished benches.

CORDELIA: *Again, Duncan, you're name dropping like readers are just supposed to know about these people. Not everyone lives the circus life. They probably don't know a thing about our world.*

DUNCAN: *Nothing? Weird. So, Boris is a brownie. And no, I don't understand why they're called that since they usually have pale skin. Although some do have brown hair.*

CORDELIA: *Duncan. Tangent. Get off it.*

DUNCAN: *Right. At Zin's, Boris is the lead brownie. Brownies work as a circus's cleaning crew. It's very important you don't anger a brownie or forget to pay them their extra allotment of cream, because they will turn on you and make a mess of things. Which I suppose you could just clean up yourself instead of expecting someone else do it for you.*

Yes, yes, Cordelia, I know, tangent.

Anyway, Zin's also has a small team of gremlins, headed up by Gregg, who work as our technical and maintenance crew. Need new lighting? Call a gremlin. Broken caravan axle? Call a gremlin. Need some trickery done with the power...

CORDELIA: Not yet, Duncan.

DUNCAN: Oh, right. Got ahead of myself there. Back to the story?

CORDELIA: Definitely.

The center ring not only was a perfect vantage point, it was also the largest of the three rings where performances and practices took place. Above the ring to my left, the Flying Flynns had already started practicing their high-wire and trapeze act. This bit of derring-do impresses the audience to no end.

The Flying Flynns are a breed of shape-shifting elves who pass a good deal of their leisure time in squirrel form. Their act, however, is done in their human form. But since the Flynns spend so much time flitting from tree branch to tree branch as squirrels, the high-wire act is little more than playtime for them. They hardly needed practice, and sometimes I think the Flying Flynns showed up early and trained well into the afternoon for the sheer fun of it.

Unlike the centaurs in the ring to my right, who despised certain aspects of their training sessions.

It's a well-known fact across the region that centaurs do not like to be ridden. I mean, how would you like it if someone jumped on your back and told you to "Giddee up"? Wait, sorry, don't answer that. I know you humans can be odd.

Regardless of your own personal tastes between consenting adults, centaurs do not like a human on their back. However, they do like the gourmet oatmeal cookies provided by Pepper, who was under strict instructions from Zin not to provide the centaurs these fiber-filled treats unless they went along with the acts as planned.

Which is why the miniature Shetland centaurs tolerate giving children rides, and why the full-size centaurs withstand galloping around wearing silly feather headdresses and ribbons in their tails while human females dressed in skimpy, sparkly outfits stand on their backs. To tell you the truth, I think the centaurs like the headdresses and feathers, but don't tell Conrad I said that.

And before Cordelia gets on my case, Conrad is a centaur and he's married to Flora.

In the center ring, Porter put me through my paces as a warmup. This mostly involved jogging in circles as he cracked a whip. The whip was far too short to ever touch me, but it did sound really impressive to the audience.

Once properly warmed up, I expanded to my show size, then Porter coaxed me to stand on a platform that was only about as wide as your average-sized human foot. It was a challenge of balance and was a great core workout. My wings flapped as I nearly toppled over a couple times, but once on the platform, the idea was for me to stand to my full height, spread my wings, then curl them forward like a hawk while fixing a menacing stare on Porter.

"That's it, Duncan. You've got it," he encouraged as my wings came around. This was the tricky bit as it threw off my center of balance. I concentrated as the leg I stood on shook with the effort. I curled my wings into position. Now it was time for the stare.

Porter tilted his head to one side as if appraising me.

"That's hardly menacing, old boy,"

If I did speak to humans, this was one thing I would tell Porter to stop calling me. I'm not old and I wanted to let him know that seventy-five wasn't even middle-aged for a dragon.

But dragons don't speak to humans. It's just better that way.

CORDELIA: *You going to explain that? It's kind of vague.*
DUNCAN: *Not yet. I'm building curiosity. Adding questions in the readers' minds. It's a writer thing.*
CORDELIA: *Oh, that's clever.*
DUNCAN: *I thought you read all those books on novel writing.*
CORDELIA: *Well, I started a bunch of them, then mostly just skimmed them.*
DUNCAN: *Which is why we aren't co-writing this book.*

I was just getting my menace on when shouting came from outside. Then the sound of a hard punch landing somewhere soft. The Flying Flynns didn't pause for a moment in their mid-air leaps and twirls, but I hopped off my platform, pulled myself down to my smaller size, and waddled after Porter as he and the centaurs ran out of the Tent to see what was happening.

And, no, I don't waddle because I'm overweight. It's just that I'm a reptile and we don't exactly have the skeletal structure for graceful running.

Chapter 4
The Bogart Battle

Once outside, we discovered two small creatures who were apparently trying to tear one another's limbs off. I recognized one as Boris. The other was unfamiliar but had — when I could catch sight of him amongst all the tussling — the snarled face of a bogart.

It's not as if bogarts ever look pleasant to my eyes, but this one's face was particularly ugly since it appeared to have received more than a couple whacks from the broomstick Boris was wielding. Boris, on the other hand, had an ear that had lost its pointed tip and was bleeding all over his crisp white shirt. Well, it used to be white.

No one dared step in. They're typically docile, domestic creatures, but once a brownie picks a fight, he or she becomes a force of nature that's liable to rip a foe's arm off, then use it as a weapon against them.

I slipped away from Porter and sidled over to Helga, one of Boris's brownie crew. She was cheering on her boss, but I didn't miss her casting an appreciative eye over his opponent.

"What's happened?"

"Well, there's been a lot of screaming, so it's a little tough to tell. Oh good one, Boris," she shouted as Boris hit the bogart in the back of the knees, knocking him to the ground. "But from what I can gather, the bogart— He's kind of dreamy, isn't he?"

I couldn't tell a dreamy bogart from a nightmarish gremlin, so I just grunted in a way I hoped sounded agreeable.

"Yeah, so the bogart came in and made a mess of the ticket booth and the areas around the caravans that Boris had just had us clean. But you can't blame him, can you?" I wasn't sure which 'him' she meant, so I stayed silent. "I mean, it's in their nature to go making a mess. Probably just a poor lost soul."

It's true. Bogarts came in like hurricanes and would wreak havoc on the cleanest spots they could find. It's one reason we were always careful to do a full bogart inspection of all the circus's belongings when we arrived to a new town and when we packed up at the end of a run. Somehow, this one had missed inspection when we arrived the previous day.

The bogart was up again and charging toward Boris.

"Nice move!" Helga bounced and applauded with glee when Boris stepped aside, swept out a stubby leg, and caught the bogart by the ankle, dropping him once again to the ground. Boris then leapt on his enemy and started punching his face with a vicious ferocity.

"Boris, you're going to kill him," Porter shouted.

"We should all live in peace," said Flora. The lead female centaur was quite spiritual. Annoyingly spiritual.

But the incense she burnt when she "cleansed" a new location did smell nice.

Someone had just called for Zin, when from the direction of Benny's mud wallow came the tiny, red-haired whirlwind also known as Cordelia Quinn. Without a second thought as to how impossible it was to get a limb replacement, she jumped into the fray and pulled Boris off the bogart. Boris swung out a few times, but being only a few feet tall, his reach wasn't exactly prize fighter distance.

"Let me at him," Boris shrieked as he writhed under Cordelia's impressively strong grip.

"No," Cordelia said, "look at him. I think he's learned whatever lesson you were trying to teach him. Unless you were trying to teach him not to bleed all over the place."

By now, Zin had joined the crowd. He pushed through to the front of the sidelines, but stopped abruptly when he saw what was going on.

"Can you calm yourself?" Cordelia asked Boris. "Or do I have to do it for you?"

She said this while holding up her free hand and making a pinching gesture with her index finger and thumb.

See, if you pinch a brownie's ears in just the right spot, it puts them into a trance state. Like scruffing a kitten, the ear pinch calms them instantly and you can make them do almost anything in that state. Needless to say, they absolutely hate having this done to them.

"No," Boris said, angling his head away from Cordelia's fingers. "Just let me go."

The bogart had sat up, but he swayed woozily. Cordelia released Boris, who glanced at his shirt and cried out in horror at the state of it. "I cannot be seen like this. *The Brownie Handbook of Cleanliness and Composure* states that someone in my position is required to maintain a certain level of pride in his appearance. I cannot go against the *Handbook*. I have to go change immediately."

Boris tried to hurry off, but Cordelia blocked him and made the pinching motion again. "You'll wait right there," she said, then squatted down next to the bogart. "Anything broken?"

"Them get good hit in," the creature said, almost admiringly. "Few teeth gone, nose don't feel right, but been worse."

"Both of you apologize to the other."

Boris looked off into the distance as if the horizon might save him from such an indignity as speaking to a bogart. The bogart, while stealing darting glances at Boris, had crossed his stick-thin arms over his chest.

"Do it now, Boris," Cordelia commanded, "or I will write to the authors of that handbook and tell them you attacked someone during working hours. And you," she said to the bogart, "should be ashamed of ruining the hard work of your fellow creatures."

Boris scowled and looked vaguely in the direction of the bogart. The bogart tightened his arms and puffed out his scrawny chest. As one, from their lips came the most reluctant, the most unenthusiastic words of apology you've ever heard.

"And shake hands," said Cordelia.

Boris pulled up short, standing rigid with his chin jutting upward. "I will not touch this degenerate. He and those like him are an embarrassment to their species."

A statement which I think even Boris realized was nonsensical since brownies and bogarts are the exact same species.

And before Cordelia raises a stink about me making vague statements, bogarts are simply brownies who don't have proper employment.

See, brownies are a little like their close cousins, the dwarves: Both have a compulsive desire to keep busy. They barely sleep because they hate giving up any time during which they could be productive. Which is why they do most of their deep cleaning in the wee hours of the night.

And I'm not exaggerating about their need to stay occupied being compulsive. If they're plagued by a sense of boredom for more than twenty-four hours, brownies become destructive. They turn into bogarts. I don't know why this is, but my best guess is that they're trying in a misguided fashion to create work for themselves to tidy up.

Also, just in case you were thinking of bringing a brownie onto your household cleaning staff, even brownies who are employed and kept busy will revert to this bogart-like behavior if they aren't rewarded with proper pay, heavy whipping cream, and fresh cookies. Preferably gingersnaps.

"Really?" asked Cordelia dubiously. "Because you didn't seem to mind plowing your fists into his face. Or were you somehow punching him without touching him?" Boris grumbled his response. "I'll take that as a no. Now shake hands." And the way she said this left no room for waffling over the matter.

Boris walked stiffly over to the bogart and held out his hand. The two shook and Boris even helped tug the mangled creature to his feet. Maybe with a little more force than necessary, but still.

"Now, put him on the cleaning crew so he has proper work to keep himself occupied."

"You don't have that authority, only Zin—"

"Give him the job," Zin insisted. "Do you still have your stash of dukie books, or do you need a new one?"

Boris's mouth opened, looking for all the world like he was on the edge of arguing. But then sense and reason took over. If he argued with Zin, he'd be out of a job, he'd have no more crisp white shirts, and he'd get no more of Pepper's gingersnaps filled with chunks of candied ginger. He would be no better than a bogart.

"I've got some," Boris said through clenched teeth. He fixed a scowl on the bedraggled bogart. "Come on, then. I suppose you don't even know how to work a dust cloth," he complained as the two strode off together.

"I better go make sure he's okay," Helga said, her eyes trained on the bogart. "He might want his wounds tended, shown around his new workplace, don't you think?"

Since there were a fair number of humans milling about by then, I merely nodded and gave her an encouraging smile.

Zin strode over to Cordelia with a look of surprised

respect on his face. I thought he might be ready to offer her a better position than behemoth handler as he said, "I just want to—"

"If you don't mind," Cordelia interrupted, staring him defiantly in the eye, "I've got a behemoth to clean, and the sooner I get it done, the sooner the air around here will smell a whole lot sweeter."

And then Cordelia — a new hire, mind you — made a dismissive, get-a-move-on motion at Zin. I grinned as Zin stepped aside.

When Cordelia marched off toward Benny's wallow, I caught sight of Porter hurrying after her. Still in the training mindset, I followed him. When he caught up to her, he clapped a hand on her slim shoulder to slow her down. She whipped around, and I swear if she'd had Boris's broomstick in her hand, she probably would have whacked Porter upside the head.

CORDELIA: You make me sound awful. Dear readers, I'm really not the violent sort, as you just witnessed with the brownie fiasco.

DUNCAN: You can put up a good fight, though.

CORDELIA: Well, yeah, you don't live and work among circus folk without learning a bit of self-defense. Some of those people can be, well, let's say "grabby" and leave it at that.

DUNCAN: Yeah, but you didn't like Porter.

CORDELIA: I didn't like that he had the job I'd dreamed of, no.

"That was really impressive back there," Porter told her.

Cordelia's jaw muscles flicked with tension and I just bet she had a snippy retort she was biting back.

"We're not friends," she said. Which I thought was pretty stupid because if she made friends with Porter, maybe Porter would have let her work with him in some capacity.

"I only meant it takes guts to step into a fight between brownies," he said, not for an instant daunted by the daggers shooting with wild abandon from her eyes. "I don't think I would have done it. You've got some real fire in you. It's just what this place needs."

Cordelia shifted, twitched her lips to one side, then brushed past Porter, muttering that what the place needed was her as dragon handler.

Oh, and that dagger-eye thing isn't just an expression. I did once work with a banshee who could shoot daggers from her eyes. It was stupendous, and she had great aim. Could hit a target at fifty paces. Great draw for Seton's Spectacular.

Unfortunately for Seton, the banshee died of a nasty eye infection. Which is why I always say, keep your equipment clean. It quite literally could save your life.

CHAPTER 5
AN UNWELCOME GUEST

Once the fracas was over, Zin ordered all of us back to our preparations for Opening Day.

Molly, the Shetland centaur I perform with, joined us back in the Tent so we could practice our trick where I pick her up with my teeth.

Supposedly, since the audience likely assumes I would just love to chomp down and swallow the mini-taur whole, this feat shows them how much control Porter has over me, how cowed I am by his awesome human brain, and just how brilliant they were for choosing to come to Zin's Circus of Unusual Creatures rather than stay home and listen to the static on their radios.

The truth is, I've never had an appetite for horse. Some dragons, those Old Ones who were alive in medieval times and snacked on mounted knights when the mood struck them, will give into their cravings for a Mustang or an Appaloosa on occasion. But the Old Ones are rare these days, especially in America.

Plus, I've been mostly vegetarian for the past couple decades. I don't mind a bit of chicken now and then, and

I've nothing against eating bugs (especially chocolate-covered crickets). But show me a properly cooked cheese omelet with a dab of truffle oil and I'm your dragon.

CORDELIA: Duncan, you're drooling.

My point is, despite the supposed danger Molly was in, the only true risk was that I might spit her out when the blonde tendrils of her bouffant wig tickled my nose.

Although he's seen all the acts a thousand times, Zin often likes to come watch us practice. He offers tips on where we can add a little more flair to the routine or how we can make a stunt appear more dangerous when it's really not.

Take, for example, the Flying Flynns' high-wire act. Zin often suggests ever-increasing amounts of flips and feigned near misses, but even if one of the Flynns did fall (which so far has happened only twice), their costumes hide webbing that, once extended, allows them to soar down to safety. Unless a mouse nibbles holes into their kit, they're as safe as hen's teeth if they fall.

CORDELIA: I don't think that's right. The hen's teeth. It's 'as safe as houses', isn't it?
DUNCAN: That makes no sense. Houses can be broken into, burned down, or destroyed by earthquakes.
CORDELIA: But hen's teeth?
DUNCAN: Exactly. Hens don't have teeth. So if a hen bites you, it's not going to do any damage. Hence, it's as safe as hen's teeth. It makes perfect sense.

CORDELIA: I— Never mind.

Molly and I had been doing our act together for a couple months, but during the trek between our last show in Dayton to our current one in Sherwood, Zin had come up with a way to enhance it and really wow the audience. Which is why, as Zin watched from the sidelines, Porter was explaining to Molly that she'd need to balance on my foot. I'd then flip her up in the air like a horsey ball, and on her descent, I'd catch her in my mouth.

See? Same trick people might have come to expect, but with a new flair. Zin knows his stuff.

For a miniature horse-lady, Molly's quite the ham, and was usually game for anything. She looked about ready to suggest something to add to Zin's idea when his attention was distracted by the man who'd just strode in as if this were his big top.

With seats and lighting still being put into place, people were continually coming and going from the Tent, so someone entering shouldn't have caught my notice. But something prickled along my dorsal spines, and when I glanced over, I couldn't stop the growl that rumbled up from my belly.

The cushioned tip of the hook touched my foot. When I glanced down, Porter was glowering at the newcomer.

"Stay calm, old boy. I don't like him either, but you're safe." Porter then signaled me to lower my head and gave me the most delicious scratch behind my ears.

Still, I kept my attention fixed on the newcomer who might just rival Molly for flamboyance.

He stood out like a peacock that shoots fireworks from its tail feathers. It wasn't just his gleaming silver hair or his wiry, wraith-like frame. He was dressed in a pair of deep purple trousers with a jacket to match. The black shirt underneath glinted with diamond-studded buttons that, despite my dislike of him, sent my treasure-hoarding instincts singing.

My attention broken from my training, I realized it wasn't just me staring. Most of the acts had stopped to watch. Those who were still at it were either in their own little world, like Flora, or had slowed down enough to observe what was going on.

Zin's often a bit stressed on Opening Day Eve. Given we pull up roots and travel to a new location every week or so, you'd think he'd be used to the haphazard routine of getting everything in place. But the tension on his face, in his shoulders, in his clenched fists was far more intense than his usual fretting over whether the gremlins might forget a bolt in one of the kiddie rides, or if Reinhart had remembered to put up flyers around town to advertise the show.

Zin, his body held rigidly erect, marched over to confront his visitor. Damian Ratcher swept off his purple top hat (which had a delectable silver band) and bowed dramatically.

"We should practice, old boy," said Porter. "Something easy, shall we?"

I can't recall exactly what tasks Porter asked me to do. My mind was too distracted by Ratcher's presence and by my desire to eavesdrop on the conversation.

"Ratcher," Zin said in greeting. "It's a bit early for the show. You're letting in all the riff-raff these days, Reinhart."

Sorry, I should have mentioned that shuffling just behind Damian Ratcher was Reinhart, dwarf and promoter-slash-accountant for Zin's circus. Through his contacts, he made sure signs were posted around town ahead of our arrival to drum up business, he tallied the ticket sales each night, and he distributed our wages.

Reinhart also manned — or is it dwarfed? — the ticket booth and entry gate. Like a bouncer at a club, he decided who could enter the grounds. And unless you were a paying customer or someone making a delivery he couldn't carry himself, Reinhart would put his foot with its four splayed toes down and block your entry.

"Sorry, boss, he said he had a proposal and I think maybe we should consider it."

"He's not for sale," Zin told Ratcher.

"You didn't even wait for me to make my speech," said Damian. "As I was telling Mr. Reinhart here, my offer would be beneficial to both you and Brutus. You would see a fair profit over what you paid for him, and he would have the comfort of being amongst his kind. You have to be aware that my circus now maintains the largest dragon herd in the region."

Sorry, another interruption. I promise these will get fewer and fewer as you start to understand the circus world. See, dragons in the wild prefer the solitary life. There are the orcadons who swim in family groups called pods, and some land-dwelling species such as the kanga-ryu will pair up, but these social species aren't common.

However, in a circus environment, especially circuses with those bad handlers I mentioned earlier, dragons take comfort in being around one other. It can be a hard life, especially for those of us with wings. The clipping is a disheartening thing to have done, but if you know you're going to go back to a stable of companions who have endured the same treatment, it takes a little sting out of the wound. The metaphorical sting, that is. The actual sting lasts at least a week unless you can drown out the pain with wine.

"His name's Duncan," said Zin firmly, "and he's perfectly happy here."

Well, I wouldn't mind slightly larger omelets, but he was right. I was more content than I had ever been. Because if you end up with a good handler like Porter and an understanding owner like Zin, a dragon doesn't need his own kind.

"Ely," Ratcher said in an overly friendly manner that made the skin of my wings crawl. He wrapped a long, lanky arm around Zin's broad shoulders and steered him away toward the half-assembled seating. "My proposal would be good for us both."

Zin looked to Reinhart, who said, "He costs a fortune to feed."

"Duncan, focus," Porter insisted. I snapped my attention back to Porter and immediately increased myself to my show size. "Molly, go on, if you're ready."

"I was born ready, Sugar," Molly said, then climbed

45

onto my foot. I balanced on one leg while holding out the foot Molly stood on. Which was not easy since centaurs, even miniature ones, have a strange center of gravity that's a bugger to find. Plus, I was still distracted by Zin's conversation.

"He's also our main draw. If I lose him, I'll likely be out of business."

"Yes, that would be awful," Ratcher said insincerely. "But I'm offering you enough that you wouldn't need to keep running this circus. You could retire. Find a sylvan glade and cavort around, drinking and dancing with others of your kind."

"First, you can take your stereotypes of satyrs and stick them up your purple-clad backside. Second, I've no interest in retiring to a sylvan glade or anywhere else. This circus is who I am. My life. My family. And third, since when did Duncan become so valuable? You cast him off a decade ago, and only twelve months ago he was in the bargain bin of circus acts. The dealer practically paid me to take him."

"Look, I'm aware of his history. I've had my own trouble with him, as you well know. But his handler seems to have worked wonders with him. I'd want him too, by the way. Package deal."

"No deal."

"Zin," said Reinhart, who'd been mumbling some calculations to himself, "have you seen the books lately? The cost of eggs alone is about to bankrupt us."

"So purchase some chickens instead of letting Pepper buy those fancy-breed eggs from the farmers' markets."

Zin narrowed his eyes at Ratcher. "No deal, Damian."

"Ely," Ratcher said, drawing out the name in a let's-be-reasonable way.

"No. Deal." Zin's voice dropped an octave when he said this, but Ratcher merely arched an eyebrow and grinned at the threatening tone.

"And if Porter comes to me? I pay the best wages in the region. I've already made him an offer."

"And he said...?" Zin asked, losing his confident air for the first time in the conversation.

"He didn't say no."

"Then that is Porter's decision," said Zin, his words crispier than a fresh head of lettuce.

"Duncan," Porter barked and gave me a gentle smack on the thigh with the hook. I whipped my attention back to him, the touch of the hook leaving me tense and ready to do whatever he asked. Trust me, I was very conditioned to the hook after my past handlers, including one who had worked for Ratcher. "Come on, Molly's waiting."

My gaze briefly flicked to where Zin and the others had been. Zin was still there, staring out the open tent flap, but Reinhart and Ratcher were gone. A sense of relief washed over me until I saw Zin heading in our direction.

"Porter, a word," Zin said, his hands clenched by his sides and his head held as if he was ready to ram someone with his horns.

"Can it wait? We just got started. It's that new act you suggested where Duncan—"

"No, it can't," Zin said so harshly I flinched and

knocked Molly off balance. Luckily, she's nimble and leapt to the ground, throwing her arms up in a gymnast's flourish as her glittering blue eye shadow sparkled under the lights.

Told you she was a ham.

"Work on what we talked about, Duncan. Want this, Molly?" he asked as he held out the cushioned hook.

"No, silly. Duncan's a big ol' sweetheart. Ain't no need for that."

Oh, if you knew how hard it was for me not to blurt out and correct her grammar, you would give me a shiny new medal for my treasure hoard. *Isn't any* need. *Isn't any* need. *Isn't any* need.

Porter and Zin moved so they were just inside the entrance of the Tent. With the centaurs in the ring to my right having resumed work on timing their steps to their music selection, and the Flynns to my left chattering orders to one another, I couldn't make out what was being said. But I guessed it wasn't a discussion of what flavor of cake Pepper should make for Opening Day Eve.

Zin loomed over Porter as he spoke. Porter responded, his brow furrowing as he emphatically shook his head. Zin then raised his right fist. Another low grumble rippled through my belly. But Zin did nothing more than wave Porter out of the Tent so they could continue their discussion outside.

"Duncan," whispered Molly, "we should practice."

I agreed, and we worked a little more on her balancing on my foot. We then moved on to me picking her up in my jaws, then setting her down. We did this several times to make sure I was gripping hard enough with my teeth to keep her from falling, but not so hard that I'd end up with a mouth full of mini-taur blood.

"How's it going? Ready?" Porter asked when I'd set Molly down for the third time. He tried to keep his tone light, but his dark cheeks were blazing.

"We sure are," said Molly, who didn't seem the least bit fazed by what had just taken place. "Come on, Duncan. Let's do this."

I readjusted my foot. Molly climbed back on board with the world's biggest grin of anticipation on her face. I gave the lightest twitch of my leg muscles. She went soaring and managed an impromptu back flip that produced a delighted laugh from Porter. Then, as she descended, I caught her gently between my teeth.

"Did you see that, Duncan?" she said, wriggling with delight. "I was a pegasus!"

With Porter standing right next to us, I didn't reply.

And not just because it's rude to talk with your mouth full.

CHAPTER 6
GOSSIPING CENTAURS

Despite her telling me to write these stories as I see fit, Cordelia is pestering me to hop right on over to an interesting conversation I had with the centaurs Conrad and Flora after my training session.

But since I am the one hunched over the typewriter and wearing down my poor claws with all this typing, before we go leaping anywhere, let me give you a tiny bit more information about dragons and our relationship to humans to shed some light on that quizzical final sentence in the previous chapter.

Now, while we will speak to human-type creatures such as satyrs, elves, and dwarves, dragons don't speak to humans. No matter what species of dragon we happen to be, we keep our tongues tightly tied around humans.

Wait, not "*tied around*" humans like a death grip or anything. Although there are a few pythonodon dragons in Florida that will do that. What I should have said is we keep our tongues tied *in the presence* of humans.

For some dragons, such as pyrodons like myself — that's the genus who can breathe fire — this silence is voluntary. We can speak; we just choose not to. Other species, especially those in the vermidon genus (those are the wormy ones who most typically live in swamps and lakes), have lost their ability to speak entirely. I'm no biologist, but I guess they figured they weren't using their larynxes much anyway, so they opted to swap out the ability to speak for the ability to breathe underwater.

Still, even if we can talk, we don't speak to humans. Ever. And it's not as if we wouldn't love to give some of you two-legged primates a piece of our minds.

The thing is, dragons can't lie. We can embellish, we have the mental dexterity to work wonders with a half-truth, but we can't utter outright fibs. I don't know why we can't. It's not as if we have any ethical objection to lying. In fact, it seems like a marvelous talent to possess. And of course, you've probably heard about some of the horrible things my forebears have done to peaceful villages, so you know we're not exactly the most moral beings on the planet. We simply don't have the power to lie. Somehow, the untrue words get waylaid on their way from our brains to our tongues.

And this inability to lie is why we've found it safer not to speak to humans.

Because humans will do anything — as many dragons discovered before the Dragon Delegation adopted the No Speaking Rule of 1274 — to get their hands on our treasure hoards. Before that decree, humans would ask us the location of our goodies, and we couldn't stop ourselves from telling them the exact whereabouts of our treasure. As if stealing our hoard wasn't bad enough, they

51

would often kill us before waltzing in and taking the entirety of our collections.

Other creatures are aware of our lying handicap, and they don't hesitate to ask where our coins and jewels are stashed. But other creatures aren't like humans. They don't have the instinct for greed. They'll thank us for the information, seek out our hoards, then only take what they need or what they can carry. Goblins always go for the coins, elves just adore sparkly things to decorate their hair and clothing, while dwarves want the precious metals for metalworking. But no other creature except for humans will kill us and take everything.

And so, in 1274, it was decided we'd all be safer if we stayed silent around humans.

After over six hundred years of us not saying a word to them, today's humans now assume dragons can't speak at all. But intuitive ones like Porter sense that we do understand exactly what's being said to us.

Speaking of Porter, let's get back to what was happening in the Tent.

After a few more test runs with Molly just to make sure that first attempt at the flip-and-catch wasn't a fluke, Porter had me finish up with a little strength work and stretching. Sometimes training sessions involved getting out for a good jog, but being so close to Opening Day, I had to be kept a mystery. I mean, if the townsfolk were able to see me strutting my stuff on the streets for free, why would they hand over their money to Reinhart to watch my performance?

Okay, yes, I suppose they might want to see Benny or

the Flying Flynns, but let's be honest, the people of Sherwood would be coming to see me.

CORDELIA: Ego, Duncan. Tame the ego.
DUNCAN: What? I just told them I couldn't lie.
CORDELIA: One of those half-truths wouldn't go amiss, though.

Having also just wrapped up their training session, Flora and Conrad joined me in the center ring. Neither of us said a word until Porter left. At the same moment Porter reached the Tent's flaps, Fergus stepped through and the two narrowly avoided colliding into one other. As ever, Fergus had a cigarette between his lips. But unlike his typical devil-may-care look, the unicorn gave my handler the wickedest stare I'd ever seen as Porter elbowed his way out.

"What's up with that?" I asked Conrad.

"I shouldn't say anything."

Which was Conrad's way of saying he had news he was dying to tell me. For such an upstanding, stalwart centaur, he really is a terrible gossip. I think he might even seek out these saucy tidbits, in contrast to his wife who takes everything in stride and lets any negativity flow past her while claiming all is sunshine and rainbows.

I gave Conrad my best spill-the-dirt look.

"Gladys told Fergus she couldn't leave Porter for him. Then, when she caught sight of me, she said she'd kill me for eavesdropping. As if it's my fault I was passing by and happened to hear them."

Somehow, I'd bet the passing by had been done at a very slow pace. But that wasn't my concern. What concerned me was that my handler's marriage might be in trouble.

"Fergus and Gladys?"

"Seriously, Duncan," said Conrad with a dramatic roll of his dark eyes, "if you weren't so big, I'd think you lived under a rock. Yes, Fergus and Gladys. She's been letting him lay his head in her lap for months."

I'd heard Gladys had strange tastes, but she and Fergus? My heart sank for Porter. He and Gladys weren't the closest couple, but he did genuinely love her from what I'd gathered. He always brought her a little something after a day of work, made sure her crystal ball and tarot cards were safely packed when we traveled, and never once looked at the scantily clad humans and pixies who performed feats of balance on the centaurs' backs as they galloped around their ring.

"So," continued Conrad, "Fergus is feeling a bit put out by it. Gladys told him the affair could continue, but she wouldn't leave Porter for him."

"We should all love one another," said Flora as she stepped over to us.

"Woman, if you start loving anyone in this circus but me, I'll give him a kick right to the head."

"Violence is never the answer, dear. And of course I wouldn't love anyone but you, my sweet pea."

I snorted a laugh, and a tiny bit of fire escaped. I recoiled at the sight of it.

"Still dealing with that problem?" Conrad asked.

"It's fine."

"I have some oils that could help with your paranoia," Flora offered. "And I've been reading about pressure points."

"Thanks. I'm fine. Really. Lunch?"

We emerged from the Tent to an intense blaze of heat. It was only early June and should have been mild, but an unseasonal heat wave for the Pacific Northwest had been lingering around for the past few days. It was turning everyone grumpy and frazzled by mid-morning, and moods weren't improved by the last-minute work that still needed done before the gates opened the next day.

As if to prove my point, a scowling Reinhart ignored us as he tramped by, grumbling to himself a list of things that he needed to check on. And from the direction of Benny's wallow, Cordelia shouted a volley of curses.

The centaur couple and I headed to the Cantina. The actual working kitchen was nothing more than a cramped caravan Pepper had inherited from her grandfather. Inside the small space was a deep fryer (mostly for the food the circus's guests craved), a grill about the size of a doormat, an icebox that was mostly taken up with the block of ice she picked up each week, an oven that was no bigger than a hatbox, and a two-burner hot plate. I have wondered if Pepper might not have a little magic in her to make so many meals for us with such a limited amount of equipment. I'm not complaining, though; I'd give my left wing for one of her omelets.

Outside the kitchen stood a popcorn machine and a

cotton candy maker, both of which were operated by gnomes since Pepper had to draw the culinary line somewhere. The dining area of the Cantina was shaded with a broad canvas awning and consisted of several tables and chairs for the humanoid-shaped beings, plus an area to the side with tall tables where the centaurs stood and where I sat on my haunches to eat.

My stomach growled at the scent of the basil-and-mozzarella omelet Pepper had already started for me. I'd put my order in when I'd picked up my breakfast, but I walked up with Conrad and Flora just in case my lunch happened to be ready.

In front of us, Cordelia stood at the caravan's wide window, reaching out to take back her dukie book from Pepper, who would have noted the meal on the Expense page.

Dukie books, which I'll explain soon enough, are so ever-present in a circus, I wouldn't have normally noticed the exchange, but Cordelia's book did because it bore a blue cover whereas mine, and everyone else's I'd seen, had a red cover.

And, well, I then suddenly wanted a blue dukie book because I didn't have one. It's a treasure-hoarding thing.

When Cordelia moved aside to wait for her order, she collided into my chest and dropped her dukie book. When it landed, a photo poked out from the pages. No, sorry, not a proper photo, but a picture clipped from a newspaper article, and it caught my eye because I was in the picture.

CORDELIA: Of course that's what caught your eye.
DUNCAN: Shush.

I should have said, the image caught my eye because I was in it and I recognized it from an article written a few months ago by Sigmund Starky for the *Northwest Circus Circular*. The article described (in terribly embellished terms) Porter's work with such a deadly dragon as yours truly.

To show how masterful Porter was as a handler, Snarky had us photographed with Porter's elbow propped on my knee. While I stared down at him with a fearsome glare that would have had the knights of old shaking in their suits of armor, Porter casually rested his head on his hand, looking like he hadn't a care in the world.

But Porter's wasn't the face in the clipping. Instead, Cordelia had pasted a photo of her own head over that of my handler's.

Before I or Conrad could do our gentlemanly duty of picking up the dukie book for her, Cordelia was already swooping down to grab it. Book in hand, she stomped over to an empty table.

"Interesting picture," Conrad muttered cheekily as he gave me a nudge with his elbow.

"You gonna order, or you just gonna stand there chewing your cud?"

"We don't chew cud, Pepper," said Conrad. "We're part horse, not part cow."

"Fascinating. Now, what'll you have?"

Conrad ordered a mushroom-oat burger with a side

of oats, and Flora ordered her usual wildflower salad with, of course, a side of oats. They really do like their oats, those centaurs.

While we stepped aside and waited for our meals — Pepper had spewed some vicious words when Boris once suggested she provide table service — Reinhart marched up to us, his brow scrunched into several rigid rows of flesh.

"Oh, you do not look well, Reinhart," said Flora. She then hovered a hand near his face. "Tummy troubles?"

"No, damn it. I've got one of my headaches. The heat does it every time. Can I get some of that lavender hoohaw? Worked last time."

"Omelet, wildflower salad, order up," shouted Pepper.

The thing with Pepper is that, while she makes fanciful gourmet specialities most people had never even heard of, you do not want to delay one second when your order is ready. After all, she's a cyclops, and they aren't exactly a species known for having a gentle temperament. Fergus once took his time picking up his slow-roasted, hand-blended Arabica coffee, and she gave him nothing but watered down instant coffee for the next three months. He finally begged forgiveness and swore to always respect her efforts, no matter how many gorgeous laps were nearby to distract him.

"Well," Flora said hesitantly, as she glanced at the waiting plate, then back to Reinhart as if debating with herself whether to help a patient or stay in Pepper's good graces. "You know where it is, don't you? The caravan's unlocked, so feel free to go take what you need."

Reinhart thanked her with a sneer on his face, then

trudged off, rubbing his temples and muttering to himself that he didn't have time and he'd have to get it later and why couldn't Flora bring it to him instead of making him traipse...

By this point, he was out of even my own keen earshot and heading toward the main gate.

CHAPTER 7
THE HANDLER'S WIFE

"Heard Ratcher wants to buy you," Fergus said when we'd all gotten our food and joined him. He'd selected a tall table farthest from where anyone else was sitting. I squatted down on my haunches with my back turned to the other tables so it would look like he, Conrad, and Flora were the only ones speaking. Although, with the prospect of the omelet before me — which Pepper had garnished with chopped fresh tomatoes — why would I want to waste time chattering?

"Zin's not selling me," I said as I shook out my linen napkin and placed it on my lap. "I'm too valuable to him."

"Don't be too sure of that. Reinhart told me Zin's not on the most stable financial footing."

"Are you kidding? Look at this stuff." I pointed to the high-quality food on our plates, the fresh strawberry juice being served in carafes, and the finery of our flatware. I didn't know of any other circus whose cook served food on real plates with shining silverware. "You can't tell me Zin's in dire straits if he can afford stuff like this."

"It comes out of our dukie books, though, doesn't it?"

Fergus said, then shifted his cigarette to one side as he took a sip of his coffee through a bamboo straw.

Since they keep coming up, I should explain these dukie books. They're used throughout the circus business in the Northwest. Every creature is issued one when he or she starts at a new circus. When it's issued, the book is signed by the circus owner to make it official. Although Zin, in a rush of excitement when he first inherited his circus, went on a mad spree with a case full of dukie books and signed them all the day they arrived. He still has a scar from the blister he developed from holding the pen.

Anyway, how it works is at the start of the week or month — depending on how the circus you're working for runs things — your salary is entered on the Income page. Then, over the week or month, whenever you purchase something within the circus, such as your meals or new gear for your act, it gets noted in your book on the Expense page. These costs then get subtracted from your salary balance and you can either carry that forward to the next pay period or cash out. Overspend and the amount is deducted from your next week's salary.

"Well, not really," I said, because Pepper had a habit of 'forgetting' to note more than half of our meals. Thankfully, otherwise her gourmet tendencies would have put most of us forever in debt to Zin.

"True," said Conrad. "I've heard Porter complain more than once that Gladys would kill him if he didn't take her out for a meal. So then he does, and she complains that he's wasting their money since the prices at the Cantina are nothing compared to what's being charged in those greasy whatchamacallit places in town."

"Spoons," Fergus said.

"What about spoons?" I asked, then took a bite of eggy, tomato-studded goodness.

"They can make beautiful music," Flora said through a mouthful of the viola garnish on her salad.

Conrad and I exchanged a look. He then smiled dotingly on his wife.

"Anyway," I said, "regardless of the food, paying customers swarm every show Zin puts on. How can he be in trouble?"

"It's a problem going around the region," replied Conrad. "From what I hear, the smaller circuses are shutting down. You know Seton's Spectacular and Yu's Emporium are considering closing their tent flaps for good, right?"

"Well, sure," I said, "but Seton and Yu are both over a hundred years old, well past retirement age. Hell, a decade ago Seton had dementia so bad he didn't even know where the center ring was. I can't believe he held out this long."

"It's more than that, though," said Fergus. "Ratcher's buying up or buying out all the independent circuses and putting them under one big umbrella."

"Wouldn't he put them under a tent?" asked Flora.

Fergus slurped his coffee, perhaps in an effort to stop a snide retort around Conrad.

"Yes, my smart little filly, he would," Conrad said, patting his wife's hand. He then said to us, "Circuses are big business. We're the only real entertainment for people. And Ratcher wants to control that."

"I don't get it." The whole conversation was making my head ache. I may be the star of Zin's show, but I'm not the creature to turn to for knowledge on business matters. "Don't more circuses mean more business? More entertainment for everyone? More job opportunities for us?"

"No, more circuses mean more competition," Fergus said, speaking to me like I was a dimwitted hatchling. "Ratcher wants to get rid of that competition. I also heard he's buying up any circus that has a dragon act. I guess he figures if he can't have the biggest dragon, he'll have the most dragons."

Something about this didn't sit right with me. More dragons meant more work, more trouble. As I said, we come to rely on each other's company when we're in a circus situation, but get too many of us together and it'd be like three other chefs attempting to cook in Pepper's kitchen. They'll try to get along, but it won't be long before trouble ensues. Rivalries start, jealousies take over, egos abound, and that's not a good combination. I couldn't imagine willingly subjecting yourself to such a mix, nor spending vast amounts of money to obtain it.

Then again, even in their best moments, most humans don't make sense to me. It's why I liked working for Zin's troupe. As a satyr, he was one of the rare owners who was one of us, who wasn't human. He had his quirks, but certainly not as many, nor as problematic as those of a human.

On my last bite of omelet, Flora whispered, "Incoming," in a surprisingly catty voice for a centaur who usually speaks as dreamily as a sylph. She darted her eyes to her left, and I followed her gaze.

Gladys was raging in like a tidal wave toward us.

"Dear Pegasus in heaven," Fergus sighed, "would you look at that lap. My horn's going to burst if I can't—"

"Fergus, please," Conrad and I groaned.

Gladys was a tall, slim-hipped woman. For her act she wore a wig of stringy black hair topped with a purple turban made of silk. But when she wasn't conning the masses with her predictions, she wore her long, blonde hair tied back in a loose braid, as if she was doing everything she could to look like the maiden in one of those European unicorn tapestries.

Her gaze flicked to Fergus, who was staring at her like, well, like he stared at most any human female: lustily.

"Where's Porter?" The question snapped from her lips like the crack of a whip. "I've had lunch ready for him for an hour. I swear if I've wasted my time in the kitchen, I'll kill him."

First, for some reason, Gladys had insisted on making Porter's meals for him for the past several weeks. I'd like to think it was because she wanted to care for and spend time with him, but this was Gladys we're talking about, so I'd bet you dragons to donuts that it was a control thing.

Second, I don't know where Gladys went to school, but somehow she'd learned that every statement needed to be punctuated with a threat to life and limb.

My table companions all muttered that they hadn't

seen him since he left the Tent. Before Gladys could decide which of us she'd like to kill first, the sound of arguing came from somewhere in the direction of Benny's mud pit. We each turned or angled our heads to gawk at what was going on.

"Is that the new hire?" Gladys asked. "The behemoth girl?"

"That would make an excellent name for an act," said Conrad. "Ernesto's Exposition used to have a fat lady. We could have Behemoth Girl."

"Just think of the size of her lap," Fergus said, clearly forgetting that the owner of the lap he was currently enjoying was standing right next to him. Luckily for Fergus, Gladys was too distracted by the sight of her husband trading verbal punches with Cordelia to notice the comment.

"Yes, that's the new hire," Flora answered. "Her aura shows so much red. I should really offer to help her realign her chakras."

"What's he yelling at her for?" Gladys asked. "He better not be two-timing me with her or I'll kill him."

Said Gladys, who apparently thought herself the model of fidelity. Humans are so confusing.

The argument was a fair distance away, so I couldn't make out exactly what they were saying. But as chance would have it, Porter had caught sight of Gladys and started to walk away from Cordelia, who was having none of it.

"Clipping their wings is cruel," she insisted when she'd darted in front of Porter, blocking his attempt to reach his wife. "Did you know that every time you clip their wings, you steal a year of their life?"

Was that true? I just thought the clipping was a demoralizing way to control us. I suddenly felt an ache in my knees and a squeezing sensation in my chest and was convinced I had sudden-onset arthritis and heart failure.

Porter crossed his arms over his chest and stared down at Cordelia, looking like someone having to revisit an old argument yet again.

"Clipping their wings only affects their life span if you cut down too far."

This made sense, and the twinges of arthritis and cardiac arrest both eased, only to be replaced by a terrible recollection.

During my first weeks at Ratcher's, I'd been forced to witness a dragon having her wings completely removed. She developed no infection and had no heavy loss of blood. Nevertheless, she died after three weeks of misery.

Thankfully, although most medicines you'll find around the region are nothing more than quack tonics, purging oils, or mind-altering drugs to make you think you feel better, veterinarians who work the circuses have been able to perfect the surgical reattachment of dragon wings. Done within twenty-four hours of the removal, it's a miracle cure that halts the death sentence, even if the wings never do flap quite right again.

"You know nothing about it," Cordelia accused. "How would you like it if someone cut off the ends of your fingers to control you?"

"I do cut off the ends of my fingers." Porter uncrossed

his arms and waggled his fingers in her face. She batted his hands aside. "They're called fingernails, and as yet, I've suffered no ill effects from trimming them. The wings of dragons under my care are only clipped once a year. The removed bits grow back. No harm done. It's better than one flying off and getting into trouble."

"If they like you," Cordelia said without missing a beat, "if they trust you, they won't fly off."

"There's no arguing with you, is there, Quinn? I've been handling for forty years." Porter took a deep breath, then continued in a rigidly calm tone. "My dragons have been my friends, my companions. I do them no harm and they trust me. But I'm not about to risk a circus owner's investment by having one get spooked and soaring away. Now, if you ever get your own circus, you can run it as you like. In the meantime, leave the handling and the dragon advice to those of us whose job it is to care for them."

"Care," Cordelia said dubiously. By then, Gladys had approached the pair and was sneering judgementally at Cordelia.

"Gladys, my darling." Porter pecked his wife on the cheek. "I think I'll skip lunch today. Something has ruined my appetite."

Looking proud to have gotten the last word in, Porter turned away from Cordelia.

"You're not coming back to the caravan for lunch?" Gladys asked.

"Nah, I'm going to go help Reinhart with the ticket booth. That bogart did a real number on it. See you this evening."

Once he'd gone, Gladys smoothed down her skirt. Fergus watched her hands slide along what would be her lap if she'd been seated.

"I suppose I'll be alone for the next few hours," she said, catching Fergus's eye before walking away, her hips swaying an eye-catching rhythm. Fergus's cigarette sizzled out when it fell from his gaping mouth and into his coffee.

"Well, beasts," Fergus said after she'd passed out of view, "I should really go, um, practice my prancing or something."

"Or something," Conrad said and lit the new cigarette Fergus had dropped down to his lips. The unicorn then trotted away, seemed to think better of appearing too eager, and changed to an overly casual saunter as the smoke wafted up and around his horn.

CHAPTER 8
OPENING DAY EVE

"Everyone, we've got a show opening tomorrow at eleven," Zin said to start his Opening Day Eve speech. Even if there was no news to report, reprimands to deal out, or praise to be lauded, he made one speech before the start of a run and another at the end. For this speech, we'd gathered in the Tent, since it was the only place where we could all fit. Plus, it gave the gremlins a chance to make sure the lighting had been set up properly as they shined a spotlight on Zin.

With me and Molly set to perform a new stunt for this run, we were standing in the center ring with Zin. Joining us was the bogart Humphrey — although I suppose since he was now employed, he should be called a brownie once again. He shifted nervously on his skinny legs as his bony arms clutched his new dukie book to his chest.

His new *red* dukie book. Red, just like mine and everyone else's. Everyone's except Cordelia's. Granted, a dukie book wasn't terribly valuable, but she had a blue one. That made it different. And that meant my treasure-seeking instincts were still contemplating where she'd gotten it and whether I could get one for myself.

"Let's all try to make sure this run goes as smoothly as the last," Zin said, yanking my attention away from thoughts of blue goodies. "Again, I commend you for the hard work at pulling the Dayton show together so well. And the Vancouver one before that. And the St. Helen's one before that. We're on a streak of great shows coming off without a hitch. Let's keep that up.

"Now," he glanced up to the operations booth, "can we get the light on Duncan?"

The request was barely past Zin's lips when there was a snap from above, and I was suddenly blinded by the spotlight. This happened every damn time. And the thing that annoyed me was that the sound was a dead giveaway. Plenty of warning that the light would be coming on and I should close my thick lids to protect my golden eyes. But did I? No. If I had the hip structure to kick myself, I would.

"Duncan and Molly," Zin continued, "have a new trick they've been working on. It just goes to show you there's always room for innovation here. And we also have a new hire who might not have had the easiest start, but who Boris promises me will fit in. Even better, his last employer was none other than Damian Ratcher." A round of boos and jeers came from the audience. "Exactly. We're always glad to welcome someone who has put Ratcher's Ringside behind them. Humphrey, take a bow."

The spotlight next blinded Humphrey. He startled at the visual assault, then with eyes firmly shut, he bowed awkwardly.

"We also have another new hire, but Cordelia Quinn has opted to remain with Benny rather than join us. Let's just pretend that's not because she's antisocial, but because she's showing dedication to her new job. Anyway, we've got Abbott's Aerials three miles to our north, and Curie's Curiosities five miles to our south. But they don't have what we have. Keep up the good work and let's make this our best run ever."

Each run was supposed to be our best, and I was never sure what we had that the other shows didn't — besides me — but the speech always produced a roar of cheers from the troupe.

"Just don't drink too much tonight." Zin shifted to stare me straight in the eye when he said this. I gave him my most innocent smile. Which, given the fangs, never seems to come across as intended.

As the centaurs, who had been watching from their side ring, headed out of the Tent, Zin waved Conrad and Flora over. They started toward him just as Reinhart approached.

When Zin's attention shifted to the dwarf, Conrad caught my eye, made the money sign by rubbing his first two fingers against his thumb, then raised his eyebrows as he looked meaningfully back at Zin.

"You coming, sweetie?" Molly asked me. "The centaurs have just uncorked a new batch of their oat beer."

I nodded that I was on my way, but remained focused on Zin. Could he really be having money problems? And why did he want to speak to Conrad and Flora? Zin and Conrad had grown up together and were practically like brothers. Surely, he wouldn't fire them to save a few bucks, would he?

"Can I talk to you at your place?" Zin asked the centaur couple.

"You're welcome anytime," said Flora. "I can see your aura is troubled. I have some lemon balm oil that might clear it up."

Zin grimaced at this. After a tonic that promised to make his leg fur more luxuriant had left him with bald patches on his knees, he'd been skeptical of any supposed cure.

"Come on," Conrad said. "We'll mix it into a bottle of oat beer. You joining us, Reinhart?"

The dwarf grunted a reply, and the four headed off.

"Have you seen Porter?" I asked Molly when I caught up to her. I whispered the question just in case any humans were within earshot.

"No. And Gladys didn't come to the speech either. I do hope they're making up. There just ain't no reason to be arguing, you know what I mean? Speaking of, have you noticed…?"

We'd come into view of the Cantina and she pointed to a table where the brownies had gathered around a large pitcher of milk.

In case you're not aware of brownie physiology and behavior, they never touch alcohol. Their systems simply don't process it the same as most creatures, so to them, even the strongest moonshine has no more effect than water and tastes of nothing other than rotted fruit, grain, or whatever's been tossed into the boozy concoction.

What does get them buzzing, however, are milk products. Allow brownies to dive too deep into a jug of milk and they'll turn into drunken hooligans.

At the table Molly had indicated, Humphrey had been given pride of place. And trying to squeeze into the seat next to him was Helga. When she found the seat taken, she resigned herself to sitting opposite him. From her vantage point, she fixed a relentless doe-eyed stare on the new hire.

Perhaps sensing this burning ogle, Humphrey glanced up and met her eye. His cheeks lost what little color they had, and he instantly dropped his gaze to pay very careful attention to his cup of milk.

"I don't think he's interested," I said as we made our way over to join Fergus, who was standing at the end of the table next to Boris.

"Oh, he is," Molly said, confidently full of knowledge on the ways of the heart. "He just doesn't know it yet."

Fergus and Molly drank their cups of oat beer while I slurped mine from a bucket. We snorted with laughter as Boris told a tale of a particularly smelly, and hairy, pair of socks he once found. I was just pondering a refill when Porter wove his way through the crowd of revelers.

Even now, I can't describe the exact look on his face. Angry? Frustrated? Discombobulated? Some sort of negative emotion that I'm sure would have had Flora eager to realign Porter's chakras. Whatever was eating at him had wiped away his normally kind and open countenance.

And of course, I couldn't ask him what was wrong.

"Duncan, a well-wisher just sent me a small keg of wine. Let's go blow off some steam, shall we, old boy?" I lapped up the last few drops of my oat brew, then stood up to follow Porter. "You're welcome to join us, Molly," he added, pointedly leaving out Fergus.

"You two go right on ahead, darlin'. I think there's a story of a pair of boxer shorts that got up and walked away coming next, and I wouldn't miss that for the world."

"Well, we'll be in the Tent if you tire of your current company."

I gave an uncomfortable farewell grin to my two companions. Before Porter and I had gone very far, my ears picked up Fergus making excuses that he had an appointment to get to. Before I ducked past the flaps of the Tent, I glanced back to see him slipping away from the others.

CHAPTER 9
A FEW BUCKETS OF WINE

DUNCAN: And where were you during all this? Pouting?

CORDELIA: No, not pouting, smart ass. Flora invited me to join everyone, and I did kind of want to go, but I'd just gotten Benny clean when you were all heading into the Tent for Zin's speech, and I'd be damned if I was going to let him roll over and get mud or other fluids all over himself.

DUNCAN: That's right. I passed you two on the way to the speech. You'd really buffed him to a high polish. Seriously, readers, Benny's skin shone with the healthiest pink hue I'd ever seen on him. And he wasn't giving off any hint of behemoth stink.

I'm going to go on record here and say that Benny never looked, nor smelled so good as he did under Cordelia's care.

CORDELIA: Aw, thanks, Duncan. Now, enough of this gushy silliness, and get back to the damn story. We're almost to an important bit.

Porter took a seat in the lowest row of the stands. I don't know if he'd done it before he sought me out, or if it had been placed there by whoever delivered the wine, but the mini-keg had been set a couple rows up from where Porter sat, providing easy access to the spigot that had been knocked into it. I looked from it to Porter, tilting my head questioningly.

"I know you like hammering the tap in, but Charlie saw me wheeling the keg in here and wanted some, so I did it myself." Charlie is our resident chimera. He's at least eighty, nearly always in a foul mood, and since he's got many deadly body parts, we tend to do as he wishes. "Next time, though, old boy."

Porter patted my flank, then filled a bucket for me and a large cup for himself.

Now, I might be fussy about my omelets, but when it comes to wine, beer, or most any other alcoholic beverage, I'll take whatever's on offer. However, even my any-booze-will-do palate raised a few questions when I lifted the bucket and caught the scent of cooking oil. Used cooking oil.

I sniffed again and wrinkled my snout.

"You smell it too?" Porter asked. And I wanted to say that I probably smelled it about ten times more strongly than his human sniffer, but you know, the whole not-speaking thing. "It's on the barrel. Must have been used to store cooking oil at some point. Bad choice, but it doesn't seem to have affected the wine. Cheers." He held up his cup, drank it down in one gulp, then refilled it.

Not wanting him to drink alone, I cautiously lapped up my own drink. He was right. It tasted just fine. A white wine, not too sweet with grassy notes. Would have gone perfectly with a chanterelle omelet.

Porter, meanwhile, tossed back a second cup of wine, then quickly went for a refill. "Zin," he grumbled, "I told him, you know?" I didn't know, but I'd learned to be a good listener around humans. So I listened, continuing to drink as Porter vented. "I know he's got money issues, but it's his own fault. He said so himself. He can't get the numbers to add up right, so I don't think any of this should be my problem."

The cup emptied again, and I will say by this point, his words were getting pretty darn sloshy. Still, I didn't complain when he filled my bucket after topping up his cup once more.

"I tol' him I would work for less, but not for free. If he wanted a handler for free, he'd have to fire me. And he says firing wasn't what he had in mind, that I was being stubborn. Me! Stupid Zin can't do math, and so he thinks I'm gonna be a pushover?"

Another cup went down his gullet.

"But this whole day is stupid. People around me got no common decency. Even my own wife, know what I mean? Duncan, you're the best people I know."

After this soppy statement, Porter's drinking slowed down slightly (mine didn't) and he switched to ever more elaborate ideas he had for tricks we should try out before our next run. I gathered Zin had asked him to take a wage cut, but he never did divulge what he meant about Gladys. Or at least I don't think he divulged what he meant. The night got a little fuzzy after my fourth bucket.

I lost track of how many cups of wine Porter had, but

at some point, he curled up on the bench seating and fell asleep.

Some sort of drunken need for camaraderie took over me as soon as Porter started snoring. I had the absolutely brilliant idea (so it seemed at the time) that Cordelia and Porter should be friends. I mean, they both liked me, right? So obviously that meant they'd become bosom buddies in no time. And Porter's new best friend shouldn't miss out on our Opening Day Eve festivities.

I ladled some wine into my bucket and marched out to take it to her.

CORDELIA: You just said you couldn't lie.
DUNCAN: But I can manage my way around a half-truth. But yes, you're right, I staggered out. Or at least I think I did.
CORDELIA: You were most definitely staggering.

This probably won't come as any surprise, but a staggering dragon is a potentially hazardous thing. We've got an awkward gait to begin with, plus we've got these big tails slapping around behind us. But somehow I wove my way through the smaller tents and displays and other circus what-have-yous to Benny's wallow without destroying anything.

Cordelia wasn't at her post, but Benny was awake, so I sat down with him. We each took drinks from my bucket and somehow, in very little time, the contents evaporated.

At this point things had turned as blurry as a painting

by a sufferer of cataracts, but I do recall thinking Benny was a genius when he had the idea to roll over onto his back and go to sleep. Not wanting to be left out, I flopped over and watched the moon disappear as my eyelids drifted shut. The next thing I knew, a small, red-haired woman was yelling at me and poking me with the handle of her push broom.

My eyes didn't immediately respond to my brain's command to open, but when they did, the moon had shifted just the tiniest amount to the left. Not much time had passed, but apparently it had been long enough for Benny to have made a mess of himself.

And somehow that was entirely my fault.

"What the hell have you done? Why are you even here?"

I held up the wine bucket, hoping to share its tasty contents and appease the angry little human. Also, full disclosure, I only know some of what happens next because Cordelia related it to me later.

Cordelia leaned over and peered into the bucket.

"Seems to have evaporated."

I snorted, delighted at how much we thought alike, and thinking again of what great pals she and Porter would make. Then again, I was at that drunk stage when I believed all the world would be the best of friends if only they could sit down over a nice Riesling.

"You think you ought to get back to your caravan?" she asked. I shook my head. "Suit yourself, but you're getting up early and helping me clean Benny."

She said this grumpily, but I think she was pleased to

have me for company. I mean, I am Brutus the However That Title Goes.

Anyway, I wish I hadn't had so much wine. I would have liked to remember that night more clearly. It certainly would have helped with the investigation.

Chapter 10
A Rough Morning

The next morning came way too soon, way too bright, and way too noisily.

Also, way too odoriferously.

I grimaced as I rolled over in the squelching mud of Benny's wallow. During the night Benny had shifted to sleep on his belly rather than his back and had produced a three-inch deep puddle of drool. Behemoth saliva has an odd scent like roasted almonds and pineapple, but on this morning Benny's was tinged with the sweet odor of marshmallow. Odd, since he was normally only allowed to have such treats when visitors stopped by.

Benny grinned at me. Although the shape of his mouth always makes it look like he's grinning, so it's hard to say for sure if that grin was his usual expression or his amusement at my disgraceful state.

The gates wouldn't open for another few hours, but Zin would already be doing his rounds, making sure all was in order and shouting demands while everyone scurried around, eager to make him proud.

I was not making him proud. I could tell by the way he

was standing next to my head and staring wickedly down into my eyes with his arms crossed over his chest.

He then squatted down on his goat-y haunches to be nearer my eye level as he said, "Duncan, unless you've fallen in love with Benny, I hope you have a very good explanation for why you're here. Porter!"

Zin was right next to my ears when he shouted this. I winced as my head threatened to burst.

Porter, wisely enough, didn't appear on command. Unlike me, he had the benefit of not being a large reptile and he hadn't fallen asleep in the behemoth wallow. Hiding for him was proving a far easier feat than it was for me.

Zin was working up another bellow when, from the Tent, came a high-pitched scream. Charging through the Tent's flaps, Flora galloped out with Conrad chasing after her. He raced forward, cutting her off, then wrapped her in his arms as she produced a round of horsey sobs.

Something entirely unrelated to the alcohol I'd consumed the night before made my gut clench.

I got to my feet. Benny swung his massive head to look in the direction of the action, then rested his head on his front paws to watch.

I leaned down. Everyone was rushing to see what had upset Flora, so I was in no danger of being overheard. I was, however, in danger of passing out from the smell of the mud pit. How did Benny stand it? How did he maintain that contented grin? How did Cordelia do her job without the benefit of a clothespin over her nose?

"Where's your handler?" I asked.

"Not seen her yet," Benny replied in his glacially slow drawl. "She gave me some marshmallows last night, then you showed up, so both of you were here. I was so happy not to have to sleep alone that I slept very sound indeed. I woke up when Zin shouted at you. Rude way to wake up, that."

"Indeed."

I scanned the area for Cordelia, then caught sight of her auburn head over at one of the water troughs. She was filling two buckets and had two push brooms propped up next to her. I vaguely recalled her threat from the night before of having to scrub Benny clean. Despite my pounding head, I pulled myself out of the wallow, shook off the mud, and hustled over to see what was wrong with Flora.

She was just containing a round of sobs that made her sound like a braying, asthmatic donkey. Conrad still had an arm around her, but Zin was tapping his left hoof impatiently.

"What is this all about?"

"In there—" Flora gestured shakily toward the Tent.

"Yes, I gathered that."

"Zin, give her a moment," said Conrad. "She's had a shock. You know she's sensitive."

"Then maybe *you* could tell me what happened." Zin's dark face drained of half its color. "Don't tell me one of the Flynns has fallen. I can't afford—"

"Don't worry. The Flynns' biggest risk right now is choking on a piece of peanut cobbler." Conrad pointed to the Cantina where the squirrel-shifting elves were gobbling down their breakfast. A few were saving some for later by cramming as many nuts as possible into their cheek pouches. It's a rather disgusting sight and explains why no one wants to dine with them. "And no, I don't know what she saw. She was already inside. I had barely entered when I heard her scream, saw her gallop past me, and went after her to make sure she was okay. You are okay, aren't you, Snickerdoodle?"

I wasn't the only one pinching my mouth shut to keep from tittering at the pet name.

Flora nodded.

"Then maybe," Zin said very tersely, "you could tell us what's going on?"

"The, the— Oh no, it's too horrible. I knew I should have added more sage to the cleansing incense when we arrived."

Zin's cheeks darkened, and he glared at Conrad in a way that said, *If you don't get her to talk this instant, I'm going to geld you.*

"Snickerdoodle," said Conrad, "I know it's tough, but it would be very cleansing for all of us if you would tell us what you saw."

Standing taller than everyone else, I peered over their heads and toward the Tent. I don't know why Zin didn't just walk in and see for himself what was in there. I was about to slip inside and let poor Flora off the hook when she finally blurted, "I think one of the brownies has killed Porter."

"Oh, great galloping griffins, woman." Zin clutched his head, his horns sticking out from between white-with-tension fingers. "Have you been dipping into your essential oils again?"

"No, I've been on a strict regimen of oat grass smoothies for breakfast. But he's in there. He's not moving. And one of the cleaners was standing over him." This was all the composure she could muster before breaking into braying sobs once again.

Porter? Not moving? Killed?

It didn't seem real. It couldn't be real. He'd probably just had too much wine. And, since Zin wasn't yelling in *his* ear, was likely still sleeping it off.

The bargaining part of my brain kept trying to convince itself all was okay, that there was nothing to see, that Flora was over-reacting. But my feet had a mind of their own and were plodding heavily toward the Tent. Zin told me to stop, but I didn't listen.

I had to see for myself. I had to prove to myself that my handler, my friend, was alive and well. Or at least alive with a horrible hangover.

CHAPTER 11
WHAT'S THAT SMELL?

Porter was sprawled out on the floor about halfway between the center ring and the bench where we'd been knocking back drinks the night before. Flora had been right: He wasn't moving.

Except during times past when I purposely defied a bad handler, I've never had a stubborn side. But seeing Porter like that, I stubbornly insisted that my handler had only passed out, that we'd imbibed too much and now we were both paying the consequences.

 This streak of self-deception slammed to a halt when I realized that not even the drunkest of drunks could remain asleep while a brownie stood right next to you shouting accusations to his new hire who was flinching as if the harsh words were striking him like hail pellets.

"What's going on?" I asked Boris after darting a glance over my shoulder to make sure no humans were around.

"This one claims Porter was like that when he got here." Boris glowered at Humphrey. "Do you really expect me to believe that?"

"Is true," said the bogart. He had a thick accent that was made even tougher to understand thanks to his nose having been broken by Boris in their fight the day before. "I finds them. I just checking them, see if they okay, and then lady horse screams and my heart nearly pop out of my nose with fright."

"Them?" I asked, looking to Boris. Was there another body? Had Porter collapsed on and crushed a pair of pixies?

"Doesn't seem to have the best grip on pronouns," said Boris.

"So, is he—?" My throat closed up as I pointed to Porter.

"They has go bye bye from the world, yes," replied Humphrey, his ears drooping sympathetically.

Zin burst through the flaps and charged up to us. He jerked to a stop next to me, huffing with anger and exertion, but he didn't seem real. Like a mirage or a hallucination or like I was seeing him through Fergus's ever-present cloud of smoke. Porter was the only thing that came through with perfect clarity. Porter's unmoving body.

"Did you do this?" he accused the bogart. Then, not giving Humphrey any chance to respond, directed his irritation at Boris. "You are responsible for all the workers under you, so if he's done this, you're out of here."

"Zin, that's hardly fair," said Conrad's soothing voice of reason. I hadn't noticed him enter. When I glanced past him toward the Tent's opening, Flora was peering in, wringing her hands as Molly and a couple full-size female centaurs said soothing and cajoling things to her.

87

"Fair?" Zin's voice pitched high with the word. "Fair? It's Opening Bloody Day. I do not have time for one-half of one of the most crowd-drawing acts to be dead. We have gates that are supposed to open in less than two hours. We have people who expect to see a dragon show, people who may have only come to see a dragon show. And we have no handler to conduct that show. So don't talk to me about fair." He squatted down, rested his elbows on his bald knees, and clutched at the horns on his head as if he wanted to tear them out. "We can't miss a show. Whoever did this will suffer." He looked up and stared directly into Humphrey's wide-with-fear eyes.

"I no do. Not me. I only find." The bogart twisted his skeletal hands together, and his pointed, oversized ears trembled.

"Actually, I believe he's telling the truth," said Boris, who had been poking and prodding Porter while Zin ranted. "Porter's cold, so it couldn't have just happened, which means Humphrey couldn't have done it. Seeing Porter like that, I overreacted. *The Handbook* always says to think before accusing an underling."

Boris passed an apologetic smile to Humphrey, who nodded to show all was forgiven.

"I don't care about your stupid handbook," Zin barked. "How can you know he didn't do it?"

"Humphrey slept in the brownie caravan yesterday. Someone would have known if he'd gone out alone. Since then, he's been learning the ropes and has either been with Helga, who won't let him out of her sight, or myself. He only came in here about ten minutes ago when I asked him to start dusting down the benches, which means he has an alibi the entire time since Porter was last, well, you know." Boris paused, then swallowed hard. "Since he was last seen."

"What do you know of alibis?" asked Zin, standing now and looking about to throttle whichever small creature got within punching distance.

"I was in service at a detective's house before I came to your show. I know a thing or two about crimes and bodies and all those shenanigans."

Bodies.

Okay, maybe the self-deception wasn't entirely done, because I couldn't think of Porter as a *body*. He was just sleepy. Really, really sleepy. I wanted to kick him, to bite him, to dig a claw into his backside, anything that would wake him up and prove my point. He could not be a *body*.

"There's something else," said Boris. "Take a whiff."

Zin bent down. He's a satyr, which means only his lower half is goat-like. His upper half still has all the sensory limitations of being mostly human — although he is quite strong and can twitch his pointed ears at will.

I, on the other paw, had a dragon's olfactory prowess and didn't need to get close to smell Porter. Now that Boris had pointed it out, I don't know how I missed the scent earlier.

I flicked out my tongue to confirm what my nostrils had already detected. Almonds. Pineapple. Marshmallow.

"Benny?" Zin asked, looking completely bewildered as he stood and shook out his shaggy legs as if to wake them back up. "Benny did this?"

89

I should probably have mentioned this earlier, but although Benny is a gentle beast, behemoths can be dangerous. Their saliva is poisonous and if they ever encounter a leviathan, the fight that will ensue could mean the end of the world. I do have a bugger of a time imagining our Benny fighting anything worse than a cold, but I suppose he might just be resting up, conserving his strength for the big match.

"Probably not," said Boris. "Maybe if we'd found Porter in Benny's enclosure we could assume he'd staggered in there by mistake. But Benny's not exactly one for getting up and roaming around."

"Are you saying Porter consumed behemoth saliva?"

"It could be that. Suicide's not uncommon in humans his age, especially ones with family troubles. But it could have also been slipped into something he ate or drank or even applied to his skin."

Boris let the implication hang in the air. The wine barrel was still perched on the bench. All eyes were on me as I went over to it and tried the spigot. Nothing. Okay, so maybe I had more buckets than I'd remembered. I rocked the barrel, but there was no sound of sloshing, no sound of any liquid that could be examined for traces of poison. But if the wine had been poisoned, wouldn't I be dead too?

I turned back and shook my head. Zin released a heavy sigh. "I can't deal with this right now," he said to no one in particular. "If Duncan doesn't have a handler, there'll be no dragon act. Do you know how angry people are going to be if they show up and—"

"I can do it." Cordelia strode toward us, shoulders

back, head held high, full of confidence. Zin's eyes lit up, and not in a good way. More in the way of a harpy who's just found a ripe piece of roadkill.

"Conrad, restrain her," Zin ordered.

Conrad looked uncomfortable at the request, but he stepped in behind Cordelia and deftly, despite her sinewy struggles, pulled Cordelia's arms behind her back and held tight to her wrists.

"What are you doing? You're crazy. Let me go."

She leapt, she twisted, she writhed, she kicked, but Conrad maintained a firm grip on her. Eventually, he got tired of her antics and kicked out his horsey front leg, gently hitting her in the back of the knees in a way that dropped her into a kneeling position. Conrad let go of Cordelia's hands when three other centaurs emerged from the sidelines to block her escape.

"You are all complete psychopaths," she shouted.

"And you are a murderer," Zin said. "I really thought you might be an asset to this place. Instead, you've probably ruined me."

"I don't know what you're talking about, you stupid piece of goat dung."

"I'm talking about that," Zin stepped aside, giving Cordelia a clear view of Porter. Of the body.

On seeing Porter, Cordelia's brow furrowed, and she tilted her head as if she wasn't quite sure what she was looking at. It was the same expression I've seen on more than one face when Flora shows us one of her latest artworks. Except for Conrad, who always looks on his wife's work with pure adoration.

Cordelia, confusion having calmed her a bit, met Zin's eye.

"Is he dead?"

"Obviously. And you killed him so you could have his job."

"That's ridiculous." Cordelia got to her feet and brushed the dust off the knees of her dungarees. "He's almost twice my size. How exactly would I have gotten the drop on him?"

"It has been ascertained," said Zin in a strangely formal and haughty manner, "that behemoth poison was involved. And you're the behemoth handler."

"I'm not certain, but I think that's circumstantial evidence," Boris, speaking in an undertone, told Zin. Zin ignored him. He'd found his culprit and that was that.

"Conrad," said Zin, "get your centaurs to take her to the Cells. We've got to get this— Sorry, we've got to get Porter somewhere else so we can get ready for the show."

Conrad nodded to the trio of centaurs who'd been guarding Cordelia. They stood nearly twice as tall as her. Although she dodged then squirmed away from their grasp, centaurs are very nimble and it didn't take long for one of them to snatch her hands behind her back and lead her away. This time, Cordelia's curses weren't so amusing. But they were plentiful. If nothing else, she had an extensive vocabulary of curse words.

"I'm not sure about this, Zin," said Conrad, watching Cordelia being escorted out of the Tent.

"It doesn't really matter, does it?" said Zin, his shoulders slumped. "Whether she did it or not, Reinhart's been promoting Duncan and Porter's act like a siren luring a sailor. People are going to expect to see Brutus Fangwrath being tamed by Porter. If we tell them the show's off, they're going to demand their money back. And we absolutely cannot lose a day of sales."

Some of the human performers were lurking around, so I couldn't speak for myself. Conrad glanced to me. I nodded in response to the questioning look in his eyes.

"Look, Zin," he said, "people don't come to see Porter. They come to see Duncan. And Duncan knows the performance inside and out. No one's going to question if you play the part of handler for a day or two until we find someone else. Abbott's is only a few miles away. He's got those dragon twins who alternate their performances daily, which means their handlers only work every other day. I'm sure he could lend us one of them."

"But I don't know exactly what Porter had planned."

"Molly can fill you in. Don't worry, Zin, it'll be fine."

Fine? It was *not* going to be fine. The self-deception had not only vacated my head, it had run away with the speed of a spooked thoroughbred.

Porter was dead.

Porter had been murdered.

And while I didn't know who did it, I had a deep down dragon-y feeling that Zin had sent the wrong person to the Cells.

CHAPTER 12
THE GRIEVING WIDOW

Damn, I just realized I sort of glossed over the Cells in that circus tour I gave you earlier.

Now, while the circus world at the time I'm writing about wasn't exactly a land of freedom for creatures who weren't part human, things were far better than they had been fifty or sixty years previous. Back then, anything that wasn't fully human, or at least elven, was seen as a potentially vicious beast who had to be chained or locked up.

Because of this ridiculous mindset, there's plenty of caged caravans around the region. While most circuses now use these cages to lock away the wine and beer so the troupe doesn't drink all the provisions in one night, a few circuses still use the cages for their original purpose: Restricting the movement of non-human creatures such as dragons, manticores, and chimeras as if we'll run away or eat all the humans and pixies if we aren't kept behind bars.

The Cells at Zin's, even though we use the plural, is actually just a single caravan that came with the circus when Zin inherited it from his father, and had once been used to house a particularly nasty manticore (another inheritance gift from Zin's father).

The Zinzendorfs have always been loathe to get rid of anything that might have a purpose one day, so even though the grumpy old beast — the manticore, that is, not Zin's dad — died during Zin's first year of managing the circus on his own, the Cells stayed.

Thankfully, Zin realized long ago that if they're kept happy and fed, most creatures, humans included, have no interest in escape or in devouring their co-workers. Of course, that doesn't stop Zin from having my wings clipped, but he's pretty progressive in most other regards.

Not long after the manticore died, Zin figured out a purpose for its old cage: a place to keep visitors who'd been caught stealing or had gotten too aggressive (oat beer often hits humans the wrong way, let me tell you). The Cells were also used for the rare occasions when one of our own needed to be dealt with.

As with the barrier, Zin worked his satyr magic on the lock of the Cells, making him the only one who could undo the latch. And believe me, many a nimble-fingered pickpocket have tried their best on that lock only to be left reconsidering their mastery of their profession.

The Cells itself had no interior furnishings or decoration, although Flora often suggested painting it a soothing shade of pink with some lavender oil mixed into the paint for an extra calming effect. What it did have were solid walls on three sides, a solid metal roof, rough oak plank flooring (made rougher from the manticore's claws), and a front made of thick iron bars.

The thing wasn't built for comfort, and judging by the heat of the morning sun on my wings before I entered the Tent, the day would be even hotter than the last few had been. The Cells would be sweltering. It was no place to store any creature. Not even a human.

CORDELIA: *You know, you could have helped me out. Besides being hot and uncomfortable, the brownies don't clean the Cells. The inside of that thing made Benny smell like a heap of honeysuckle.*

DUNCAN: *I do feel bad about it, but speaking out would have put me at risk of serious trouble.*

CORDELIA: *I guess that's why they don't call you Brutus the Brave Heart.*

DUNCAN: *You've been saving that one up, haven't you?*

CORDELIA: *Maybe.*

Cordelia, now outside the Tent with the centaurs, was still howling her curses. I was wrestling with my own conscience about what to say, or more correctly, *if* to say it, when the Tent's flap fluttered open and Gladys entered. She paused, perhaps waiting for her eyes to adjust to the dimly lit interior, then fixed her gaze on Zin and walked toward him with a determined stride. Moving with quick steps, Flora followed after her. No doubt she was already formulating what oils or herbs Gladys might need to handle her grief.

Boris had told Humphrey to get some of the other brownies to help move Porter. They hadn't returned yet, so my handler remained sprawled out on the lightly sawdusted floor.

"Tell my lazy husband to get up," Gladys said, refusing to look at her lay-about spouse.

"That's going to be a little impossible," Zin replied.

"That drunk, is he? Why am I not surprised?"

"No," said Boris as he stooped down and shifted Porter's head. Gladys's jutting chin lowered ever so slightly. "Not drunk. Dead."

"Well, doesn't that just figure." Gladys rolled her eyes, and her right hand went to her hip in a pose of utter annoyance.

Boris lifted Porter's upper lip, pressed on the exposed teeth, nodded to himself, then met Zin's eye. "And it is behemoth saliva. The teeth get soft from the stuff."

"Wait," said Gladys, as if finally taking in the implications of what was going on, "should you all be traipsing all over this...?" She fluttered her left hand vaguely at the area before her.

"Oh, great minotaur bollocks!" cursed Boris. "I'm always forgetting the crime scene thing. We should have checked for footprints."

"We still can," Flora suggested. "And I could offer up chants to Gaia to bring the circus back into harmony as we look around. I believe clockwise circles would be most cleansing."

"That's not exactly how it works, you ditsy creature," Gladys snipped. "I saw a detective film last month — wild centaurs can't keep me away from anything starring that William Warlock — so I know all about these things. You have to look *before* everyone's been tromping about.

There might have been a telltale clue left behind."

"What's it matter?" Zin said. "We've got our culprit."

"You do?" asked Gladys warily.

"Yes, locked up and ready to be dealt with at the appropriate time. Which is not now. We need to move Porter and get things ready for today's show."

"Well, that's very efficient," Gladys said stiffly. She'd already taken several steps back, as if trying to make a subtle retreat. "I should go finish doing my makeup, getting into costume, and all that. The show must go on, right?" She said this with an oddly flippant, tittering laugh that set my fangs on edge.

Gladys swayed her slim hips out of the Tent, walking in that way that looks for all the world like a person's trying not to run.

I caught Boris's eye, put my forepaw to the center of my head, then stuck my forefinger straight out like a horn. He nodded once to show he understood.

"Has anyone seen Fergus?" he asked.

No one had. The last time anyone had seen him was the evening before. Molly told us he'd said his good nights soon after I left, which confirmed my seeing him leaving the revelers when I went to join Porter.

"He probably went to Gladys," said Molly. "We'll have to interrogate her. That's the right phrase, isn't it, Boris?" He agreed it was and that we would have to question Fergus, too. "Golly, but this is exciting. Except for, well, you know," she added guiltily when she seemed to realize her enthusiasm was about as misplaced as a crystal chandelier over Benny's mud wallow.

"I do think we should keep an open mind about who the culprit is," said Boris. "I don't like that Fergus isn't around."

"That's ridiculous," said Zin. "Where would Fergus have gotten behemoth saliva? It's obviously the newbie. Thought I was being clever hiring that one. Stupid me."

"Cordelia Quinn is the most obvious solution, but my detective always advised me to look deeper."

"Yes, yes," said Zin impatiently, "but I don't think we should waste much time on the matter right now. Opening Day? Remember?"

"I can't believe what I'm hearing," said Flora. "We're supposed to live in a country of guilty until proven innocent."

CORDELIA: Are you sure you noted that correctly?

DUNCAN: Innocent before guilty? Oh yes, I suppose that does make more sense, otherwise I would have wanted to correct her.

CORDELIA: You do know people think you're an annoying know-it-all when you do that, don't you?

DUNCAN: Well, I wouldn't have to do it so often if some of your human sayings had a bit more logic to them. Raining cats and dogs? That would be physically impossible, not to mention dangerous. Although it could rain frogs and fishes, if a tornado sucked them up from a lake bed.

CORDELIA: Sometimes I do marvel at how your brain works.

DUNCAN: Thank you.

CORDELIA: It wasn't a compliment, Duncan.

Flora was right: Suspects are supposed to be presumed innocent. Although that kind of seems to go against the whole definition of the word *suspect*.

But Cordelia was now in the Cells, presumed guilty, and with the gates opening in a couple hours, it didn't seem as if a fair or extensive investigation was going to be launched anytime soon. If at all. Zin wanted it hushed up, taken care of, and off his mind so we could rake in ticket sales and keep the coins rolling in.

Something needed to be done, the matter had to be looked into. Trouble was, I didn't know exactly what I could do about it. I could tell Conrad about the night before, but the only thing I knew was Cordelia had shown up to the behemoth enclosure some time after I left Porter.

I read any detective novel I can get my claws on and the words of Christie, Doyle, and plenty of others told me that not being able to pinpoint a suspect's exact location during the time in question was never good. Which meant if I told anyone Cordelia had been absent when I'd arrived, it could only make things worse for her.

Then I'd gone and passed out. But if the position of the moon was any indication, I hadn't been out long before Cordelia appeared. Then again, it probably doesn't take much time to poison someone. Where had Cordelia been? Had she met up with Porter to apologize for their argument? Or to take revenge for his having the job she desired? Without knowing for sure, I worried if I said anything about last night, it would only make Cordelia seem more guilty.

CHAPTER 13
THE NO-SPEAKING RULE OF 1274

Eight brownies from Boris's crew finally showed up. With Helga at the lead and looking for all the world like she was relishing her new role of authority, they arranged themselves around Porter like tiny pall bearers. On Helga's count of three, the group lifted my handler and carried him away.

When they left, I noticed Humphrey hunkered down at the edge of the stands, staring at his knobby knees and muttering to himself. I went to him, glanced around to make sure the humans had skedaddled, and asked, "You alright?"

Humphrey looked up. At the sight of me, he startled and scrambled back.

"It's okay, I'm not hungry," I said, trying to make a joke. A really bad joke, but I wasn't at my peak performance that morning. Heartache and hangovers will do that to you.

"Too much like last circus. Ratcher place."

"Someone died there too?"

The tips of Humphrey's ears flopped back and forth when he nodded.

"Is why I leave. I see Ratcher beat dragon. Beat to death. I scared, so I run. Then I cause trouble here but I taken in anyways. Then I like here, and now here just like before."

"I don't think this is just like before." Not at all, in fact. But I didn't want to criticize a creature who looked worse off than I felt. "Why did Ratcher beat the dragon?" I asked, my stomach churning at the image, at the memories of how Ratcher's circuses were run.

"Dragon no talk. Ratcher think dragon can talk, so they..."

Humphrey trailed off. He didn't need to say anything more. The dragon had been beaten because Ratcher wanted information. And I doubt it was information about the secret ingredient in the dragon's chocolate chunk cookie recipe.

Let me explain.

It all relates back to the No Speaking Rule of 1274. See, dragons hold a pretty big secret. I mentioned the hoards we gather as youngsters. Piles of gold and all kinds of sparkly things that we guard with our lives. That treasure we collect might be enough to buy a small town or even a small country, depending on how ambitious a dragon has been.

However, there's also the True Hoard. A hoard of treasure, yes, with loads of all those shiny, glittery goodies that humans and dragons crave. But hidden amongst the True Hoard's treasure are the eggs from every dragon that has existed since 1274. Every girl dragon, that is. Boy dragons just, well, never mind.

Anyway, when the Dragon Delegation got together in 1274, it was noted that our numbers had been dwindling. Knights were really getting into the dragon-killing game and could slaughter us far faster than we could breed.

So, during the same Dragon Delegation that crafted the No Speaking Rule, a ruling was made that each dragon donate an egg to the collection that would be kept in a safe location known only to dragons.

Those ancient dragons foolishly believed humans might soon get over their killing spree and matters would improve for all animals. When that day came, the eggs would be hatched and a whole new age of dragons could begin. Which sounds way more fantastically cool than it really is. I mean, think about it, we're basically overgrown lizards with attitude.

So far, even with knights no longer getting stabby while dressed up like tin cans, humans have refused to accept they need to share the world with other beasts. So, while our numbers have continued to dwindle, the True Hoard has continued to grow. And humans have continued to seek it out.

Since evolution decided it'd be a hoot if it took away our ability to lie, if someone learns that I or any other dragon can speak, all they have to do is ask, and we'll be singing like operatic fat ladies about the location of the True Hoard.

So what, you say? It'd be fun to have more dragons in the world. I agree, but dragons have a quirk that could spell trouble if our eggs are found by the wrong person.

Dragons are a bit like ducklings and will imprint on the first creature they see when they hatch. I once knew an amphibodon who hatched right when a crab had been crawling over his egg's shell. Poor guy could never give up the habit of walking sideways.

Anyway, because of this imprinting, the person who finds our hoard of eggs, the person who hatches the dragons within those eggs, will easily be able to tame and control and manipulate creatures that are rapidly becoming rare commodities.

In other words, ladies and gentlemen, getting your hands on a clutch of dragon eggs could be extremely profitable if you're corrupt enough to enter the dark — and immensely profitable — world of dealing dragons to circuses, zoos, and private collectors.

And this is why, even though Porter had been the best handler, the best human friend I'd ever had, he was still human. Since the base nature of even the best humans contains enough greed to drown out their good side, as much as I trusted and liked Porter, I simply could never work up the courage to risk speaking to him for fear of stirring up that greedy inner demon.

CHAPTER 14
THE SHOW MUST GO ON

I sat with Humphrey for a long time, doing nothing but staring at the spot where Porter had been. The Flying Flynns soon bounded in, smelling of peanuts and chattering away about the order of their stunts and who would be partnered with whom for the grand finale.

I wanted to leave. I wanted to sulk in my caravan and perhaps lose myself in another vat of wine. But soon enough, Zin stood before me, tapping the padded tip of the hook against the side of his thigh. My scales bristled at the sight of Porter's hook in Zin's hand. Where had he gotten it from? Had he already rifled through Porter's belongings? Did he realize how much I wanted to knock the tool from his grasp?

"I know this is weird," he said, and I did a double take at his sympathetic tone. "Maybe it seems cold of me to make you go on with this show, but you have to do it, Duncan. You understand why, don't you?" I nodded, and the motion jostled the tears from my eyes. I blinked them away, patted Humphrey reassuringly on the shoulder, took my spot in the center ring, then increased myself to my show size.

Zin was right. We had no choice. To keep the troupe paid and the visitors from complaining, the show quite literally did have to go on. Reinhart had done his job of drumming up business and by half past ten, people were already lining up to get their tickets.

I suppose they wanted to get their money's worth, since on Opening Day we were only open until the dinner hour. We also had limited hours on Closing Day when the gates didn't unlock until late afternoon. While Closing Day was when all the stops were pulled out and we gave our showiest performances, Opening Day was sort of a rehearsal day to make sure all the equipment was in order and we had all the kinks worked out.

So, why did people come on Opening Day rather than wait until the next day when we'd be open from eleven in the morning until well past sunset? Especially considering tickets cost the same regardless of which day you visited?

Because these guests didn't want to miss out on any bragging rights. See, Reinhart would go around touting that you absolutely had to be there to see the Opening Day acts because otherwise your friends and neighbors might see them before you, and you wouldn't want that, would you?

Seems odd to me, but the humans in nearly every town we toured through ate up the pitch. They didn't want to miss out. They didn't want to hear about the acts secondhand. They wanted to be first in line to see Zinzendorf's Circus of Unusual Creatures when we came around that year.

As I've said, humans are weird.

"Duncan," Conrad called from a screened off area in the Tent where props were stored and where performers could change or adjust costumes. He waved me over, an urgent look on his face.

"Where's Fergus?" he asked when I reached him. "He's supposed to do his thing under the Flynns and no one can find him."

One of Fergus's roles in the circus was to cavort around under the high-wire act with a few of the mini-centaurs or, more often, with the Dumble family's clown act. It gave a spot of comic relief in case anyone in the audience started feeling woozy from watching the Flynns flipping around in mid-air.

Although lights were shining on the stands so our audience members could find a seat without falling on their faces, the rings were still cast in darkness and I was in no danger of humans seeing me speak to Conrad.

"Can't Charlie fill in?"

Charlie was our chimera, and since it's far more nail-biting to have a foul-tempered lion-eagle-goat beast prowling under a bunch of rodent-like people, he usually only worked the evening performances that were deemed more serious, more daring, more adult than the afternoon shows that were geared toward the kiddies. But stick a pink saddle on him and have one of the pixies ride him while wearing a jester's hat, and you've got a perfect diversion for the youngsters.

"Charlie's a bit under the weather today. Stomach ache."

This wasn't surprising, given that Charlie would devour any random piece of meat he came across. From road kill to round steak, if it once ambled, flew, or did the backstroke, he'd eat it.

"How's Flora, by the way?" I asked.

"Better. Took some chamomile tea and did some mediation, so she's feeling more centered or something. I am worried about Fergus, though. He's a rogue, but he's not irresponsible when it comes to work."

"Is he with Gladys?"

"I went to her caravan, but no one was there. But you know what she had been doing?" He paused just long enough to build my curiosity. "Packing. And," he added waspishly, "it looked like she was making a quick job of it. Hangers left scattered on the floor, drawers gaping open."

"Getting rid of Porter's stuff already? That's a bit cold."

"No, not Porter's stuff. Unless Porter's taken to wearing wispy gowns and silk headscarves." I arched an eyebrow at him. "I didn't snoop. When I showed up, there was a big suitcase open on the bed, already half full. Two smaller cases were waiting by the door with stuff sticking out the sides. But when I got there, there was no Gladys. And given there was no hint of cigarette smoke, I'm guessing Fergus hadn't been there recently."

I let Conrad's gossip settle into my foggy brain.

"I don't think Cordelia did anything to Porter," I said.

"Yeah, me neither."

"I wish I could remember more about last night. All that stupid wine. What if I missed something?" Conrad didn't say anything, which of course spoke volumes. Music started playing, announcing the show would soon begin. "I better get to my ring and let Zin think he's a natural-born dragon handler."

Zin proved to be not too terrible a handler.

Of course, Molly and I knew our act front and back, so his role was more like someone in the audience of a classical music concert waving his finger around and pretending to conduct.

Even with Porter, the padding comes off the hook for a show. Unfortunately, while Porter had a deft hand with the tool, Zin was clumsy with it and scraped me more than a few times. Still, I knew the injuries weren't done on purpose, and to be honest, I was too numb to feel much of anything except for the pain in my heart whenever I looked down, expecting to see Porter only to find Zin flourishing the hook like he knew how to use it.

Except for the grand finale, when I had to catch Molly in my teeth and concentration was vital, I spent most of that Opening Day performing by muscle memory alone. The cheers didn't please me, the gasps didn't make me want to grin, and I couldn't even delight in Molly later giggling about a man in the audience who had passed out when I flipped her up into the air.

By the time the gates closed on Opening Day, Fergus still hadn't reappeared. Zin was livid, but he was also a quick thinker and had asked the Cuttles to step in to do their act under the Flynns.

The Cuttles are actually part of Stanislaus's Strange Sea Life performers you'll find touring along the coast.

This six-member family is another breed of elf shifters who can morph into cuttlefish if they do their act in the water. Since Stanislaus had temporarily closed to recuperate from an emergency surgery (orcadon bites can be nasty things), those of his troupe who could perform on land, such as the Cuttles, were doing their acts with other circuses for the next few months.

On land, the Cuttles retain their elf shape, but just as they do in water, they produce the most dazzling, ever-changing patterns on their skin. In the dimmed lights of the Tent their skin show is mesmerizing. It's certainly not as fun as Fergus and the Dumbles, nor as edge-of-your-seat as Charlie, but the Cuttles' shimmering skin display does the trick for people whose kinked necks can no longer crane upwards to watch the Flynns.

As soon as they got the message, the Cuttles stepped in to help Zin without hesitation. This was no surprise. Most people would have done the same. Zin was just one of those guys who could rally people to pull their weight.

But, I wondered, what happened to people who didn't do as Zin asked? I then immediately felt a wave of disloyalty. Zin had taken me in when no one else wanted me. He'd cut the manacles and chains from my legs and body, then tended to the wounds my bonds had left.

Still, Zin wasn't perfect. He was sometimes quick to anger. He and Porter had argued. Porter had turned up dead. Murdered. And now Zin had Porter's hook. An unbidden growl emerged from deep within my throat.

Once the day's crowds had left with bellies full of popcorn and deep-fried foods, and arms filled with cheap trinkets they'd won or purchased, Zin called a meeting in the Tent. Since he normally only made speeches on Opening Day Eve and Closing Night, it took some time to get the troupe's speculative prattle to die down before he could begin.

"As you know, Porter Kohl was found dead this morning. His wife is in mourning and has asked we leave her to her thoughts." I guessed then that Zin didn't know Gladys had packed her *thoughts* into her suitcases and had likely already done a runner. "I made a rash call this morning by accusing a newcomer of the murder."

Murmurs and gasps came from my co-workers as if they didn't know a thing about the goings on earlier that day. And here I thought rumors spread faster than fire in Zin's circus.

"But I have to admit, I shouldn't have made that accusation." And for just a moment I thought Zin was about to confess that, in a moment of rage, he'd done something stupid. My lips twitched into a snarl as I glared at him.

"With Fergus disappearing the very night of Porter's death, I think we have to assume he is the real culprit. Boris has alerted brownies in other circuses and households in the area to be on the lookout. They will, in turn, alert others of their kind. We will find Fergus."

"Find me for what?" said Fergus.

Again with the murmurs and gasps. Mostly gasps. And a few shrieks of terror. After all, we supposedly had a lusty, murdering unicorn heading straight for us.

CHAPTER 15
THE LAP OF ZOLA

Alongside that murdering unicorn was a human female who was wearing the most shockingly short shorts. Barely more than underpants. The bit of fabric she had on her lower half reminded me of shorts I'd seen on the strongmen of other circuses. And her legs were nearly as big and muscly as those strongmen. Thanks to Fergus's incessant observations of human laps, I could tell he would think hers a good, if firm, one.

"Arrest him," shouted Zin.

A pair of centaurs — full-size ones, not miniature ones, that would just be silly — rushed up to Fergus, smoothly got between him and his muscly friend, and blocked him in so he couldn't get away.

"Zin, I'm really too tired to deal with this." Fergus took a drag on his cigarette, not appearing the least bit bothered by his confinement. "I just wanted to introduce Zola to a few people before we settled in to some of Pepper's cook—"

"Fergus," Boris said, stepping up and taking charge, "you are under arrest for the murder of Porter Kohl."

"Porter's dead?" The cigarette fell from Fergus's lips. One of the centaurs instantly stomped it out with his hoof. Fergus then flicked his head, and the cigarette lodged behind his ear dropped into his mouth. "I didn't think the bitch had it in her. Anyone got a light?"

Everyone was silent. Which doesn't happen very often in the Tent. My skin itched with the eeriness of such silence. Or maybe it was a reaction from spending the night in Benny's wallow.

"What?" said Fergus, after taking in everyone's quizzical expressions.

"Where have you been since last night, Fergus?" asked Boris.

"With Zola." He tilted his head toward the sturdy woman he'd shown up with. "I needed a break, so I trotted over to Abbott's. You've seen his posters around, right? The ones announcing the Superhuman Skirskis? Zola's pictured front and center on those posters, and well, I couldn't help but admire her lap."

"Fergie," said Zola, shyly tucking down her square chin. "Stop it. You embarrass me in front of people."

"It's true, Sugar Thighs. Trouble is, Zola's family is protective of her. And I am not exaggerating in the least when I say she's got some huge brothers. And parents."

"And cousins," Zola added.

"So I figured, to not risk getting my horn pulverized, I should get in good with them first. And boy, can those Skirskis party. All damn night. Man, we had a great time."

"Well, while you were having a great time, you missed

Opening Freaking Day, Fergus," Zin said, fists clenched and shoulders tensed. "So unless they kidnapped you—"

"Horse-napped," someone volunteered, but Zin's scowl quickly shut up any other commentary.

"Look," said Fergus, "by two in the morning, I'd had way too much vodka to feel safe trotting home, so I stayed the night. In the morning, I tiptoed over to Zola's caravan — being the Skirskis' only daughter she has her own place — and she let me—"

"Fergie, don't tell them," said Zola, blushing like a schoolgirl who's just come face to face with her centaur crush. Fergus gave her an indulgent look, then turned to Zin and shrugged his withers while a what-can-you-do smirk slipped over his lips.

"And what time did you, did this—? What I mean is, what time did you go to her caravan?" Boris asked.

"Must have been nine in the morning. Yeah, that sounds about right because Abbott's opens at ten and by then…well, you know. I mean, can you blame me? Just look at that lap."

Cue more blushing and chin tucking from Zola.

"We found Porter at seven," Boris said to Zin. "Sounds like Fergus has plenty of alibis. I can check them if you like, but I think we need to follow our first assessment. Cordelia Quinn may indeed have killed Porter."

"The one with the little lap?" Fergus asked. "Yeah, I could see that. She had a chip on her shoulder, didn't she? Not sweet like my Zola."

I wanted to gag, and I'm not sure whether it was due to Fergus's lovey-dovey talk, my still-raging hangover, or the idea that they were going to lay the blame on Cordelia. Then again, I could have just been hungry.

"Cordelia Quinn?" asked Zola just as she leaned over one of the centaur's backs to light Fergus's cigarette. "Hair like fire? Itty bitty thing?"

"That's the one," said Fergus. "Don't worry, Sugar Thighs, she's got nothing on you in the lap department."

"No, I know name. She work for Abbott for little time. Very little. She claim to be dragon handler. Abbott find out she lie, so he fire her."

"I knew she couldn't be a handler," said Zin. "Thinking she could come in and handle Duncan. Ridiculous."

Zola had more giantess features than human ones, but since, "*Are you a giant?*" isn't the nicest thing to ask a woman you've just met, I decided it was safest to assume she was human and not speak around her. I nudged Conrad and mouthed, "*When?*"

"When was this?" Conrad asked Zola. "The thing with Cordelia."

"Oh, maybe ten, twelve years ago. I have good memory for names. She not even good liar."

"Let him go," said Zin, sounding both defeated and relieved. Fergus had been with Zin's circus for at least a couple decades. He was truly one of the family, whereas Cordelia was new. No one had gotten attached to her yet. She was an outsider, and now she was a known liar. All of which made her more easily disposable in Zin's eyes. Like a human hankie.

"We'll have to call in the Kailin," Boris said.

Yep, this announcement brought another round of

murmurs and gasps. Except from Fergus, whose mouth gaped open, tongue practically lolling.

"The Kailin," he sputtered. "What? Now? I need to untangle my mane, I need some mints, I need to—"

Zola stared at him. I don't know if humans can strength train their faces, but enviably brawny muscles rippled over the massive woman's cheeks, nose, chin, even her eyelids.

CORDELIA: Remember what I said about exaggerating, Duncan.

DUNCAN: No, you didn't see it. Ripples. Like the flanks of the centaurs when they're running at a gallop.

CORDELIA: Oh, I remember Zola now. You're right. She can do some scary things with her face when she's mad.

DUNCAN: Fergus is probably lucky those centaurs were still close to him.

"You stinking beast," Zola growled.

"I— No, Sugar Thighs, I just mean, that we should all look nice for the Kailin. She's very important."

"Not what you mean. I could—" She lifted her hands, holding them as if ready to strangle Fergus as another set of freakishly toned muscles danced along her forearms. After a moment, during which even the centaurs guarding Fergus looked about ready to bolt, she lowered her threatening mitts. "You not worth time. Tiniest horn I ever see."

More muscles rippled and flicked along her legs and backside as she stomped out of the Tent. Those of us left behind practically deflated with our sighs of relief.

"Should I go get the Kailin, then?" Reinhart offered, already pulling a woolen cap from his back pocket. He always wore one when going outside the circus grounds, claiming the human townsfolk treated him more like an equal when he covered his pointed ears. This cap was one I hadn't seen before: black with the silhouette of a circus tent in red, in the center of which was an R. It was nicely done and I wondered if he'd made it himself.

Once Zin grunted his assent, Reinhart trundled away, tucking his ears under his cap.

The Kailin, for those of you who didn't get a full education in mythological creatures of the world, is a unicorn with ancestors from the East. Unlike Fergus's horn, that's maybe about the length of a human forearm with a nice little spiral to it, the Kailin has a meter-long, slender, saber-like horn that's as smooth as a coffin nail. A real coffin nail, that is, not one of Fergus's cigarettes.

The Kailin works alongside a regional judge. Judges travel to hear local cases and can often come to a decision on their own. But in some cases, the judge can't quite sort out the loose ways humans and other non-dragon creatures have with the truth. This is when the judge relies on the Kailin.

Now, what I'm about to tell you might upset the kiddies out there who picture unicorns as delicate, peace-loving creatures. But you've already met Fergus, so I suppose that stereotype's already been shattered.

Through some sort of ancestral power, the Kailin knows the truth behind a person's words, and she is merciless with liars and the unrepentant. If by the end of a hearing, a defendant continues to try to lie about what he's done, or if a defendant has shown no remorse for his crime, the Kailin will surge forward and use that smooth length of horn to stab the person in the gut, eye, neck, or other vital body part.

Her victims never survive. But before you get the idea that the Kailin is a bloodthirsty beast who's just salivating for a lying bastard to cross her path, the Kailin also maintains order by correcting judges who have misread a witness. And if the judge has been corrupted, well, he just better hope he remembered to put on his steel-plated robes, because the Kailin is all about justice.

"With this new evidence," said Boris, "I think we should search Cordelia Quinn's sleeping quarters."

Again, Zin gave his grunting assent.

Once Boris had left with a small team of brownies to check over Cordelia's caravan, and Reinhart had gone to fetch the Kailin and whichever regional judge she was working with, no one seemed to know what to do with themselves and began milling around doing whatever busy work they could find.

I didn't mill around. I left the Tent. And no, not to get an omelet. Although I did want one.

I can't explain why, maybe it was some secret dragon sense, but just as I was more than certain Cordelia hadn't killed Porter, I knew that despite what Zola said, Cordelia hadn't lied to Zin about her qualifications. She had been a dragon handler at some point.

I needed to go see Cordelia. I didn't know what I was

going to do or if I could do anything, but I didn't think she should be left feeling as if she had no ally.

CORDELIA: And you figured a mute dragon with a drinking problem and omelet addiction was going to make the perfect ally?

DUNCAN: I did just admit I had no idea what I was going to do.

Chapter 16
The Prisoner

I left the Tent and, forgetting how long the sun stayed up in late spring, squinted against the brightness outside.

Even if I were new to Zin's circus without any idea of the Cells' location, I'd have had no trouble finding it that evening because Cordelia was shouting herself hoarse about the indignities of her being locked up, about the need for a fair trial, and about having no reason to kill Porter.

When I strode up to her—

CORDELIA: Wait. Strode up?
DUNCAN: Okay, fine...

After I *tripped* over a hose someone had left out — the main water spigot was located behind the Cells — I regained my balance and lumbered toward the bars at the front of the makeshift prison. Cordelia stopped shouting, but her face remained a scarlet beacon of fury. And the sight of me didn't ease that fury one bit.

"You! You know very well I was with Benny all night. You know I didn't kill Porter."

I nodded, my throat itching to speak to her, to tell her I believed her. But a lifetime of staying silent around humans kept my mouth clamped shut.

"What are they going to do? Minotaur?"

I shook my head vigorously, hoping to convey that horrible possibility hadn't even been brought up. Yet.

The minotaur punishment is reserved only for someone who is clearly guilty of murder, as in witnessed doing the deed. It's a guaranteed death sentence once the person is locked inside the minotaur's enclosure.

I know I just said we're all tame and civilized, but not minotaurs. Those half-man-half-bull monsters are sixty-five percent rage, and thirty-five percent insatiable hunger for living flesh. For a minotaur, every day is a bad day, and every hour is lunchtime. Put anything with a heartbeat before them and they'll rip it to pieces, then gobble up those pieces like candy.

"Expulsion?" Cordelia asked hopefully since compared to a minotaur, expulsion did seem the better alternative. Then again, I'd already gathered that much of her life had been spent in circuses. Nearly the entire region's economy turned on circuses. If she was expelled from Zinzendorf's, she would never find work in another circus in the Northwest. I'd seen a few expelled circus workers in my time. Something vital in them had died. Perhaps being devoured by the minotaur might be the kinder choice.

"This is ridiculous. They're only blaming me because I'm new. Just the usual circus BS. You're an outsider," she said in a mockingly snide tone, "you must be a horrible person."

Some of the fight went out of her. Her shoulders sagged and I could smell a nervous tang wafting off her. She began pacing the cage like a bored polar bear in a zoo.

"I just can't believe they think it's me. But you know what the worst part is?" She stopped and stared at me as if waiting for something. "Not knowing. It's like a form of torture. If I knew what I was going to face, maybe I could prepare. Maybe I could fill my head with thoughts that are productive instead of racing around in circles."

I could tell she was fishing for a response, and I did want to say something. To tell her the Kailin was coming. The Kailin was scary, but at least you knew you were getting a fair trial. Cordelia watched me with a curious glint to her eyes, which were incredibly green. Like lush, verdant forests would be jealous of that green. Why was she looking at me like that? Did she see my lip muscles twitch? Did she sense I was on the verge of blurting out what she wanted to know?

"I mean," she said, resuming her pacing, but with a more casual air, "there's two other likely suspects for the murder. Porter's wife, for instance. I've only been here a couple days and even I know she's going around behind his back with that Ferdinand beast."

"Fergus," I said before I could stop myself.

Cordelia stopped in her tracks, her mouth gaping wide.

"You *can* speak. I knew it! I knew I saw your mouth doing more than just chewing when you were at the Cantina the other morning."

I shook my head, drawing an imaginary zipper over my mouth with my clawed fingers. After all, this was a human under duress, and stress does strange things to human brains. Maybe she would assume she had imagined it.

Unfortunately, even my body language can't lie, and soon my insistent head shaking morphed into a nod.

"You can't tell anyone," I said once my traitorous head stopped moving.

"But you could save me. You know I was there all night with you and Benny. You practically crushed me."

"I did?"

Honestly — because I am, if nothing else, honest — I barely recalled the journey from the Tent to Benny's enclosure, let alone what happened between then and Zin shouting in my ear at dawn.

"You don't remember?"

"I'd had a lot to drink."

"Great, my only alibi was blind drunk."

"And can't speak for you at your trial. Oh," I said brightly, "it's the Kailin. You're going to get the Kailin."

"Seriously?" Relief softened Cordelia's face. "That's good news, at least. She'll know I'm innocent. Since my alibi won't vouch for me," she added meaningfully.

I shifted, looking at a particularly pretty pebble next to my toes. The trouble was, all judges were human. That may change one day, but that's how it was and it's why dragons never gave testimony no matter what we knew. I finally looked back to Cordelia, who, even though she had every right to be, didn't appear to despise me for my silence.

"Is there anything I can do in the meantime? Get you an omelet, perhaps?"

"You need to find out what Gladys and Fergus were up to last night. It's got to be one of them. Yesterday, I even heard Gladys telling Porter she would kill him."

"Gladys always tells people she'll kill them. And Fergus was at Abbott's last night with the Skirskis. Did you really lie about being a handler?"

"I take it you've met Zola." I nodded. "I tried for a job at Abbott's when I was starting out. He had just gotten those twin dragons, and I saw in the *Northwest Circus Circular* that he needed a couple handlers. I figured it would be a great way to learn the trade. He'd hire me along with some seasoned handler who could train me.

"But owners don't like to hire inexperienced handlers, so I told him I had worked with dragons over at Ernesto's. And technically, I didn't lie. I did have experience, I just didn't mention that my experience was as a lackey — bringing water and food to the dragons, cleaning up after them, that sort of thing.

"Anyway, the Skirskis also worked for Ernesto, but left and joined Abbott's about a month after I'd started working there. I'd already learned a ton, but Zola saw me, said something to Abbott about the wisdom of letting a lackey handle a young dragon, and I was out of there."

"That's it?" I asked incredulously. "You've only got a month of handling experience?"

"No, because luckily that other handler Abbott had hired had a brother who kept a few retired dragons. He told me to go to him, and that's where I learned the ropes, got references, and I've now handled dragons at Costello's, Yu's, and a few other circuses."

"And didn't have to kill anyone to get the job?"

Cordelia smiled at my quip.

"Not once. Anyway, I still think it's Fergus or Gladys. They're going to be there when the Kailin comes, aren't they? She'll get the truth from them. Or kill them," she added with a dismissive shrug.

"I don't know. Fergus showed up this morning with Zola, so he's got a solid alibi, and it seems Gladys has taken off."

"That's it. A clear sign of guilt. It has to be her." This was followed by a long silence as I struggled with the thought of what might happen if Gladys wasn't the murderer. Cordelia must have been thinking along the same line. "Anyway, I hope you end up with a good handler."

"You don't want the job anymore?" I said, then realized I didn't want her to go. Maybe it was that dragon-y sense kicking in again, but something told me we'd make a great team. I mean, it's not every day I speak to humans, and those I choose to speak to (which so far was one) are those I feel a connection to.

CORDELIA: Aw, I think I just got a cavity that was so sweet.

DUNCAN: Are you making fun of me?

CORDELIA: A little. And by the way, I did see your lip twitch. I messed up Fergus's name on purpose to test you.

DUNCAN: Devious little human.

"Even if I can prove my innocence, I doubt Zin is going to want to keep me. People are going to talk. People are going to question whether I can be trusted. And Zin really threw me under the omnibus. I've heard people talk about Zin, nearly all of it good. I really didn't think he'd be one of those owners who treated newbies like dirt. Then again, he did stick me on behemoth duty."

"Zin's a good satyr. Bit of a grouch, but he treats us well. And I think—"

Just then, the murmur of human voices came from a couple caravans down the line. I tightened my lips and met Cordelia's gaze, my eyes begging her to keep my secret. Whether or not she would, I couldn't be a hundred percent certain. She was human, after all, and her life was on the line.

CORDELIA: Thanks for the vote of confidence there, Duncan.

DUNCAN: Hey, I learned a long time ago that humans gonna human.

CHAPTER 17
AN OPEN-AND-SHUT CASE

After such a blazingly hot day, the sunset brought a sky full of pink and orange streaks along with a welcome coolness to the evening air.

Conrad, Flora, Molly, and I were at the Cantina when Reinhart returned from fetching the judge. He pulled off his cap, stuck it in his pocket, and presented a large, sweating man to Zin, who had been impatiently loitering near the gates since Reinhart had left.

Now, before you start thinking how convenient it was that a judge just happened to be nearby, circus folk are well aware of who's in the towns we're closest to thanks to the *Northwest Circus Circular.*

In addition to circus news and job announcements, the *Circular* lists which shows are headed to what towns using a schedule that's spelled out every year at the Annual Unusual Circus Conference.

This schedule keeps shows from hitting an area too frequently and keeps us from rolling into the same town at the same time — a problem from decades ago that nearly started a circus war. The *Circular* lists this schedule but also updates it when changes need to be made due to illness or, as is often the case lately, due to shows shutting down completely.

The *Circular* also tells us what other traveling services such as doctors, suppliers, and, yes, judges are in the nearby towns. It's all very organized, and I'm not sure how some of the scatterbrains I've met from the *Circular* manage to put such an informative and reliable paper together on a biweekly basis.

Anyway, that's all just a long way of saying we knew a judge and the Kailin were hearing cases in the town that sat only a mile away from where we'd set up.

"Judge Judge Javert," said Reinhart as he presented a very corpulent man.

Zin had stepped forward to shake hands with the judge, but then came up short. His eyebrows raised with concern as he looked at Reinhart. "Are you feeling okay?" he asked the dwarf.

"Fighting fit," Reinhart said and stood up taller, pushing out his barrel chest. "Why?"

"I've never heard you stutter before."

The judge chortled. I don't normally use the word *chortle*, but he was a very rotund man so *chortling* seems appropriate here.

"A common mistake," the judge said, dabbing away the sweat on his pasty forehead with a silk handkerchief. "My mother picked the name Judge, I suppose with wishful thoughts of what I might do with my life. You should have heard the jokes I put up with during my three months of law school."

Standards for the legal profession were slightly lower in those days.

"What are they saying?" whispered Conrad. The upper portion of centaurs is human, albeit with upper body strength that could rival most strongmen. However, along with that human portion comes human ears and the limitations of human hearing, something that's often an obstacle to Conrad's gossip gathering. I waved vaguely to signal to him to stay quiet and allow my amazing dragon senses to pick up the conversation.

"And where is the Kailin?" Zin asked.

"Away on other business," said Judge Judge with a darting glance back toward the gate.

My four-kilo heart plummeted to my toes. Although it was common for judges to hear cases and make rulings on lesser crimes, such as pickpocketing, without the help of the Kailin, in tougher cases such as blackmail and murder, the Kailin made sure all was conducted fairly. Without the Kailin, if someone presented false witness, there would be no one to dispute their statements. It also meant that if evidence was flimsy, as it was in this case, there would be no one to dispute the judge's decision.

I didn't like the situation. I did not like it one bit.

"We can't—" Zin started to say.

"Look, Zin," said Reinhart, "judges charge by the hour, so maybe we should get moving on this. It's open-and-shut, isn't it?"

"Yes, I hear there's some clear evidence," the judge stated before Zin could respond.

"You're right," Zin said as he moved conspiratorially

closer to the judge. "Reinhart, I need a moment. Why don't you tell the others to gather around. I'm sure they'll want to be a part of this. It'll keep them from having to gossip about it later."

Even my ears couldn't pick up what was being said between Zin and Javert. Zin reached into his vest pocket, then seemed to be handing the judge something. Since he had his back to me, I couldn't see what Zin was holding, nor could I interpret his facial expressions as he spoke. Judge Javert, however, had donned a pleased smile as he and Zin shook hands and stepped back from each other.

"Come on," I said to the centaurs. "Let's get over there before everyone else does."

Once most of the troupe had gathered, Javert told Zin to present his case.

"The culprit, Cordelia Quinn," Zin said, shifting on his hoofed feet and fiddling with the fur on his hips.

"Cordelia Quinn, did you say?" interrupted the judge.

"Yes," replied Zin, "a new hire. Why? Do you know her? Has she done something like this before?"

"No, no, not that I can think of, but the name does have a ring of familiarity about it. But go on, you were saying?"

"Ms. Quinn was overheard speaking ill of the deceased, Porter Kohl. She tended the behemoth, and it's been determined that Porter died by behemoth poisoning. She may have also lured the dragon Duncan to the behemoth enclosure."

"Why would she do that?" Javert asked.

"Dragons imprint on people," Zin explained. "When

their handler dies, they'll attach themselves to the first person they see next."

I rolled my eyes and, because of the human standing right next to him, had to fight down the urge to correct Zin. This handler attachment notion is a rumor based on that habit of imprinting at birth I mentioned earlier. So far, I've yet to come across a single dragon who has any evidence to prove the notion's true. Unfortunately, no one in the rumor department has asked about my research.

Zin continued, "Making sure Duncan woke where she spent most of her time is a clear indication that Ms. Quinn wanted to be the first human Duncan saw after his old handler died."

"Or that said dragon just passed out in the mud," muttered Fergus, who had been pouting ever since Javert had said the Kailin wasn't coming.

"I see. Yes, it's all very interesting. Very open-and-shut," the judge said, his pudgy hand slipping over his jacket pocket.

Open-and-shut? Even I knew the evidence was circumstantial at best. We needed the Kailin. Of all the times for her to have other business to attend to.

"Sir, if I may present my evidence," said Boris as he pushed his way to the front of the crowd. In his hand I saw the photo of me and Porter that Cordelia had altered. I tried to talk Boris out of this gambit when he discussed it with me earlier. Now, after seeing the judge's style, I could only imagine it backfiring.

See, when Boris found the photo after searching through Cordelia's belongings, he reasoned that if

Cordelia really hated Porter enough to kill him, she would have used his face as a dartboard, slashed it with a knife, or damaged it in some other manner. But she hadn't even crossed it out with a black marker. She'd merely pasted her photo over it. This, according to Boris, clearly indicated that Cordelia was not a violent offender.

I had my doubts whether Judge Judge Javert would understand the subconscious symbolism Boris had interpreted from the photo's condition.

"No, no," Javert protested, "I'm coming to a decision. I cannot be having my mind cluttered with too much information." He pondered for all of ten seconds before saying. "Yes, as I said, this does seem open-and-shut, but as much of this evidence is only circumstantial—" A wave of relief made my legs tremble. The case would be dismissed. Or delayed until it could be heard by the Kailin. "—I cannot rule to bring the full punishment of the minotaur down on the defendant."

He stopped speaking, and we all watched him, waiting for more. Reinhart nudged him. Javert gave a little start and shook his head as if only just realizing he had yet to deliver the sentence.

"As I said, the evidence is circumstantial at best. I do not have the means to take her with me now, but you have her secured?" Reinhart said we did. "Then keep her there. I will send someone to collect her in, let me think, the jailor is off for a— Well, he called it a *yoga* retreat. Not sure what that is exactly, but nevertheless, he's due back in three days and can come collect her then. What you have said and what Reinhart has told me leads me to understand the Quinn woman wants to work with dragons." Zin nodded. "Then she will have her wish. I'm sentencing her to the Pits."

There weren't any gasps this time, but there were a few groans of disgust.

One of the region's main fuel sources, in addition to water mills, is dragon dung. I'm not proud of it, but what can I say? Even the smallest of us is a big creature and what goes in must come out. In a slightly altered and much stinkier form. But that end product—

CORDELIA: Hind-end product?
DUNCAN: Good one.

The end product can't simply be fed into your furnace or your steam-powered jalopy. It has to be sent to what are known as the Pits, a work camp where dragon waste is processed. This involves the smelly, back-breaking, and dangerous work of spreading it out, drying it, turning it, then compressing it into bricks. The bricks can then be transported to retailers to sell at a profitable margin to customers who burn the bricks to fuel their furnaces, lamps, ovens, and more.

There's also a new system being worked on in which the poop is placed into sealed vats that collect the gas, which can then be piped into people's homes for lighting. But even this modern marvel involves someone going into the vats and turning the foul stuff to keep it doing its thing.

Regardless of how the poo is handled, let's be clear on one thing: No one willingly works at the Pits. Not in the processing department, anyway. I'm sure administration and shipping are perfectly pleasant places to spend the working day.

Despite being a nasty process, dragon dung is big business, second only to the circuses. Since the owners of the Pits are as greedy as humans get, they do whatever they can to keep the Pits' substantial amount of profit for themselves. Which is why a couple decades ago, the owners turned the hard labor over to convicts. After all, you don't have to pay convicts, and you definitely don't need to bother treating them well or provide them safe working conditions. And if one of your convicts injures him or herself (easily done in a job that requires frequent use of pitchforks), gets an infection, and dies, there's always another convict to take his or her place.

My point about the Pits is, you don't want the person you think might be your next handler, possibly your friend, to be sent there. I had to do something to clear Cordelia's name.

CHAPTER 18
SLEUTHING DRAGONS

Judge Judge Javert didn't even bother to go over to the Cells to tell Cordelia her fate. He left that up to me.

Okay, he didn't specifically ask me to inform her. He probably assumed Zin would relay the news. But as soon as Javert left, everyone seemed worn down. Instead of the usual buzz of excitement on the night of an opening day when we'd gather at the Cantina and jabber on about how the day went, what visitors to watch out for if they came back, what acts did great and which could use just a bit more polish, there was an uncomfortable hush over the grounds as the troupe went their separate ways.

I watched the dispersal, wondering who would go to Cordelia to explain the judge's rushed ruling.

No one did.

As such, I took it upon myself to deliver the verdict. Not wanting to draw the attention of any humans, I waited until long after moonrise when I was sure most people had gone to sleep. And as I waited, I wished I was an orcadon, because if speaking meant having to deliver this kind of news, I'd prefer to be one of those species of dragons who've lost their ability to speak.

"You have got to be kidding me," Cordelia said. She kept her voice lowered, but there was still plenty of fire in her words. "The Pits? That judge didn't even hear my case. He didn't even let the Kailin take a single look at me. How can I be convicted? It's a death sentence. You know that, don't you? I'm as good as dead."

She then blurted out more of her curse words. They sounded less adorable now and more like the roars of a desperate chimera. As she vented, she paced her cell, pounding her fists into the walls before each turn. I tried to say something, but she just kept on with her angry ramble.

Finally, she let out a loud huff and dropped down to sit on the wooden floor with her legs twisted into a pretzel shape. Maybe she'd finally run out of curse words.

CORDELIA: Never.

"The Kailin didn't come," I said a few seconds into the break of her verbal storm.

This caught her attention. It should have caught everyone's attention.

"Judges don't work without the Kailin," Cordelia said. "I mean, maybe for an offense like driving a caravan with an expired license, but not for big cases like murder. No one brought this up?"

I shook my head. "The judge just kept saying it was open-and-shut."

Cordelia gripped her head, then scratched at her

copper-colored hair that was inexpertly chopped into a pixie cut.

A little side note here... You should avoid the term *pixie cut*. At least in front of an actual pixie, otherwise they'll go on for an hour about how the expression is an offensive stereotype, and that not all pixies wear the same hairstyle.

Even though they do.

See, pixies are impatient creatures with short attention spans. This means the future beauticians among them rush through their training and only manage to learn one style of cut. Unfortunately, they also blaze through their lessons on how to avoid clipping off their clients' ear tips and I've seen more than one pixie leaving the pixie parlor with ears that look far more human than elven.

But back to Cordelia.

"Something's not right here, Duncan. Which judge did you say it was?" I told her, and she mulled over the name a bit. "It's got a familiar ring," she said, almost an echo of Judge Javert upon learning Cordelia's name. She mulled it over a moment longer, then shrugged. "Nope, won't come to me. You've got to do something, Duncan. I didn't do this. You believe me, don't you?"

"Yes, I just wish I could remember more. That wine was crazy potent. Maybe it was Roman. Did you know the Romans made their wine strong to reduce their shipping costs? Then, when it was delivered, you were meant to water it down. Not everyone did, and I bet those were some wild nights." Cordelia was staring at me. "Sorry, I have a thing for trivia."

"Where did the wine come from?"

"I don't know. Porter just said a well-wisher sent it. Probably some townie gave it to us. Handlers are always getting gifts from fans. But you probably know about that."

Cordelia nodded, a slight smile at the edge of her lips as if recalling a fond memory. She then asked, "Did anyone else have it? The wine, I mean."

It took until just then for me to remember that the barrel had been tapped without me. And why.

"Porter gave Charlie some before he found me, and I shared some with Benny, but other than that, it was just me and Porter. I think he wanted to be away from other people for a bit. He was bothered by something."

"Did he say what?"

I shrugged a shoulder. "He was annoyed with Zin about an offer Zin had made him. I think Zin wanted Porter to work for free because of some money issues with the circus. But it was more than that. He seemed really rattled. Said something about people having no common decency. I'm guessing that was probably something to do with Gladys. Maybe they'd had a fight."

Cordelia pondered this, then asked, "Whose caravan is next to theirs? Would anyone have heard them arguing?"

I did a mental scan of the circus. While the arrangement of the grounds is fairly similar wherever we stop, the exact placement of caravans can shift depending on who wants to be neighbors with whom. And who doesn't want to be neighbors, which is probably more important to get right if you want to keep the peace in such close quarters.

"I think Molly's set up next to them. Not sure why. She and Gladys used to be close, but the two fell out over Fergus during our last run."

"Molly used to be with Fergus?"

"Dear dwarf dung, no. Molly can't stand him, which is saying a lot because Molly gets along with everyone. She just can't figure out why anyone would want to be with someone like Fergus. I wonder if it's because she doesn't have a lap?" Cordelia was looking at me like I was an insensitive idiot. "Right, moot point."

Cordelia stood up again, paced the Cells a few more times, then stopped in front of me, her face peering out from between the iron bars.

"Duncan, you need to listen. I can't get out of here unless you can pick a lock."

"Zin locks the Cells." I waggled my fingers like a sideshow magician to show her it wasn't a key Zin had used. "Lock picking's pointless with his satyr security system in place."

"I suppose it would only make me look more guilty if I escaped and fled. I need your help. You're going to have to find out what had Porter so upset. I'd bet it was to do with the Gladys and Fergus situation. Talk to Molly, see if she heard anything. If she did, get her to tell Zin or that brownie fellow."

"Boris?"

"That's the one. He seems like he likes doing things by the book. He'll want this done according to the law."

"He was a little annoyed the judge wouldn't listen to the evidence he found. Although, it might not have helped your case if he had."

"What evidence?"

"They searched your things and found the picture of me and Porter. The one with your head pasted over Porter's."

"A silly picture isn't exactly proof that I would poison someone."

"That was going to be Boris's argument. He wanted it made clear that the picture wasn't showing anything violent, just wishful thinking. I'm sure he wants to find out what's really going on. Maybe not as much as you do, but still."

"Good. We'll count him as an ally. Now, you also need to find out what made Javert come out here without the Kailin. It just strikes me as being suspicious, like someone was trying to hurry the case along. This is murder we're talking about. Any other judge wouldn't have come at all if he didn't have the Kailin with him. And he certainly shouldn't have been able to deliver a ruling and sentencing without her."

"But how do I do that? I can't exactly go wandering around town asking questions."

"I have no idea," she said, stepping back from the bars, her shoulders sagging. The dejected look left me feeling both eager to get to the business of clearing her name, and doubtful that a large, supposedly mute dragon who wasn't allowed to leave the circus grounds would be able to manage it.

Cordelia sat again on the wooden floor and again made a pretzel of her legs as she crossed them under her.

"I suppose I'm lucky the region's jailor is on vacation. That at least gives us a few days."

"Us?"

She gave a single nod of her head.

"Us," she said with a twitch of a smile on her lips.

CHAPTER 19
MOLLY THE MINI-TAUR

The day after Opening Day would follow our normal schedule: starting at eleven in the morning and running into the night. If I was going to get anything done for Cordelia, I had to do it before the gates opened. So, resisting the siren call of the mushroom-and-gruyere omelet Pepper told me she'd be preparing for breakfast, I stopped by Molly's caravan. She was in the middle of picking out which headdress she would wear for the day's performance.

"Peacock feather, or the blue, fluffy one? I'm leaning toward the blue fluffy one. It was a gift from an admirer and they put in a note saying how much they'd love to see me in it. I'm sure they'd get an absolute kick of delight if I wore it. What do you think?"

She held both up behind her head. Just the sight of the fluffy one made me want to sneeze, so I opted for the peacock feather. She later showed up to our act with the blue fluffy one, so I'm not quite sure why she asked my opinion.

"Molly," I began, as she applied a thick layer of cream

to her face, "did you happen to hear anything the night Porter died? Between him and Gladys, I mean. He just seemed kind of upset and I never found out why."

"Oh, sure." Molly was now smoothing an odd-colored liquid over the skin she'd just smeared with lotion. "I'd been listening to albums most of the night. I just adore the new one from Duke Elfington, and I was about to start it over for the sixth time when my gosh darn needle broke."

After screwing the jar of liquid shut, she pulled out a brush and a container of pinkish powder, which turned out to be another item to apply to her face. I was beginning to wonder how she held her head up with the extra weight of all those layers.

"I knew Gladys had a record player, and I was dying to listen to the album just once more before calling it a night, so even though her and I had our little falling out, I figured our tiff wasn't bad enough to go over and ask an old friend if she had a spare needle."

"So you went over there?"

"No, sorry, darlin'. Like I said, I was about to, then I heard Porter's voice and I knew I couldn't pop by."

"Why not? Porter's a nice guy. He would have given you a needle."

"Oh, I know that, you goofball. But I'd already washed my makeup off. I couldn't let him see me with my eyes all naked and my cheeks coated in cold cream."

"But you're letting me see you without..." I waved my forefoot vaguely in the direction of her scattered piles of jars and tubes and brushes.

143

"That's 'cause you're different. You're not human. Or even part human, like me. Humans judge people differently."

She was now dipping another brush into another dish — one containing a glittering, blue powder that she swept over her eyes. Seriously, where do people learn how to manage all these tools and concoctions and steps? It's like a chemistry-meets-art experiment on your face.

"So you didn't see anything?"

"Didn't *see* anything, no." She pointed her brush at me, then gave me a knowing wink. "But I still *heard* something. An argument. And it sounded like they'd already been at it a while, likely assuming I couldn't hear them with the record player on. They probably didn't notice when my music stopped playing."

"Could you tell what were they saying?"

"Well, I think Porter said something about not granting her a divorce. The minute I heard that, my ears perked right up and I forgot about my albums altogether. He said he couldn't afford to divorce her because he'd agreed with Zin not to be paid. Gladys went livid as a llama at that bit of news. And he said, shouted really, that it was only temporary to help Zin make ends meet."

"Make ends meet? But the circus is doing okay, isn't it?"

"I don't know anything about that, sweetie. But Gladys says he should have never made that agreement without consulting her. And he said he couldn't have consulted her even if he wanted to because she was never around. And Gladys said— One tick, Duncan, this bit is tricky."

Making an odd, stretched face with one eye closed, she glued what looked like half a tarantula onto her eyelid. She blinked a few times, then did the same thing to the other eyelid. It was frightening to watch, but it did give her eyes a certain doe-like quality.

"Anyway, so she says if he doesn't grant her the divorce, she'll kill him. She'll just kill him then and there and not look back."

"Molly, why in the world did you not tell Zin this? She's the one who should be in the Cells, not Cordelia."

"Because wives are always wanting to kill their husbands, aren't they? Except for Flora. She couldn't even kill a horsefly. But when I was with my fella, I probably wanted to kill him once a week."

"But he never turned up dead, did he?" I said, wanting to shout at her and just barely holding back. I could feel the fire rumbling in my chest, struggling to get out. I swallowed as much saliva as I could muster. I didn't want to see those flames. Mainly because I've got a little issue with pyrophobia. But also because Molly was now spraying her elaborate show wig with something that smelled like it had a high alcohol content, and I'd hear no end of it if I set her caravan on fire.

"Unfortunately not. The lousy bastard. But then again, he was fine with divorcing me, so I didn't have to kill him."

"Molly, you have to tell Zin what you heard. Please. If I take you to him, will you tell him? You heard the judge. Cordelia is going to be sent to the Pits for something Gladys might have done."

"Sure. Don't worry, Duncan. I'll do it," she said sincerely. "But where would Gladys have gotten behemoth saliva? She gagged at the scent of Benny and always kept herself at least ten feet from his enclosure."

I left Molly to finish "putting on her face" and returned to the Cantina feeling discouraged and slightly annoyed with her for stating the obvious about Gladys's distaste for Benny's stench.

But as I delighted in the rich gruyere of my omelet, I began to feel somewhat hopeful. Gladys didn't have to get the poison directly from Benny. She could have gotten behemoth saliva from some other source. And no one could deny her argument with Porter was far more damning than the slim evidence against Cordelia.

I'd done it! Molly would tell Zin what she heard. We'd send word to other circuses in the area to be on the lookout for Gladys, and Cordelia would be set free.

Yes, I know, you've probably already figured out it wasn't going to be that easy.

CHAPTER 20
TIME FOR A SCRUB

I had enough time to savor my omelet while Molly finished getting ready. Once Molly had her full palette of makeup on, she met me at the Cantina and we headed over to Zin's office. *Office*, by the way, is a generous way of referring to Zin's kitchen table that's forever piled high with account books, receipts from innumerable days' takings, paper scraps with notes scrawled across them, and rolls of tickets in various colors for different days of the week.

When I peered in the window, Zin was at his makeshift desk (that being the countertop next to his sink), head in hands, staring at a sheet of paper. Nice paper too, from what I could tell. Not the rough, grey stuff we normally used around the circus, but creamy white paper with a smooth surface, a printed header, and something written by hand in black ink. I couldn't see the header, and I couldn't read the words, but at the bottom were two well-spaced lines. One of them held a bold signature I was unable to make out. The other remained empty.

"Yoohoo! Zin," called Molly as she knocked on the door. She'd wrapped her eight-inch tall wig of blonde curls in some sort of brightly colored netting. She said it was to keep the wig from getting mussed, but it looked more like a giant spider that spun neon pink silk had taken up residence on her head. "Are you in there?"

Zin startled from his papery mediation. When he saw me waiting outside the window, he jolted like a horsefly had just bit his backside. Pretending as if he hadn't seen me, he hurriedly slipped the paper under a half-full ten-pound sack of peanuts he keeps on hand for the times when the Flynns ask for a raise. Slip them a few peanuts and they forget most any other desire.

"Come in," he called and waved her in. When he met my eye again, I smiled pleasantly, as if I wasn't boiling with curiosity over what had been on that sheet.

Molly entered and Zin's eyes went straight to the sculpture that was her hair.

"You know," he said, "you really should keep the style simple so it doesn't detract from the act."

"I know, but tonight's the debut of my new song. Thought I'd do something special."

I should probably have mentioned Molly, in addition to being a high-flying mini-taur, also performs songs while the gremlins take down and set up equipment between acts. Most of her songs are about growing up poor, her working hours, or pleading with her cheating husband's lover to back off.

"And you came here to sing me that song?" Zin asked in a way that made it clear he hoped she hadn't.

"No, silly. I came to tell you something I didn't tell you because I thought it'd all be sorted with the Kailin, but then the Kailin didn't show up, and—"

"Molly, I do have work to do before we open. My head is killing me trying to figure out these stupid numbers. The sums, they just don't—" He shoved aside a stack of receipts. "Please, just get to the point."

"Right, so I heard Gladys threaten Porter the night he died and now he's dead and now she's gone. So I just think that looks miles more suspicious than some newbie who only yelled at Porter a few times. And, well, who really wanted his job."

I groaned. This was not helping Cordelia's case. But Zin wasn't thrown off by Molly's fast-pitch prattle.

"Gladys threatened him? I mean, more than usual?"

"Yep, sure as a Sasquatch poops in the woods."

"Thanks, Molly. I'll look into this, or have Boris or Reinhart look into it. I've got too much on my plate right now. You haven't seen a handler from Abbott's come by, have you? Then again, what am I going to do if one does show up? It's not like I can afford the wages Abbott pays his people. I wonder if I can bribe one of the Flynns to do it?" He gave a watery smile and gestured limply toward the peanuts.

"You know, you probably could. But sorry, sweetie, I haven't seen anyone new come by. Still, you did great yesterday. Duncan and I know the act upside down and sideways, so don't sweat it."

"Thanks, Molly." And he did look somewhat relieved. There's one thing about Molly's perpetually chipper attitude: It's hard to stay down in the dragon dung heap when she's around.

When we left Zin's, I asked Molly to tell Cordelia the good news because, well, before I left the Cantina earlier, I'd ordered another omelet and the rich scent of melting gruyére was in the air. I know, I know, a woman's life was on the line, but you didn't taste that omelet. Or the half loaf of toasted brioche slathered in butter and lavender honey…

CORDELIA: Seriously, Duncan? That's why Molly came that morning?
DUNCAN: What? It's not like anyone was barging through the gates to drag you off to the Pits just yet.
CORDELIA: We need to have a serious discussion about your priorities.
DUNCAN: Priorities?
CORDELIA: Friends before omelets.
DUNCAN: Even ones with gruyére?
CORDELIA: Even ones with gruyére.

Anyway, as I was enjoying my second breakfast, I caught sight of Zin speaking with Boris. The brownies did their housekeeping at night and never seemed to need much sleep. So, during the day, they were often bored. Which could be how bogarts happen. I mean, what better way to create work for yourself than to make a new mess of surfaces you've just cleaned? Unfortunately, their employers don't see the logic in this, especially since bogarts, while they're making those messes, tend to break things. Usually expensive things.

Boris nodded in response to whatever it was Zin had said. I assumed he was agreeing to track down Gladys since, soon after I slipped the final cheesy bit of perfectly folded egg into my mouth, the lead brownie headed out the gates with Humphrey by his side. As the two passed the ticket booth, they waved a farewell to Reinhart, who was making notations in the day's account books — and likely recording who was in the Cantina so he could compare his tally to what Pepper noted in our dukie books.

After I finished eating, I cleared out of the Cantina when a trio of brownies showed up to get the space rearranged to serve as the concessions area for the day's guests. Under Helga's command, they performed the task in record time.

At half past ten came the clang of the bell announcing the gates would be opening in thirty minutes, a signal to get our butts in place. I started toward the Tent to do some warm-up exercises, but before I'd gotten far, my nostrils twitched at an odor in the air. A behemoth-sized odor.

Now, you'd think being about the size of a train's caboose, Benny would be hard to forget, but Benny's not much of a complainer and typically accepts life as it wanders past him. Which meant, with Cordelia locked up, no one had thought to tend to Benny, and he hadn't been fed or scrubbed since yesterday morning. The entire area surrounding his wallow was thick with his pungent scent. Several members of the troupe passed by to get to their stations, pinching their noses as they cast judgmental looks at the poor creature.

When he saw me approaching, Benny bellowed a cry of hunger so pitiful I worried the animal activist people might come rushing in and shut us down.

They tried that once. One of them happened to be spying on us the one day of the year when I had to have my wings clipped. The discomfort's not much more than a pinch and a bit of a stinging sensation until Porter would put salve over the wounds. But, well, I'm not very tolerant of pain, and I might have yowled more than strictly necessary. The activist guy who saw the incident went off the rails with fury at the indignity and torture I was being subjected to.

Problem for him was, by the time he got back with a herd of his friends and the authorities, I was sitting down contentedly enjoying a treat. And it's really hard to make a claim of abuse stick when a dragon's got a curry-filled omelet and a mound of samosas before him.

As for Benny, we needed to get him fed and we most definitely needed to get him cleaned up. I enlisted the help of Conrad and Flora. The moment Benny saw Flora, he began drooling and pointing to his mouth with his broad, webbed forepaw.

"We'll do that later," Flora told him. "Now, since you've already got a head start with that empty belly, I really think you could benefit from a four-day fast to flush the toxins from your system." Benny hung his head low at the prospect. Even Conrad looked doubtful. After all, if Benny was whining this bad after one day without food, what would he sound like after several days of starvation? But Flora failed to see our hesitancy and suggested a juice fast to bring his body back into balance.

"I really don't think we have time for that," I said, trying very hard not to move my lips. "Flora, find him some greens and some grains to fill him up. Conrad, if you scrub, I'll beat my wings to help clear the air. Sound good?"

"No, it sounds demeaning," he said. Flora was already humming a cheerful tune as she cantered off to collect supplies. "But I'll do it. Only to help Zin out, though. No visitor is going to stick around or tell their friends to come here if this smell is the first thing that hits them when they walk in."

So Conrad and I scrubbed. Benny wavered between purring with the pleasure of being bathed and moaning over the agony of being hungry. Just as Conrad was getting a particularly tough spot under Benny's armpit, Flora returned with a sackful of food. The sight of the treats roused Benny. He began flopping around in ecstasy, and only stopped when Conrad and I issued a round of stern threats. I now understood Cordelia's frustration with me the morning before when I'd muddied her sparkling clean behemoth.

I don't know exactly where Flora found them, but she'd brought back clusters of grass stalks, along with a bushel's worth of calendula, lavender, and assorted other flowers I hoped weren't poisonous.

The thought of poison sent a stab of grief through me. I hid the tears prickling my eyes by concentrating on

Flora's other offerings. She'd apparently convinced Pepper to hand over as much stale bread as she could spare. Which probably meant no bread pudding tonight, but I suppose keeping Benny happy was worth the sacrifice of another egg-y indulgence.

While Flora fed a heavily drooling Benny, I helped shift him so Conrad could finish up by wiping away the gunk lodged in the webbing between Benny's toes. With my wings fluttering in the breeze, the odor of Benny's stench was soon replaced by the rosy scent of Benny's favorite soap.

We'd just gotten the chore done when Zin headed over with the first group of customers for his Monsters and Marauders Tour (a new gimmick Conrad had come up with a month ago).

"Our next stop brings us to a most dangerous beast, not to be trifled with." Zin pinched his lips, biting back a grin when a child began to whimper. The group was still positioned at the edge of a small stand for souvenirs, and they couldn't yet see Benny. "Ladies and gentleman, two more steps and you will witness the Barbaric Behemoth of the Bayou. Those who frighten easily should remain here."

Flora quickly threw a sheet over Benny to hide him. I just hoped he wouldn't wallow too much as Zin explained the horrors of the behemoth, the mangled state of their victims, and their insatiable blood lust. The whimpering child now cried in fear, one woman shrieked in horror, and all the men tried to appear brave, but I could smell their apprehension.

Then Zin guided his hesitant group around, grinned at them, then whisked the sheet back. After a momentary silence, most everyone let out a delighted, "*Awww!*" as they took in the sight of Benny, who was nibbling on a stem of daisy, the cheery flower bouncing up and down as he munched blissfully away.

CHAPTER 21
AN UNEXPECTED ALIBI

Although we would be open all day, the circus did have a sort of dinner period. After all, we put on physically demanding shows — well, except for Benny — and that physical work left us ravenous. If we didn't take a meal break, we wouldn't have the energy for the evening performances, and people would demand their money back when Brutus Fangwrath, Deadliest Dragon in the West, did little more than clutch at his growling belly.

We didn't kick people out for this respite. First, it would be a nightmare trying to round everyone up to shoo them out. Second, a ticket gave you access to the circus grounds for the whole day, and some people did indeed stay for the whole day. However, Zin had learned from his father and his grandfather that there was a lull in the late afternoon when the early birds had worn themselves out and the people who wanted to catch the evening performance for a bit of fun after work hadn't shown up yet.

The few guests who were still wandering around during this lull found enough amusement in Eisenberg's

Entertainment Alley where they could play the test-your-skills (-and-earn-Zin-some-money) games or they could whirl around on rides that we had to hope the gremlins were keeping in good repair.

Since few people could speak Gremlinian, it was always difficult to tell if they understood our instructions. They're a species who adore repairing things, but like brownies, a rogue few unleash their boredom by making a mess of things just for the fun of it. Unlike the easy clean up after a brownie fit, the damage a gremlin does can be life threatening. So far, all our gremlins seemed happy in their work, but until he found an interpreter, Zin wasn't installing any loop-the-loop rides anytime soon.

It was during our Opening Day dinner break that Gladys reappeared. Not voluntarily, mind you. Humphrey was prodding her along, while Boris told her that if she confessed the truth, the Kailin might go easy on her. To which Gladys kept declaring she had nothing to confess.

Well, and that she'd kill them both if they didn't let her go.

With Helga watching admiringly, Humphrey marched Gladys over to Zin's office. Perhaps it's because we spend our lives providing entertainment for other people, but circus folk are always desperate for an unexpected diversion. Which meant a fair number of us joined the brownies and their prisoner, taking our egg sandwiches, hay smoothies, or bowls of toasted nuts with us. Dinner and a show. A rare treat.

"We've apprehended the suspect, Ely," said Boris, standing prouder than normal. Even his ears looked pointier — well, except the one Humphrey had ripped the tip off of during their fight.

"I am not a suspect," insisted Gladys, her hair shone in a gleaming golden braid down her back.

"You were heard threatening your husband."

"I always threatened him."

"Told you so," whispered Molly.

"Yes, but this time you threatened him and the threat happened," Boris said. "And someone is in the Cells right now, someone who has been sentenced to the Pits for something she might not have done."

"And who might that be?"

"Cordelia Quinn."

Gladys nodded her head as if this wasn't the least bit surprising. "Knew it all along. Wasn't me anyway, so it had to be her."

Zin sighed and dropped into a rickety wooden chair. The thing barely looked strong enough to hold up a pixie, let alone a full-grown, two-hundred-pound satyr. The chair creaked under him and I swear the legs trembled.

"Gladys," Zin said, sounding like he was nearing the end of his rope, "please just tell us what happened and whether or not you can account for your whereabouts last night."

She glanced around at us.

"Do I gotta do it in front of all them?"

Zin nodded and fixed a look on her that said he would lock her in the Cells himself if she didn't start telling her story right then and there.

"Fine, but if any of you—" she whipped around,

pointing her index finger at us "—make a single comment, I'll kill you." She turned back to Zin. "So, here's the deal, I wanted a divorce from Porter. To which he replied that he loved me. And I said if he loved me, he wouldn't spend all his free time with that dragon. And before you interrupt, I know it's his job, but it's not like Duncan can't take care of himself now and then. It's no wonder I had to seek attention elsewhere. And when that attention turned to love, I wanted a divorce."

"Fergus, you mean?" Zin asked. "You were really going to leave Porter for Fergus?"

"Oh lord, no. Fergus was a fun distraction, but I knew he was two-timing on me. Like he really thought I didn't know he was off placing his head in the lap of a *maiden*." She said the final word like it tasted of Benny's push broom after a good scrubbing. "I know some cousins of the Skirskis, and let me tell you, that Zola he was lusting after at Abbott's hasn't been a maiden since she was fourteen."

Nearly everyone shot a look at Fergus, who pretended not to notice our stares, instead remaining focused on Gladys as she continued to rant.

"But show Fergus a good lap and he'll believe anything. I mean, I had him convinced I was only twenty-five." She stopped abruptly, perhaps realizing she might have confessed to more than she meant to. "Of course twenty-five's not a big stretch since I'm only twenty-nine," backpedalled the woman who'd had a delta of crow's feet at her eyes for at least the past decade.

"Please, Gladys," said Zin wearily, "we don't have much

time before the evening acts begin. If it wasn't Fergus you were with, who was it?"

"Alfred Abbott himself."

"He's ninety-five," Zin blurted, nearly tipping over the wobbling chair with the force of his outburst.

"Which means he's had plenty of time to learn a trick or two." Gladys looked around with her eyebrows tartly arched, as if making sure we knew exactly what she was implying. "He's also learned how to treat a lady, how to make her feel special. You know age is only a number, Zin. Anyways, I needed a divorce. Alfie had proposed to me, I love him, and I wanted to marry him."

"For his money?" A fair point. Abbott's was one of the few small circuses that was bringing in a substantial share of the entertainment profit. Gladys didn't say no to the question, but the small lift of one shoulder, the tiny tilt of her head toward that shoulder was a clear, *Perhaps.* "So what did Porter say? Why would he want to be with you after he knew what you'd been up to?"

"He stubbornly refused the divorce. He said Abbott's was a rival to you and he wouldn't give a rival the satisfaction of winning." Zin's chest puffed up with a touch of pride at that. "Then he went out with that stupid dragon, got drunk, and got dead. Good riddance to him."

"Alibi," Boris said. "You don't have an alibi. How do we know you didn't poison him?"

"The moment he left to drink with Duncan, I went straight to Alfie's. I stayed the night with him. We didn't get much sleep."

"But you were here in the morning," said Boris, since Zin was too busy looking disgusted to ask any questions.

"Yeah, I came back here to pack and to tell Porter we were through, divorce or not. The minute I got back, I went to the caravan. I expected Porter to be there, but he wasn't, so I packed up my things while I waited. I was there maybe ten, fifteen minutes and Porter still hadn't shown up.

"Well, he might not want to hear it right before Opening Day, but I was in no mood to leave the matter 'til later. I wanted it done and over, so I went to the Tent where I knew he'd be. And well, he was. Just, you know, not as I expected. Then, I suppose I panicked and took off right back to Alfie's arms. Alfie's *valet*," she emphasized the job title, driving home the point that Zin probably didn't even know what a valet was, "can confirm when I arrived, when I left, and when I returned."

"And when you came back, did you think Porter might agree to a divorce after he'd already said no?" Zin asked, sounding like he was still wrapping his head around Gladys Kohl and Alfred Abbott as a couple.

"I didn't care what he said. I was going to make sure he knew I had no intention of staying with him. Even if I was forced to live with Alfie in sin."

So said the woman who was two-timing her husband with Abbott, while also two-timing Abbott with Fergus. Wait, is that three-timing? Or do you multiply? Four-timing?

"That doesn't mean you didn't poison Porter," said Zin. "He told me you'd been demanding he have meals at your caravan instead of the Cantina for a while. You could have been putting something in his food. Slowly poisoning him. I've heard of dissatisfied wives doing that very thing."

"Um, Zin," said Boris, "we're fairly certain he died of behemoth poison."

"And?" Zin snapped.

"It's not instantaneous, but it is a relatively fast-acting poison, takes maybe an hour or two. It also doesn't build up in the system like arsenic or banshee tears. He would have had to be poisoned the very night of his death."

I wondered then, and have many times since, if Boris might not have been better suited sticking with his detective rather than working for a ragtag circus where rules were something that happened to other people.

"You know," Zin said to Boris, "you could have told me that sooner."

"Well," sniped Gladys, "how about *I* tell you that Porter never ate a thing I made him. Claimed I burnt things when everyone knows a good char brings out the flavor of food. Especially toast. Anyways, it would have been pretty hard for me to poison someone that picky, now wouldn't it?"

"That still doesn't exclude you. You could have been around that night doing—" Zin fluttered his hands in the air as if summoning the right word. "Well, doing something, that's for sure."

"Someone should go to Abbott's to confirm Mrs. Kohl's story and her timeline," Boris suggested.

Since he wouldn't be needed for the centaur act for at least another hour, Conrad volunteered to go while most everyone else returned to their stands and displays and shows, telling anyone who remained behind to fill them in on each and every detail if anything new happened.

Fergus, for his part, surprised us all by playing the better man. Or maybe he was just trying to show off. When Gladys emerged from Zin's caravan (Humphrey and Boris acting as guards), the unicorn strode up — his mane slicked back, his horn gleaming with a fresh coat of polish — and said sincerely, "Your lap was one of the best. Quite comfortable, really. I wish you much happiness with Abbott."

He then dipped his head in a slight bow, turned around and walked away, leaving behind a stunned and, for once, silent Gladys.

CHAPTER 22
THE TROUBLESOME BLUE FLOOF

Wanting to make sure Fergus was truly all right, Flora cantered over to join him as he sauntered off. I didn't catch the entire conversation as they walked away, but I did hear him ask her if the Kailin might be coming by later to review the case.

So, perhaps the mane styling and the horn polish hadn't been for Gladys's benefit.

Since Conrad had earned a name for himself in his youth by winning several long-distance races, it took him little time to make the trip to Abbott's and back. "Barely a warm up," he claimed when I walked with him over to Zin's, eager to hear his report, even though my act started in less than thirty minutes.

When we reached Zin's, Boris and Humphrey were still guarding Gladys — although I'm not sure how much guarding they were doing as they were both slumped against the side of Zin's caravan with their eyes closed.

Gladys was busy reading the palm of a very attentive

Helga. Helga jerked her hand away when I nudged Boris and Humphrey before Zin came out and caught them napping.

"The valet and a couple other people confirm what Gladys told us," said Conrad. "Oh, and Helga, your cousin says hello and wants to hear more about your new—"

"Yes," squeaked Helga, her face as red as the paint on Zin's caravan. "My new hat. She sure does love hats." She then tittered nervously as she did everything she could to avoid meeting Humphrey's eyes.

"We must let the suspect go," Boris said despairingly. I guess his first case wasn't going as quickly or as easily as he'd hoped.

"It's about time," huffed Gladys. "I'd like to kill you all for embarrassing me in front of my Alfie." She then caught herself. "Perhaps I should stop using that phrase." This was followed with a dismissive shrug. "Nah, I'll be who I want. Alfie loves me for who I am, and the rest of you can all—" She made a rude gesture, then stormed off.

There was nothing for it. The dinner break was long over, our entertainment was through, and Zin was pestering me about why the hell I wasn't in the Tent getting ready for my act. A question I could have spat right back at him if my mind hadn't been so preoccupied with the conundrum of Porter's death.

Gladys didn't do it. Cordelia probably didn't do it. But who did? Even after the show began, I so was distracted with the possibilities, I nearly missed Molly a couple times. But since the audience loved the thrill of seeing a mini-centaur nearly being splattered to bits, and since

Molly thrived on being the *centaur* of attention (her words, not mine), Zin merely scowled at me rather than reading me the riot act over my screw-ups.

For the final bit of derring-do of our performance that night, I was meant to balance on one leg, spread my wings, and hold my arms outstretched for Molly to walk across them. It was uncomfortable on a good day. This was not a good day and my arms shook with the effort of holding them steady while also supporting Molly's weight.

The trickiest part was when she needed to make the return trip. On the outgoing trip, I would tilt my head forward and she crossed from right to left arm along the broad expanse of my back. On her return journey, to make the feat more challenging and therefore more exciting, I would tip my head back. Molly would then jump from my right shoulder and land on the left one. Or sometimes my biceps if she got a bit too much momentum behind her leap.

And before you think this is the most ridiculously cruel thing you can imagine doing to a dragon, the stunt was my idea. What can I say? The audience loved it and they paid well to see it.

As she approached my shoulder and prepared to make her return journey jump, Molly chided me about needing to hold still. I did my best to focus my attention and keep my arms rigid, but the real trouble came when she made the leap.

Remember earlier I told you she had shown up with the blue, fluffy thing on her head? Well, when she leapt over my neck, the upward motion sent the floof dipping down and brushing right up against my nostrils. I'd been able to avoid the damn thing so far that evening, but this was a direct assault.

I did my best to hold back the sneeze mounting in me. The pressure built as Molly landed gracefully on my left shoulder. When she began her prancing steps toward my elbow, the tickling in my nose turned into an eye-watering prickle. Then, just as she stepped onto the crook of my elbow, the sneeze refused to be held back any longer.

I did manage to contain the majority of the force behind that sneeze, but when you're balancing a tiny horse-human on your arm, that is not the time to make jerky movements. Molly slipped. The audience shrieked. Zin cursed. Even Molly swore me to the Pits as she held onto the scaly skin of my arm with her human hands.

Centaurs might be stronger than full humans, but their arms still don't have the power to hold up the weight of their horsey bodies.

Molly's grip faltered.

The ground beneath us was covered in sawdust, but it wasn't thick and wouldn't provide much cushion. One or more of Molly's body parts was going to break if she hit the ground. To my ears the entire world had gone silent as fear focused my every sense on what I'd done.

Molly's hooves, legs, and arms flailed helplessly as she fell. Fear for her hollowed my gut, but it also sparked an instinctive need to react.

I jumped off the pedestal and swooped down to the ground. It still seems bewildering whenever I look back on it, but somehow I got under Molly, spreading myself flat on my back under her as her legs galloped in midair and her body twisted as if fighting against gravity.

Swirling sawdust all around, I whipped my wings forward, holding them so they formed a sort of canopy about a meter above my body. If they hadn't been clipped, I could have doubled them over like a cloak. Instead, they just barely met.

Someone screamed. It had a neighing quality to it, so it may have been Molly. And then came a *thunk* and a weight against my wings. The weight remained there momentarily, and through the webbing between my wing bones I saw the outline of a small centaur. There was a pause as if everyone was holding their breath. Then the weight was gone, and the audience roared out with whoops and cheers, stomping their feet so hard with excitement it rumbled through my spine.

I opened my wings and sat up to see Zin and Reinhart scowling over my nearly lethal fumble. Molly, however, was bowing in all directions to the audience. And they were eating it up. When she turned to face me, I expected to see anger. I expected to have my delicate ears riddled with reprimands. But Molly was glowing. She trotted over and gave my neck a hug. Thankfully, the blue floof had fallen off at some point. I hoped it was smashed under me.

"Best stunt ever, Duncan!"

I was too stunned to say anything. Zin said it for me. "You nearly killed her."

"And he saved me. That was an absolute hoot! Like a living trampoline. Can we try it again? Work it into a practice session?"

Zin's scowl only deepened, but he was enough of a showman to put on a performer's broad grin when he turned to the audience, who had finally quieted down.

"Thank you all for coming to tonight's performance. Tell your friends. Tell your family. Tell one and all of Zinzendorf's Circus of Unusual Creatures, where every act brings the thrill of the unexpected."

He bowed, sweeping his top hat before him as he did so. The audience cheered again as Molly pranced around me, the centaurs took their final trot, and the Flynns bounded down from their trapezes with a flourish of tumbles and twists to join in on the evening's farewell.

It always takes a while for the audience to shuffle out of the Tent. As they do so, we work to clear up the props and equipment from our acts. As I was picking up my pedestal, Zin came up to me. I tensed, expecting another tongue lashing.

"Sorry for yelling at you, Duncan," he said.

He's lucky he was standing to my side because, had he been standing in front of me, my jaw dropping to the floor probably would have hit him in the head. I knew Zin had been out of sorts lately, but this was an entire lapse of personality. Ely Zinzendorf did not apologize. Ever. I've seen his broad hoof come down on an old lady's toes and he still didn't apologize.

He gestured me over to where a backdrop painted to look like a tropical island scene had been pushed out of the way. Since I'd already reduced myself back to my usual size, it would block us from the view of any lingering humans.

"It's just that I really can't afford to pay for medical expenses," he continued. "And you know your reputation, the orders are pretty clear." Those orders being that, due to my past misdeeds, if I ever harmed a performer or circus employee or audience member, the Pacific Animal Welfare agents would put me in full chains and sentence me to the Pits' work camps on the grounds that I was too dangerous to remain free. "I don't want to lose you, Duncan. Not like that." Then, resuming his usual, financially focused manner, he said, "You're one of my biggest money makers."

"Literally," I said, trying to make light of his heavy attitude. It didn't work. He gave a weak grin. "Is everything all right with the circus, Zin?" It seemed impossible we could be doing poorly. We had better food than any other circus I'd been in, and we had well-kept equipment, a reliable crew to care for that equipment, and high-quality props, even if some of those props were a bit fluffy for my taste.

"We're barely making it." There was a tremble in his voice that made me want to hug him. He cleared his throat, then abruptly said, "Look, it's not for you to worry about." An odd statement since he was clearly laying his own worry at my scaly feet. "Just try to be careful. You want to get something to drink? I've got some dandelion wine ready."

The idea of wine didn't have its usual appeal. Zin did a double take when I said I didn't feel like drinking. After all, such a statement from my lips was likely just as surprising for him as it had been for me to hear him apologize.

"You all right there, Duncan? Is it—? Well, do you mind me being your handler?"

"No, really, it's not that. You're different, but you're okay." I was about to say I'd rather have Cordelia as my handler, but Zin spoke before I could make the request.

"Good, because any extra expense will be too much, especially the expense of hiring a new handler. It should help to have Gladys off the payroll. And Quinn too, soon enough. Anyway, I just wanted to check in and make sure I didn't need to put out any help wanted ads in the *Circular*. Good job tonight, Duncan. Those were some quick reflexes."

Among the odd conversations I've had in my life, that ranked as one of the oddest. I couldn't help but wonder what had him so out of sorts, what had happened to the circus's once-stable finances, and what could make a satyr, one who had always treated me with such fairness, blindly accept Cordelia's guilt and willingly let her be dragged off to the Pits.

CHAPTER 23
A POPCORN-FUELED CHAT

Once I'd finished cleaning things up and the gates had closed for the night, I borrowed a flour sack from Pepper and scooped out the leftovers from the popcorn machine. I then headed to the Cells. Cordelia sat hunched over a small lantern and a book. I squeezed the sack of popcorn between the bars.

"Thought you might be hungry."

"Starving." Cordelia scrambled to the popcorn. "Any cotton candy?"

"I'll check. Wait, they aren't withholding food, are they? They can't do that."

"No, a centaur named Flora has been put in charge of my care. She brought me some food, but it's all green salads and herb soup and this weird mushy stuff she says is made of soybean curds. I've been dying for something with flavor," she said, then crammed a handful of popcorn in her mouth. "She also brought the lantern and this." She held up the book. It was titled *A Beginner's Guide to Mediation*.

"Enjoying it?"

"Not really. So, what did you find out about Gladys?"

"Sorry, I should have come to tell you about that straight away, but the show..." She nodded to indicate she understood. "She has an alibi, and it checks out. Godzilla's gonads," I chuckled, "I sound like Boris. Anyway, she's off the hook."

"And I have how much time?"

"The jailor comes back the day after tomorrow."

"And tomorrow's another full day of performances, isn't it?"

"Yeah, a weekend show. We'll be on all day."

Cordelia, sounding very much like a little chimera, let out a growl of frustration.

"That's not going to work. I need to figure out who did this. And to do that, I need out of here."

"Yeah, thing is," I rubbed the back of my neck, thinking of my conversation with Zin, "I don't think Zin's going to go for that."

"Then you need to find out who killed Porter. And why. I'm not going to the Pits for something I didn't do."

"But Fergus and Gladys are the only people who would have a reason to kill Porter. Most other people liked him."

"Except for me, you mean?" I didn't answer. As Judge Javert had said, it did seem open-and-shut when you looked at it from an outsider's perspective. After all, I'd only just met Cordelia, what did I know about her past, her secrets?

Cordelia shoved more popcorn into her mouth and, unfortunately, started speaking before she was done chewing.

CORDELIA: Sorry about that, everyone. I can't begin to tell you how hungry I was.

"Where did the poison come from, do you think?" she asked. "What I mean is, how did it get inside Porter?"

I know it sounds idiotic, but I honestly hadn't given much thought to this obvious question. Boris had mentioned it could have been delivered by food or drink or a salve, but after finding the wine barrel empty, we'd all been focused more on the who, and had neglected the how of the deed. Still, in our defense, it was our first murder case.

"I'm not sure. Maybe in his food? His dinner that night? Boris said it's not the fastest acting poison, but I'm not sure exactly how behemoth saliva works."

Cordelia stood up and began pacing the confined space as if stretching her legs would loosen up her thoughts.

"It would be good to find out. I know some species are immune to it, otherwise everything in a behemoth's swamp or riverbed would be dead. And is it slow-acting to all species, or just humans? You need to learn more about it, just the basics, just to give us an idea. And then—"

I held up my forefeet, signaling her to stop this lava flow of ideas.

"Hold hold hold on a minute. Performances. Me. Tomorrow. How am I going to have a chance to do any of this? Plus," I said, using my paws to indicate my body, "I'm not exactly built for stealth."

Cordelia stopped her pacing to take a swig from a glass containing a substance that looked more like swamp muck than a beverage. Cordelia grimaced as she swallowed. She tapped her foot while pondering what was left inside the glass.

After several moments, she threw back the rest of the muck. Grimacing, she then snapped the fingers of her empty hand, pointed her index finger at me, and said, "Gremlins." I thought it was a mild curse over Flora's concoction, so I didn't respond. "Duncan, you have gremlins working here, right? I thought I saw some adjusting the lighting equipment my first day."

"Oh right, gremlins. There's a team of about ten, fifteen. It's hard to tell since they're always scurrying around, getting into places most of us never go. Are you thinking the gremlins did it? I dunno, doesn't seem their style, they're more likely to—"

"No, they're not suspects. But they could help buy some time for you to ask more questions. If they can screw up something with the main electrical box, Zin won't be able to power the arcade games or the rides, and it'll be too dark in the Tent to have any acts. He'll have to close up shop while things are under repair. That'll give us — well, you — time to investigate."

It was a pretty ingenious idea, but she should have made the proposal without mentioning Zin's name. He'd just confided in me that the circus was on shaky financial footing. He'd indicated we were keeping our heads above water, but only just. If he had to refund tickets for an entire day, what would that do to his bottom line?

"I don't think Zin can afford a whole day of lost ticket sales."

"It wouldn't have to be the whole day. He could open in the morning like usual. People come, people browse. Keep them here until lunchtime when they'll buy the concession stand's overpriced food and drinks. Then, sometime in mid-afternoon, the gremlins do their work. Zin has to shut down, but he's already sold plenty of tickets and trinkets for the day."

"And if people want their money back?"

"Some will, sure. But I've been working circuses long enough to know how our esteemed guests flow in and out of the grounds. By mid-afternoon, most of the early birds will have had their fill. They'll probably already have left anyway, or will be getting ready to. You only need a few hours, then the power can come back on right about the time when people who come for a little evening entertainment will be arriving. I'm sure you can get plenty of questions asked during the downtime."

I have to say, all this did prove to me one thing: Cordelia definitely had a lifetime of circus experience to understand the ever-changing tide of circus guests so well. She'd only missed one point.

"But some people do stay all day. And they stay because they want to get their money's worth."

While Cordelia thought about this, I stole a pawful of popcorn.

"Got it," she said, and did the finger snap and point thing again. "Suggest to Zin that the people who were planning to stick around all day can use their tickets to come back the next day. He won't lose anything, and the people won't feel like they're getting screwed over."

"Okay," I said, not entirely convinced, although her idea had promise. It would free up some time and Zin wouldn't lose out on a day's revenue. "But that still doesn't help me figure out where to begin. I don't exactly have any experience with this sort of thing."

"And you're sure you didn't poison him?" Cordelia asked as she swirled a finger around the inside of the glass to get the rest of the goop. I glared at her. A nice menacing glare that should have had her limbs trembling. But there was no knocking of knees, no rattling of bones. She merely shrugged. "Accidentally, I mean. You were pretty gone that night."

"A little wine relaxes me after a tough day. And I'll have you know, I've had nothing to drink today. Or last night," I added, surprising myself by what a teetotaler I'd become.

"Okay, so not you. Not me, Fergus, or Gladys. Anyone else have something against Porter?"

I shook my head, feeling a little stupid for not knowing the answer. I suppose the vast amounts of time I spent drinking had taken precedence over observing the personal dynamics of Zin's circus.

"Fergus and Gladys are the only ones I can think of who would have had something to gain if Porter died."

"Gain," Cordelia said, chewing on the word as she munched on another handful of popcorn. She then looked into the empty glass. I offered to get her some water, took the glass, and went off to fill it from the hose.

When I returned, she had gone back to her cross-legged position on the floor and was continuing to work on the popcorn.

"What happens if Zin can't find a new handler?" she asked.

"What's that have to do with Porter's death?"

"Bear with me here." She twirled a finger next to her temple. "Thoughts are swirling. You said Zin can't afford to close down for a day. If he's having financial troubles, would he consider selling you? Or," she said, cutting off my protest, "is there someone who *thinks* Zin would sell you if he needed the money? I mean, bringing on a new handler is expensive. There's not a bunch of Cordelia Quinns barging in and volunteering to work with a dragon with your reputation."

Yes, I had a reputation. I had a tough time in my youth with bad handlers. I fought them, lashed out at their treatment of me, and of course, there was that incident that landed me on the Pacific Animal Welfare's list of dangerous creatures, but I try not to think about that.

Still, Cordelia was right. Dragon handling was a prestigious position in the circus world, and it earned that renown for being dangerous. After all, we're talking about managing a giant reptile who could turn you into a piece of bar-be-que if you crossed him. It certainly wasn't working with something cute and fluffy and mostly harmless like the chimera kittens in the petting zoo.

The scarcity of handlers, and especially of good handlers, meant they commanded a decent amount of bargaining power. And they were rarely denied the high wages or the sign-on bonuses they asked for. Which explained why Zin might not be able to afford to bring in a new one and why he'd asked if I minded him being my handler.

Cordelia had been the exception. She had trained and worked for years to gain the experience to handle me. She wanted the job so badly she was willing to work for a Mop's low wages just to get her foot in the proverbial door. Which again made me wonder why Zin wasn't doing everything he could not to lose Cordelia to the Pits. Why was he not looking more deeply into who killed Porter? I didn't like the answers lighting up in my brain.

"Zin said he'll handle me," is all I said. "I know my routine. It's not like I require much handling work."

"Zin can't do it forever, Duncan. He's got other responsibilities. I know he has that Reinhart as his bookkeeper, but he's got the day-to-day management of the circus to consider. I've heard the paperwork alone is enough to eat up half of an owner's waking hours. If he's spending his time working with you, things are going to slip past his notice and the circus is going to suffer for it. So, again, who would gain from Porter's death?"

I hated myself for the name that sprang to the tip of my tongue. I might be the biggest draw of the circus, but I was also its biggest liability. I ate the most, I required the largest caravan, and I'd just nearly racked up an enormous vet bill to repair Molly's broken limbs.

Now that the name was there, it seemed so obvious. After all, who had seemed unfazed by the murder of Porter? Who had taken Judge Javert aside just prior to the rushed trial of Cordelia Quinn? What had the judge been patting in his pocket as he declared it was an open-and-shut case?

"Zin," I said gloomily. "Zin would gain. Porter had to go because he would never have let Zin sell me. I know that doesn't make sense, Zin's the owner and everything, but Zin's not like some owners whose word is law. He wants to keep his workers happy. But who knows, maybe he'd gotten an offer he couldn't refuse. Porter really turned me around, you know." Cordelia nodded. I was sure she'd followed my career, the good and the bad parts. "I'm a hot commodity now according to the *Circular*. With Porter out of the way, Zin could probably get enough for me to boost his bottom line for years to come."

"You need to find out what Zin's been up to. I know he's your friend, but it's not fair for Porter's killer to get away with murder. Do you agree?"

I absent-mindedly nibbled on the popcorn. What had Zin been saying to the judge? How did Zin get Porter's hook? What exactly had Zin and Porter argued about that night? Did he get rid of Porter to make it easier to sell me? Could Zin really be that ruthless and underhanded? Satyrs weren't known for their gentle nature. They could be unscrupulous and malicious louts, but Zin a murderer? I hated to think of him that way, but I also hated the image of Cordelia up to her knees in dragon dung.

"Agreed," I said reluctantly. "But what can I do? How can I find out what he's done, if he's done anything?"

"Porter was poisoned with behemoth saliva. Has anyone asked Benny what he saw that night? Or, no, it couldn't have been that night. I was with him almost the whole time. Maybe in the week or so leading up to that night. Did anyone come to him to take his saliva?"

"Dear Smaug, I should hope not. You have smelled him, right?"

"I have smelled portions of that creature that will live on in my nightmares until I die. But no one stuck Porter's head under Benny's mouth and made him swallow the drool. Someone collected the saliva and kept it until the right moment. And the right moment might have been when I showed up, giving whoever it was the perfect scapegoat." Cordelia emptied her glass and I fetched her another to wash away some of the popcorn's six kilos of sodium.

"Okay, here's what I think you need to do," Cordelia said after guzzling the water. "First, find out who might have taken Benny's saliva. Then— Oh, you see it, don't you? It's perfect."

I wondered if the overdose of salt was giving her hallucinations.

"What's perfect?" I asked, as I hooked the popcorn sack with my claw and tried to drag it away from her.

"The wine. The barrel of wine. You should find out where it came from."

I too had thought it was the wine. That's why I'd inspected the barrel on the morning we'd found Porter. But the keg had carried none of the pineapple-almond scent of behemoth saliva. There was also another problem with the wine-as-murder-weapon idea.

"Can't be the wine. I drank plenty of it. Charlie and Benny had their share too, and we're not dead."

"Again, ask someone, find a book, whatever, just figure out how behemoth poison works. Like I said, I know it doesn't affect fish or water birds. Maybe it's the same with other creatures. Once we know that, we can figure out how Porter was poisoned, and maybe that will lead us to who did the poisoning."

"You're really very good at this, you know."

"I'll do whatever it takes not to end up in the Pits."

Despite the unusually warm evening, Cordelia's arms shivered involuntarily. Seeming not to notice I'd removed the popcorn, she hunched over her book once more. When I didn't take the hint to leave, she said, "Good night, Duncan," without looking up at me.

"Good night, Cordelia."

CHAPTER 24
AFTER HOURS ENTRY

I left Cordelia to settle in for the night. I tried to sleep, but from my bed I could see the edge of Zin's caravan. Zin. What had he and Porter argued about? Why had it left Porter so rattled? Did it have to do with Zin's money troubles?

I hated to think Zin could possibly kill Porter, then let Cordelia take the blame for it. But when people are in trouble financially, you never know what they might do. And why had he told me of his troubles? Was he working his way up to a confession, or was it a warning that I might be up for auction soon?

I didn't want to leave Zin's circus. Not only did I view most of the troupe as family, but I knew there were owners out there who saw their creatures as little better than livestock. They even referred to us as *cattle*. And not pampered cattle being primped and tended to for a prize at the county fair. More like cattle that had stomped through your rose garden, kicked out your dining room window, and pooped all over your doorstep.

And yes, I have known cows like that. Lesson of the

day: Do not cross a cow, those ladies have a serious vengeful streak.

With such thoughts in my head and the lack of wine in my belly, I couldn't sleep. I turned away from the view out my window and onto my back to stare up at my vision board. This, by the way, was Flora's idea to help me identify my aims without feeling constrained by them. Or something like that. All I know is it covers up a water stain from when my caravan's roof leaked last fall.

An hour passed, and I was more awake than that time Charlie dared me to eat a pound of Pepper's Italian espresso beans. I gave up on trying to sleep and went out for a wander around the grounds. I was just making my circuit past the main gate — locked not only by Zin's magic, but by Reinhart's giant padlock — when someone whispered my name. I then caught the stench of cigarette smoke.

"Fergus? Is that you?"

"Yeah, I missed curfew."

"How did you get out in the first place?"

"Gates were still open."

"But Zin's barrier?"

Even with the main gates standing open, Zin's magic penned us all in. Or so I thought.

"Man, you can't keep a good unicorn down, or locked away with magical barriers. We've got special unicorn power for that sort of thing. Padlocks," he nudged the lock with his muzzle, "are another thing entirely. Can you get me in?"

"Why didn't you just wait to come back in the morning?"

184

"Zola kicked me out."

"For what?" I don't know why I asked, since I was sure I did not want to hear the answer.

"Oh, she was already in a foul mood when I showed up. Said I had a crush on the Kailin. As if. But I sweet-talked her a bit, and she found my charms irresistible. Then I make one little comment about her lap not being as soft as Gladys's lap, and she flies off the rails. Did she want me to lie to her? I mean, Zola has a nicely built lap, but sometimes a unicorn doesn't want that much support. A little cushion, you know?"

"No, I do not know. And," I said when Fergus looked about to explain, "I don't want to know. I guess that means you're lap-less now."

"Yeah, it's the bachelor's life for me," he said, kicking at the dirt with his hoof and taking a deep drag on his cigarette. "So what do you say? Do a guy a favor?"

"Only if you put that out." I indicated the stick of death between his lips. Fergus pulled one long drag, trying to get as much from the cigarette as he could, then spit it out and crushed it under his hoof.

In my usual size, I'm about eye level with the top of Zin's barrier. But when boosted to show size, I tower over it. Not enough to step over the thing, but enough to be able to bend forward and arch my upper body over its barely detectable edge. And by *barely detectable,* I'm not referring to the six-foot tall fencing that's easily visible even in the moonlight, but the electrical buzz in the air that extends seven feet up from the ground. A magical buzzing that makes my scales tingle and my ears itch.

Leaning over carefully to keep my chest from touching the barrier, I eased my jaws over Fergus's back and closed my mouth on him just enough to hold him in my teeth. It was the same pressure I used to grasp Molly, but Molly smelled far better than Fergus. I groaned at the taste.

"I just had my coat cleaned, so don't mess it up with those fangs," Fergus said. He started to twist as if he wanted to scold me eye to eye.

"Don' twisht," I mumbled since it's not easy to annunciate with a mouth full of ashtray-flavored unicorn.

I stood back up, wanting to gag from the smell of Fergus. Even Benny's scent was tolerable in comparison. I took two steps back from the barrier, then set Fergus down. As I returned myself to a more manageable size, he inspected his coat, which showed only the slightest indentations where my teeth had gripped him. He shook, reminding me of a dog shaking off after a bath. The motion sent a ripple along his hide that ended with a flick of his head — a motion that dropped the spare cigarette behind his ear into his mouth.

"Light?" he asked.

"No."

"Ah, come on. If you do, I'll show you how to get into the beer cooler."

"No," I said, but with slightly less conviction.

"You really gotta work on that, man."

"No, I'm pretty sure I don't."

"You're a pyrodon who's afraid of fire. I still haven't decided if that's hilarious, or if it's just sad."

"Goodnight, Fergus," I said, turning to leave him.

"No, come on, man. I'm sorry. I'm just teasing. Come on, I'll walk with you. What are you doing up, anyway?"

"Couldn't sleep. Do you know anything about Zin having financial troubles?"

"Oh sure. You didn't know? Wait, guess you didn't if you're asking."

"How do you know about it?"

"Learned it from one of the Skirskis that night I wooed Zola. What?" he asked in response to my exasperated glare.

"You make it sound like you've known for a decade, when you've only known for two days."

"That's still longer than you've known." I didn't respond. Fergus could be trying, but he was one of the few of us who mingled with folks from the other circuses. This was mainly in search of new laps to rest his head on, but there were still times when his sociability turned out to be useful. "Anyway, they were speculating about whether their circus might be under the Ratcher umbrella soon."

"But Abbott's is one of the oldest circuses in the business and he's doing really well."

"Yeah, but Ratcher keeps making these offers people can't refuse. You've seen how many of the smaller circuses have been closing their tent flaps. And Abbott has that pair of young dragons."

"What's that got to do with it?"

"Man, what rock have you been hiding under? Ratcher is keen to buy up all the circuses with dragons. First, he makes an offer for the dragons themselves, then if the

187

owner won't sell, he offers to buy up the entire show. Even if the owner hems and haws for a bit, they eventually give in. Ratcher's rarely refused."

"But Ratcher runs a permanent spot in the heart of Portland. Not everyone can get to that. If the smaller circuses, the traveling circuses, close down, what are people outside of the city going to do for entertainment?"

"If they don't have a horse that can cover the distance or one of those automobile things, they'll have to pay for the Ratcher shuttle that will bring them to the Ratcher circus where they'll have to stay the night in a Ratcher hotel because the shuttle only makes return trips the next morning. He ends up getting at least quadruple from each guest per show than any traveling circus does. It's genius, man. Genius."

"And you gathered all this from the Skirskis?"

Fergus looked around covertly. "I might have other sources."

"Don't tell me you have another lap waiting for you in Ratcher's circus."

"Dear pegasus, no. I wouldn't betray Zin like that. Nah, that little bogart fellow, Humphrey, he came to me for advice."

"Advice?" I asked dubiously.

"With the ladies. He's got a crush on Helga, but doesn't know what to do about it. He's mostly been avoiding her for fear he'll screw up. Anyway, we got to talking, and he told me about this Ratcher stuff."

I recalled Humphrey's distress at seeing Porter's body, and how he'd told me Ratcher had beaten a dragon to death for not speaking. A chill tickled the ridge of spines that run down my back.

"But what's this have to do with Zin's money problems?" I asked. And yes, I realize how stupidly obvious the answer seems, but it had been a long day.

"Because I'm sure Zin has had an offer. Either for you or for the circus itself. He could sell this place and live a pretty good life. You should have heard the argument between him and Porter about it."

"Porter knew?" The chills hit the tip of my tail and zipped right back up to my neck.

"Yeah, I think it was the afternoon before the night he died. I saw them in a wicked verbal battle. Porter was going on about how terribly Ratcher treated his creatures, asking questions about what was going to happen to people like Pepper if Zin shut down, and how could Zin turn his back on the people of the region whose only real joy is the circuses rolling into town."

"And Zin said what exactly?"

"Nothing. Reinhart butted in saying something about Porter being an employee and how he shouldn't be trying to step above his station. Then Zin tells Reinhart to mind his own business. Reinhart trudges off talking to himself like he does, and you know what Zin does?" I said I didn't. "He goes and tells Porter that Reinhart was right. Tells Porter straight to his face he's nothing more than an employee. Not a friend, not an advisor. And—"

From the caravans came a startled roar. Then all was silent again.

"Charlie," I said. "Guess he's still having those

189

nightmares despite Flora's chamomile smoothies, or whatever it is she convinces him to take. Go on, what else did he say?"

"Not much else. Zin just said if Porter wanted to remain an employee, he'd get out of his face right that instant."

"That makes no sense. Zin and Porter have known each other for over a decade. Of course they're friends. And since when does Zin not want Porter's advice? Porter's been working the circuses since he was a kid. He knows the business inside and out. Zin would be a fool not to listen to him."

"Yeah, but you know how it goes. If it's advice you don't want to hear, you don't want to hear it from anyone, friend or foe. And, like you say, Porter knew the business. Maybe he knew too much."

"What's that mean?"

"Not sure exactly, but he had to know something. He didn't like Ratcher, that's for sure."

It was true. Porter hated Ratcher almost as much as I did. And that's because Porter was a good handler. Stern when he needed to be, but never mean, never a hook user. Never like a Ratcher handler.

"You gotta dominate them," Ratcher would say to new handlers. "Make them see who's boss. They won't ever forget it."

If the handler didn't listen, Ratcher would withhold their pay. The truly good handlers would leave. The others learned to dominate us. They learned to cower us. They learned to wield a hook in the most painful way possible.

"Go back a minute, Fergus." Fergus started walking backwards. "Not what I meant. You said Ratcher is buying up dragons."

"Seems to be. I mean, you've seen the flyers, the posters for other shows. How many of them feature dragons anymore? Even a couple decades ago, nearly every show had a dragon act. Now, of the smaller circuses that are still holding onto their independence, only about a quarter of them have dragons. And I'd bet you anything all of them have received offers from Ratcher. I tell you, man, your kind are *pop-u-lar*," he said, adding extra emphasis to each syllable. "Then again, you're also becoming rarer. I guess that adds to your mystique. Unicorns, on the other hand, we breed like bunnies even in captivity. We're never going to be rare."

It was true. While we were once as common as lap-craving unicorns, so many wild dragons had been caught for circuses or private zoos, my kind were becoming as tough to find as a noodle in a haystack.

CORDELIA: *Needle. Needle in a haystack.*

DUNCAN: *But that could hurt someone. And what if it was a dirty needle? You could get a nasty infection. Drug users should really learn not to pollute.*

CORDELIA: *I think it refers to a sewing needle.*

DUNCAN: *Are you sure about that? Besides, wouldn't a noodle be just as hard to find? Unless, of course, the mice got to it first. Then you wouldn't find it at all.*

CORDELIA: *Story, Duncan. Get back to the story.*

DUNCAN: *Right.*

See, dragons don't do well in captivity as far as baby-making goes. First off, most circuses rarely have two of the same species in their collection. And while most species of pyrodon can breed with each other, some combinations result in infertile offspring. As for a pyrodon and a vermidon? Our parts don't even fit together. That's not to say some haven't tried. In my youth, there was—

Sorry, Cordelia says you don't need to know about that.

"Why would Ratcher want to buy up all these dragons, then treat them so terribly?" I asked.

"Humans, man. Humans. Can't figure them out and you'll drive yourself batty trying."

Fergus and I completed our circuit of the grounds, then went back to our caravans. I still didn't sleep. I kept thinking of what it would take to bribe the gremlins to throw a wrench into the system to stop tomorrow's show so I could help Cordelia.

Which would mean betraying Zin.

But that notion didn't bother me as much as it had earlier. After all, it seemed Zin might have already betrayed me.

CHAPTER 25
MISSING INGREDIENTS

In the Northwest, even after a hot summer day, we're usually rewarded with pleasantly cool nights. But the temperature had remained high the night of my popcorn-fueled chat with Cordelia and my uncomfortable conversation with Fergus, which meant the next day blazed in with the promise of another abnormally hot day.

CORDELIA: Just in case anyone was wondering about my well-being, the Cells do not have good air flow. If Flora hadn't sent Conrad by that morning with a block of ice, I'd have melted.
DUNCAN: And I was too hot to even want an omelet.
CORDELIA: Yes, I'm feeling very sorry for your suffering. Besides, you're a reptile, shouldn't you enjoy the heat?
DUNCAN: I descend from the British dragons of yore. We're not good with heat. Now, can I get back to the story?
CORDELIA: Go for it.

As I said, I wasn't in the mood for an omelet, but I was ready for some of the strawberry-mint iced tea Pepper made from freshly picked, heirloom berries she'd gotten from, well, wherever it was she managed to obtain her supplies. The Flynns, unfazed by the sweltering morning, were already at the Cantina, digging into thick slices of bread coated with an even thicker layer of peanut butter.

The scent of their breakfast triggered the memory of Zin guiltily hiding that sheet of expensive paper under a sack of peanuts. As I lapped up my berry-minty beverage, I closed my eyes, trying my damnedest to recall what I'd been able to glimpse on that sheet. The more I thought about it, the more I felt certain it had been a contract. The two lines. One already signed. The other waiting for a signature.

I didn't like it. Not one bit. I also didn't want to think about it, because the more I thought about it, the more Zin seemed like he could be Porter's killer. And I really didn't like that thought. So, I placed my empty tea bowl in the bin for dirty dishes, then went to distract myself by getting Benny ready for the day.

Benny isn't much of a talker. As you've seen, he can talk, but it's as slow and plodding as you might expect from a creature half the size of an omnibus and older than some American cities.

Based on the sludge in the empty bucket next to him that morning, Flora had fed Benny the same green goop she'd given Cordelia. And as usual, the green goop had moved through our gentle behemoth in the smelliest way possible. Wishing I could close off my nostrils like a deep-diving hydrodon, I picked up the scrub broom and set to work on cleaning Benny.

"Benny," I said once he'd started to rumble with pleasure, "has anyone been after your spit lately?" And yes, my brain was fighting with my lips over how ludicrous that question sounded to my ears. But I had to know. If Zin had collected saliva from Benny, I couldn't ignore my suspicions. I would have to do something. What that something might be, I had no idea.

"Flora."

A sense of relief and dismay hit me. Relief that the name hadn't been Zin's. Dismay over Flora being involved in any of this.

Benny purred and shifted so I could get to his underside. The movement sent up a plume of stink. Seriously, could we not start feeding Benny rose petals and lavender? Had anyone ever considered that maybe a change of diet would improve his overall aroma?

"Flora takes your spit?" I asked, trying to breathe in as little air as possible as I worked.

"Mmmm-hmmm. She makes a healing salve. For bruises, sprains, Porter's bad knees. My saliva. Key ingredient. Pain relief. Preservative. Good stuff." These few short words took about ten minutes to get out as he gurgled and chirruped and made all sorts of noises of animal happiness while I continued to scrub under his pits and between his toes.

I couldn't picture Flora as a murderer, but then again, no one could possibly be that nice, that "at peace" all the time. Maybe she harbored some pent-up rage that even a lengthy meditation session couldn't cure.

Or maybe it had been an accident. Maybe she'd

mixed up a bad batch. Maybe Porter had used too much of this pain-relieving salve. I didn't know much about healing, but I did know that some ingredients, like the stuff Flora extracted from foxgloves, could be good in small doses, but deadly in large amounts. I finished up with Benny and swore to find something with a more pleasant fragrance for him to eat. Lemons would be nice. A good clean scent. Maybe some pine branches. Why in the world were we feeding him what looked like half-rotted swamp greens?

It was getting late. The gates would be opening in just over an hour, and I still needed to talk to the gremlins. But I wouldn't be able to concentrate on a thing if I didn't clear up a few questions with Flora first.

When I approached Conrad and Flora's sleeping quarters, the radio was on and I could hear them moving about inside (centaurs aren't the stealthiest creatures). With trepidation digging a hole in my belly, I tapped on the door. Conrad answered.

"Duncan," he said cheerfully, "amazing show yesterday. The sneeze. It didn't even looked planned."

"It wasn't. It was that stupid floofy thing Molly insisted on wearing."

Just then, Flora strode up to us. "Are you sneezing? I have just the thing for allergies."

"No, thank you. It was just something tickling my nose. But I did wonder if I could ask you something, Flora."

Flora agreed and, due to the tight quarters of their homey dwelling, stepped out to join me in the patch of grass out front of it. Conrad joined us and commented on the heat, then I made what I'm sure was a very witty observation about the weather.

CORDELIA: Oh yes, I'm sure they were awash in your wit.
DUNCAN: What? I'm witty. Aren't I? Okay, why have you gone quiet again?

It would have been so easy to keep on with the chitchat about the weather, the show, that sort of thing, but then I pictured Cordelia sitting on the floor of her wooden cell with her sack of popcorn.

"Look, Flora, do you use behemoth saliva in any of your mixtures?"

Before Flora could open her mouth to answer, Conrad's face tightened. "Are you accusing my wife of killing Porter? Because if you are, you can get off my lawn right this instant and—"

"Dear," said Flora in her misty, soothing tone as she placed a hand on her husband's arm, "remember your mantra. Find your calm place. I don't think Duncan is accusing me. He's only curious about what happened to his friend." She fixed her attention on me, then added, "And wants to help another."

Flora may seem like a complete loon, but sometimes she can be frighteningly spot-on with her observations.

"So, do you?" I asked.

"Yes. Behemoth saliva works as a preservative because germs can't grow in its presence — that's how Benny can lounge about in that filth and never suffer an infection. It's also a strong pain reliever. The dwarves often need it. Those stout bones do suffer arthritis at an early age. And of course," she glanced worriedly at Conrad, "I put it in a salve for Porter's knees."

"Porter's been using that salve for a year now with no problem," Conrad blurted. His cheeks had gone red, and I didn't think it was from the heat. If I didn't tread carefully, I'd end up with a broken snout.

"Mantra, dear," Flora reminded him. Conrad closed his eyes and muttered a phrase to himself while inhaling through his nostrils and exhaling through his mouth in three lengthy breaths.

"How often do you collect Benny's drool, then?" I asked. Conrad now appeared the image of calm, but I wasn't taking any chances. I casually shifted and stepped back to be out of his reach.

"Let's see, generally about once a month."

"And the last time you went for a refill?"

"The saliva's most effective if gathered under the light of a full moon, so I would have refilled my supply when we first arrived to this location."

I shifted another pace back from Conrad before asking, "Aren't you worried about preparing medicines with poison in them?"

"Many medicines are just poison in a smaller dose. But you're right, I do have to be careful. Humans are incredibly sensitive to behemoth saliva. I believe it's because their chakras are often out of line. Or is it their auras?" She fluttered a hand as if waving off her uncertainty. "Either way, I don't often prescribe it to them because, if you're making a salve, you have to make sure they only get the tiniest drop in a rather large quantity of cream. Other creatures, like centaurs, can also be killed by it, but it takes a much greater quantity."

"Because of our chakras," Conrad said, with a mocking grin on his lips. Conrad is level-headed, logical. He even teaches the younger members of the circus science and math. He loves Flora to a fault, even her eccentric beliefs in the mystical healing arts, but he's not beyond teasing her about them.

"Very good, my sweet," said Flora, entirely missing the aura of sarcasm in her husband's voice.

"So it has to do with size?" I asked.

"No, now that I think about it, I'm quite sure it's the auras. After all, other creatures, including all the smaller races of elves — brownies, bogarts, and dwarves — weigh far less than humans and they're completely immune. They don't even get woozy from it. On the other hand, for bigger elves like the wood elf and moon elf, it's like a drug and they can get addicted to it. It makes chimeras feel awful, while domestic cats can lap it up like water. And of course, behemoths can't poison themselves, although another behemoth's saliva could poison Benny. It's all very interesting."

Chimeras. Charlie had complained of a belly ache the morning we'd found Porter. Maybe it wasn't just a bad piece of road kill he'd gotten hold of. I thought of how odd I felt that same morning even before seeing my handler sprawled on the floor of the Tent. Charlie, Porter, and I had all sampled the wine given to Porter. Benny had as well, but he couldn't poison himself.

"And dragons?" I asked, just to confirm my suspicion.

"Oh, dragons are a little sensitive to it. Makes your kind a bit foggy in the head, but it's never deadly to you. Oh dear," Flora fretted, "all these questions. Has someone accidentally ingested some? Should I get the antidote?"

"There's an antidote?"

"Yes, it smells like roses and honey, and I've almost considered adding it to my aromatherapy regimen. But I always mix up a fresh batch whenever I collect new saliva. It's a good habit. Here, let me show you."

Flora stepped in and, while I watched from the window, headed over to a shelf lined with mismatched jars and bottles. Some looked like something straight out of an apothecary's shop, while others were nothing more than reclaimed spice jars or condiment containers Pepper had thrown out. Running across the front of the shelf was a leather strap, put there, I assumed, to hold Flora's potions and powders in place as the caravan jostled down the road. Flora scanned the shelves, making disapproving noises as she did so.

"I told you to alphabetize them, sweetheart," said Conrad. "If you need an antidote, you're going to need it as soon as possible."

"No, I did alphabetize them. That day last week when it wouldn't stop raining, I got bored and did it. But it's missing. See, beetle powder." She pointed to a former mustard jar that was filled with an iridescent dust. After tapping her finger on two taller jars, she indicated a soda bottle half full of a red liquid that I hoped wasn't blood. "And then it jumps right to berry vinegar. Behemoth saliva and the antidote should both be in between, but they're gone."

Conrad stepped forward to double check. He opened up the two containers that had been stuck between the pulverized beetles and berry juice, but both were empty.

"They're not labeled either," he said. "Someone replaced the jars so you wouldn't notice an empty spot."

"Well, that is quite the rude trick," Flora said, crossing her arms over her chest. "I hope they know that behavior is very bad for their karma."

"I'm sure they do, dear." Conrad looked to me. "I assume you're trying to figure out who killed Porter." I nodded. "You do know Flora wouldn't—"

"No, no," I protested, "of course not, but someone got in here and took those jars. If you last collected when we first got here, it could have been anyone. Did you mix the antidote on the same day?"

"That afternoon."

"Does any of this help?" Conrad asked.

I shrugged. It helped that I now knew how Porter was poisoned and where the poison likely came from, but it didn't help ease my suspicions about Zin's role in that poisoning. An image flashed in my mind of Zin walking off with Conrad on Opening Day Eve. Zin had been in their caravan. He'd had access to the poison. But, I argued with myself, people rarely locked their caravan doors. Anyone could have wandered in at any time and taken what they liked.

"It would be good to know where that wine came from," I said, mostly to myself.

"I could ask around," Conrad offered.

"Would you?"

He agreed, and I thanked him. I needed to know more before I accused Zin. Before I accused the satyr who had purchased me out of the dragon dealer's bargain bin and rescued me from being ground into chimera food.

Plus, I had to go chat with some gremlins.

Or try to.

CHAPTER 26
WORKING WITH GREMLINS

Oddly enough, the communication barrier between dragon and gremlin broke down faster than Gladys's morals around a rich man. Apparently, gremlins do speak English, but there's so much jargon mixed in it sounds like a different language to most ears.

I also learned that it doesn't take much to bribe them, which should have been no surprise since a gremlin's natural instinct is to cause havoc with machinery. But since they've found it's tough to get paid for bunging up equipment, they've opted to use their mechanical know-how to repair rather than ruin.

I should note here as a word of warning for anyone in need of an electrical or other technical fix: There are a few shady gremlins who will gladly come out for a repair when you call them. They'll then make a minor adjustment so your whozzit *seems* to be mended. However, while they're doing that job, they'll tinker with three other things that are far more costly to get up and working again. These things then break down over the course of the next few weeks, and none of them break at the same time, leaving you stuck with a hefty call-out fee every time they show up.

So, take it from your pal Duncan, if you're hiring gremlins for any home or office repairs, be sure to ask someone for a referral. Oh, and make sure that someone isn't a wood elf. More likely than not, they're getting a kickback for the recommendation.

Anyway, the gremlin foreman, Gregg, got a shine in his eye, the likes I've only seen when Fergus has spotted a shapely lap for the first time. Gregg fought back his eagerness, but there was an excited grin lurking beneath the feigned tension in his narrow jaw.

"This is for real?" Gregg asked, his speech quick and punchy like he didn't have time to waste words. "Not a ruse? Zin's not sending you to test us, our loyalty? Heard he's looking to cut expenses, and my crew doesn't work cheap."

It was true. The gremlins demanded benefits the rest of us had never even imagined asking for. Sick leave. Double pay for emergency work. Zin reimbursing them for their tools. And they even had something called a pension fund.

"No, this is all me. I need time to find out what really happened with Porter, and having the circus shut down for a few hours is the only way I'm going to get that time. Your crew won't get in trouble, will they?"

"You kidding? We'll just make it look like mice. Done it a dozen times before. But you didn't hear that from me, got it?" I told him I did. "We'll hem and haw over it, tell Zin to adopt a mouser, then make a big show over how complicated it'll be to get things running again. How much time you need?"

"Just a few hours."

"Things'll go down about two, be back up by six. That good?"

"Let's hope so."

By this time, odd happenings and uncomfortable suspicions or not, my stomach was mounting a protest over being empty. When I reached the Cantina, Zin was leaning in close as he spoke with Pepper. I didn't want to approach. I didn't want to speak to him yet, but Pepper caught my eye and gave a nod to signal she'd get my usual order going as soon as she was done. I took a seat that put me out of Zin's line of sight — not an easy task when you're as big as a Clydesdale, but it helped that Zin seemed preoccupied as he strode off.

I was in such a strange mood over this business with Zin and Ratcher that I didn't even enjoy my omelet. Sure it was fluffy, it was full of chanterelle mushrooms, it was oozing with a nice Jarlsberg. But Pepper could have served me up a deep-fried piece of packing crate and I wouldn't have noticed the difference.

I did manage to finish my food, though. Mainly because I knew Pepper would be furious if I didn't clean my plate, and Pepper was one cyclops you didn't want to have on your bad side. After all, I'd eventually get my appetite back up to full speed, and if I didn't appear to enjoy every last scrap of what she served, that deep-fried packing crate might just be all I got for a meal the next time I showed up at her Cantina.

Flora soon joined me with a plate of oat greens topped with candied viola petals. Conrad, she told me, had gone to Boris with the wine theory, and the two were going around subtly asking questions. As Flora took a forkful of her breakfast, the flowers reminded me of the test I wanted to try out. I asked her if she could help and she was more than willing, saying it could do nothing but boost her karma.

When we finished up, I took our dishes to Pepper and asked if she had any lemon peels she wanted rid of.

"Everyone's asking for my leftovers lately," she grumbled as she dumped a pile of lemon rinds into a bucket. "Should start charging for them."

With Flora's guidance, we strolled along the barrier, picking plants that were fragrant and non-lethal. We then went back to her caravan, where she filled the rest of the bucket with dried rose petals, lavender stems, and some honeysuckle blossoms. By the time we were done, the contents resembled one of Flora's salads. Minus the oats, of course.

Benny sniffed at the offering, looked around as if his favorite swamp muck might be hiding on the other side of the bucket. Then, realizing this was the only breakfast on offer, took a tentative nibble of his fragrant salad. The nibble turned into a bite, and the bite turned into Benny lifting the bucket with his tiny arms and downing the contents.

"Good stuff?" I asked.

"Tasty."

While he ate, I gave Benny a quick scrub. His skin was

still gleaming from my earlier cleaning, but my strength and my height gave me extra leverage with the scrub broom that he really enjoyed. We'd have to wait until later in the day — until Benny's breakfast had been processed, that is — to see if the change in diet made any difference, but I have to say, I was already proving myself a pretty decent behemoth handler.

By the time I set aside my behemoth cleaning gear, the bell was clanging to signal the gates were opening. I hurried over to the Tent to get in place for my act and crossed my claws that the gremlins' meddling wouldn't cause a panic.

To an enraptured audience Zin made a show of guiding me through four of my shorter acts. These were quick things that didn't last much longer than fifteen minutes, each concluding with Zin telling everyone to come back that evening to see the real show, the death-defying feats, the most dangerous deeds performed in any circus. Do not bring the kiddies, it might give them bad dreams.

The majority of the crowd had filed out of the Tent when there came a muffled popping sound. This was followed by an electrical whine like a fan shutting down, then the interior plunged into darkness. Some of the lingering people cried out with startled shrieks, but most laughed over the others' fright. Soon, someone pulled back the wide entrance flaps, allowing in enough light for everyone to make it out safely.

Zin was cursing. And not in that cute human way. This was an angry, worried-about-losing-customers rant, and each foul word was punctuated with his shouting for Gregg to fix the damn lights.

Gregg, possibly the bravest gremlin I could imagine, came running right up to Zin.

"Everything alright? Everyone made it out safely? I was so worried." He delivered this with such sincere concern, I wondered if maybe he hadn't learned his trade in a theater.

"Yes, they're fine," said Zin through clenched teeth. "What the hell happened?"

"Someone crossed the wires on the transformer and that got re-routed…"

What followed was a bunch of that gremlin-speak I mentioned earlier. I'll just save you a lengthy paragraph of electro-jargon and again reaffirm my conviction that Gregg will have a good career as an actor if he ever gets tired of electrical and mechanical maintenance.

"What does any of that mean? No—" Zin held up a hand when Gregg took a deep breath to prepare for his explanation "—never mind. I don't need to know. Just tell me how soon you can get it working again."

Gregg's gaze shifted upward, he muttered to himself and counted on his fingers, then he met Zin's eye and said, "Should have it up right around dinnertime. Good timing. No guarantees, though. Pepper should plan on sandwiches for our dinner break, and—"

"It is far from good timing. We've only been open for two days. This is the weekend show. We can't run it in the dark, and we certainly can't do it with torches." He was right. He'd tried torches for lighting once and it not only burnt part of the Flynns' trapeze equipment but also left me cowering in a corner. "Generators?"

"Not powerful enough to light the Tent. I put in a request for a bigger one, but Reinhart never approved the expense. That thing we have now? Barely enough power for the popcorn maker."

Zin pinched the bridge of his nose, a relaxing technique I'd seen Flora show a few people. It didn't seem to help.

"So we really have to close down until dinnertime?"

"It's the wisest course. We might be able to get it up and running earlier, but this is a messy job. It's going to take me at least an hour to go into town and get the supplies I need. The fuses. Completely fried."

"No, you stay here and sort this out," Zin said, his jaw shaking with impatience and frustration. "I'll get someone to go into town for you. Just please get started with what you can."

Zin turned, ready to get away from Gregg's bad news.

"Not just yet, Zin." Zin took a deep breath. With fists clenched, he faced the gremlin again. Gregg didn't waver a bit under Zin's furious glare. "Like I said, crossed wires might be the culprit, but I also noticed some spots where mice have nibbled away at the housing. Even if it didn't cause this meltdown, it's a problem waiting to happen. You really ought to get a mouser. Actually, while you're getting my supplies, bring back a cat. No, a kitten. We can train him up."

"Anything else I can get you?" Zin asked in that way that said any further requests would be met with a goatish head butt.

"Nope. I've got to get started unraveling the mess or it'll be dark before I'm even—"

"Just bring me a list of supplies, then go do whatever it is you need to do. Conrad and Flora can get what you need. No doubt she'll want to examine the kittens' damn auras before selecting one," Zin said with pure exasperation, then marched off, shaking his head.

Gregg, wearing the happiest grin you'd ever seen on a gremlin, gave me a conspirator's wink. At least one person was being made happy by this fiasco.

CHAPTER 27
A DISTURBING DISCOVERY

It took little time for Gregg to come up with a list of various types of wires and fuses and clamps. He also added a reminder to get a litter box, cat food, and a scratching post for our new mouser. Something was telling me that Gregg might have had a scheme like this in mind already. Specifically, a scheme to make it look like we had a mouse problem.

What tipped me off? First was the smiley face he added below the list of cat supplies. Also, he'd written out a detailed, and clearly well-researched, description of the best and worst ingredients to look for on the cat food labels.

With Conrad and Boris taking advantage of the break to hunt down some information about the wine barrel, Flora off gathering more sweet-smelling plants for Benny, and Reinhart nowhere to be found, Zin was in a right rage when he finally gave up trying to find volunteers amongst us "ungrateful, lazy louts" and clomped off to town himself. He might have asked one of the Flynns, but there was always the risk of them getting distracted by a general store that carried peanuts, walnuts, or hazelnuts. They were amazing performers, but were not the most focused shoppers.

Once Zin left, I pictured myself creeping up to his caravan and slipping in like a cat burglar. But my size quickly put a damper on any dreams of creeping, skulking, or burgling. Instead, I grabbed my dukie book and walked straight up to Zin's caravan for all to see. My book was full to the last page, so I had the perfect excuse that I needed a new one if anyone asked what I was doing rummaging around Zin's stuff.

Of course, since I was fully prepared with an excuse, no one stopped me. Figures.

Our caravans are basically boxes on wheels with no insulation to speak of. Fully closed up, on a sunny day they can turn into giant bread ovens, so most circus folk keep their windows open to allow air to flow through. This makes them more like warming ovens rather than bread ovens. Every little bit counts, right?

Zin's caravan was no different. To keep the papers on his desk from flying away (not that you would notice amongst the other mess), he'd only left the windows open a crack, but it was enough for me to slip my claw under and lift the sash the rest of the way. I had no intention of trying to climb in. That would only result in me getting stuck halfway through with my hind end sticking out. Not exactly how I want to be remembered.

When I poked my head in, the sack of peanuts was still slumped in the same spot, and I had to hope the piece of paper was still tucked underneath it. I lifted the nuts, then took the pile of papers, holding them carefully to keep them in as jumbled a condition as Zin had left them. With my left hand (okay, yes, I have *paws*, but they're very dexterous, so I often think of them as hands), I kept a hold of the papers, then used my right hand to flip through the stack.

I had imagined myself instantly recognizing the high-quality paper I'd seen before, but the stack I held contained all manner of paper, from newsprint to cardstock, making me wonder if Zin was stealing samples from stationery shops everywhere we went.

I recalled the two lines at the bottom of the document, so I checked the lower portions of the papers. Or what should have been the lower portion. Unfortunately, Zin seems allergic to the concept of *tidy* and the papers were turned every which way. I got through the whole stack without seeing any lines. After glancing over my shoulder to make sure Zin wasn't coming, I started again, this time paying attention to what should have been the top half of the sheets.

About a third of the way through, I found the two lines. One signed. One empty. The signature was sharp, with letters like little daggers stabbing through the vacant line. And those letters spelled out Ratcher's name. I eased the sheet out, then replaced the stack.

At the top of the sheet was the Ratcher logo. Something about it tickled a nerve, like seeing someone you think you know but can't quite place. Then again, Ratcher's was the biggest, brashest name in the circus business in those days, and his billboards were roadside eyesores no matter where you travelled in the region, so it was little surprise the logo felt familiar.

The sheet was full of legalese language, but what it amounted to was an offer to buy out Zinzendorf's Circus of Unusual Creatures intact. Zin would be allowed to keep his personal belongings, but Ratcher would take control of all the other equipment, creatures, caravans, acts, tents, and the various other stuff that goes into keeping a circus running.

The offer was comprehensive and substantial. Zin would lose everything he'd inherited and everything he'd built up from that inheritance, but he would have enough money to start a new life in style. How could Ratcher afford this?

Circuses are the region's primary source of entertainment and there's high demand for that entertainment. Demand that explains how so many circuses could travel around the region and still stay financially afloat. We each kept to the circuit arranged during the Annual Unusual Circus Conference, going from town to town and maintaining at least three miles distance between each show. This spreads out the circuses amongst the small, scattered towns of the region, keeping us close enough to a town so its people could walk to the show, while also keeping the circuses from stepping on each other's toes.

Because while the circus owners might make a show of being rivals with each other, there was little true competition. The truth of the matter was people craved circuses, and if they could afford it, they would attend each and every show that stopped nearby.

The owners had long ago made an unwritten agreement to keep entry prices low (concessions and trinkets, however, were fair game), so even people who lived paycheck to paycheck only needed to set aside a tiny amount to make a trip to the circus when a new one rolled through. Circuses were life's little diversion, and there once used to be so many that you could go to a show each week of the year and never see the same one.

But then Ratcher came along.

Over the past few years, Damian Ratcher had been snatching up circuses like the Flynns snatched up nuts. I thought of what Fergus had told me he'd learned from Humphrey and what I'd seen myself. A disturbing answer to how Ratcher might afford his extravagant offers crept over me.

Ratcher was buying up dragons. He'd killed a dragon while Humphrey was there. He'd killed that dragon while trying to get it to speak. Did Ratcher know our secret? Had he gotten one to speak? More than one? How many hoards had Ratcher stolen? How many smaller circuses had been purchased using the treasure of my kind? And how many dragons had died for his greed?

Or maybe I was just being dramatic, and Ratcher was getting his money by some other means. Still, I'd just bet those means were corrupt ones.

I glanced over the paperwork once more. Ratcher wanted everything. Including me. And Porter must have known. Maybe not the full details, but he would have known any deal with Ratcher was bad news for dragons.

Porter had stood up to Zin, and now he was dead. I shuddered. I was half-tempted to tear the document to shreds, but if there was this one, surely there was a matching one in Ratcher's office. It would be a simple matter to send over a new contract if Zin claimed he lost his copy.

I slipped the sheet back into the stack, noticing the logo for Ratcher again and feeling once more that sense of foreboding familiarity in my gut. I didn't dwell on it. There were more things to worry about than a logo. Namely, my possible torture and demise at the hands of one of Ratcher's handlers.

With shaky hands, I rearranged things as they were, grabbed a new dukie book, and slid the window back down.

CHAPTER 28
COTTON CANDY THREATS

After leaving Zin's, I tossed my dukie books onto the table of my own caravan, then went to the Tent to find the cotton candy vendor — a gnome named Percy, in case you were wondering. After promising him a couple credits from my dukie book, he agreed to my offer.

"For me?" Cordelia said, as she eyed the box filled with fluff-topped paper cones.

"Figured there's only so many salads you can handle." I tilted the box, and she selected a pink hunk of candy floss.

"Flora thinks the greens will improve my aura, since apparently it's a little too red at the moment. Gee, I wonder why." She swept her hand to indicate her surroundings. The hand was holding the cotton candy cone, and the ball of unnaturally colored fluff went flying. Luckily (depending on how much you hate your teeth), there was more where that came from, and Cordelia plucked out a purple replacement. "So, I notice you didn't bring any keys. Guess that means things aren't going well?"

"Zin's had an offer to sell the circus to Ratcher. I saw the paperwork and Fergus confirms that Porter argued with Zin the afternoon of the day he died.

"Zin," she pondered, her lips already purple from the candy coloring. "Do you think he could have done it?"

"I'd like to think not, but he made this weird sort of confession that the circus is having money trouble."

"All circuses have money trouble. It's like a requirement."

"Yeah, and a lot of those circuses are solving their money woes by selling out to Ratcher."

"That gangly bastard's ruining the circus business. And I've heard how he treats his dragons."

"What have you heard?" I'd gathered plenty of gossip and now there was Humphrey's tale, but like someone addicted to horror stories, I always craved just one more tidbit to remind myself how horrible it would be to find myself back in Ratcher's troupe.

"Dragons don't survive long. Even healthy ones barely last a year. Accidents, infections from beatings, or just outright killing them for the tiniest bit of aggression. It's no place for you, Duncan."

"Thanks, Cordelia. But I don't know what I can do to avoid it if Zin agrees. I'd almost prefer he sell just me rather than have everyone lose their jobs when Ratcher buys the place and gets rid of the people he doesn't need."

"That's the problem with Ratcher snatching up circuses. The dragons, the workers, and the townsfolk who need the shows as a bit of escape all get screwed over." Cordelia took a large bite of her purple floss.

HOARD IT ALL BEFORE

"Ratcher's going against everything the circuses stand for: cheap, variable, and easily accessible entertainment."

"I don't get it. If the circuses have agreed to a set entry fee, why wouldn't Ratcher's entry be as cheap as the rest?"

I realized how naïve that sounded even before Cordelia gave me her you're-an-idiot look.

"Once people are left with no other choice of circus for their entertainment, he can charge whatever he likes. And once you pay that high price, you're not done giving over your wages to Ratcher. Not in the least. A drink that costs a day's wages? Pay up or go thirsty. Want to see the dragon show or have your palm read? Oh sorry, that's not included in your ticket, you'll have to pay extra. And don't balk, young man. You wouldn't want to appear cheap in front of your date, would you?"

She popped the final piece of purple fluff into her mouth and reached for another. Blue this time. She was going to have a hard time explaining the strange coloring on her face to Flora.

"It would be best if Zin didn't sell at all," she said. "He can't be doing that bad, can he? I know I've only been here a couple days, but it's the busiest circus I've ever worked in. And Zin's has always been on people's lips whenever a circus I've been with rolled into town."

"How do you mean?"

"I've done odd jobs for plenty of small time circuses. You know, those ones that have a sway-backed centaur act, a gang of drunken clown dwarves, and a couple rides with half the bolts missing." I nodded. "People love any circus and they'd go to those half-ass shows, but when

219

they'd show up to the gates, they'd always be asking if we knew if Zin's might be coming early that year, saying how they'd been saving their money for a day at Zin's, going on about how Zin could charge double and they'd still find a way to go to his shows. People sense something about this circus. Some sort of connection between the acts and the owner and even the workers." Cordelia gave a funny look at the empty cotton candy cones scattered around her. "I think I might throw up if I eat another one of those." She then considered her plate of half-eaten salad. "Is there any popcorn?"

"I'll look for some, but you better wash up. Flora's going to wonder what happened to your aura if she sees all those colors on you."

I filled her cup with water, then left her to clean her face while I hunted down the elusive popcorn machine.

As I wandered over to where the concessions were fried, spun, salted, stuck on sticks, or coated in sugar, I thought about what Cordelia had said. Maybe it took an outsider to see it, but she was absolutely right. Zin's should not have been in any financial trouble. Tickets sold out nearly every day.

Sure, we had expenses such as buying the food for the concession stand, but that was sold to visitors at a decent profit. As far as feeding the troupe, well, I still had no idea exactly where Pepper sourced some of her more fanciful ingredients from. She did buy some produce and other goods on trips to local farm stands, but a fair portion of our basics like flour and oats were donated in exchange for behind-the-scenes tours of the circus.

Other expenses such as tents, caravans, and the like had been paid for long ago by Zin's great-grandfather, who began the show. Gregg's team did a great job maintaining that equipment — most of the time. And thanks to Reinhart's keen scrutiny of our dukie books, our wages weren't breaking Zin's bank. So even if he wasn't about to be listed as one of the region's wealthiest satyrs, Zin's circus should have been on stable footing.

I had just gotten two massive boxes of about-to-be-discarded popcorn when Conrad found me.

"Got a minute?" he asked, looking around as if worried someone would overhear us.

"My place. I can take these to Cordelia later. I don't think they go bad, do they? Or deflate?"

"Not that I've seen, but don't let Flora see you with those. She'll have you on a cleansing fast faster than you can say *starvation*."

When I slid back the door to my caravan, on the floor there was a piece of paper that had been shoved through my mail slot. The paper was the usual cheap stuff we used around the circus for notes and notices, so I assumed it was another of Boris's flyers about how to stay organized to make the brownies' work more efficient. I picked it up and set it aside along with the boxes of popcorn.

"Did you find out anything about the wine?"

"Yeah," said Conrad, still speaking quietly. "It didn't come from anyone in town."

"Are you sure about that?"

"None of the farms around here have vineyards, and while a few people make bootleg moonshine, no one knows a thing about wine making. And this isn't exactly a wealthy area. They wouldn't have had the extra money to buy a barrel of wine just to give it away."

"So where'd it come from?"

"I asked Pepper if she knew about the wine barrel's delivery and she said it had come that very evening Porter had died. She had to sign for it and noticed the shipping address was from Portland. That's not to say it came direct from there. There's distributors who send their product to local warehouses. It could have come from any of them."

"But if it wasn't a gift, someone had to have ordered it, right? Or could someone from Portland have sent it as a gift?"

"Maybe, but I'm not sure how we'd find out."

My gaze landed on the dukie books I'd left on the table. It made me think of Reinhart's close scrutiny of our expenses.

"If someone in the circus ordered it, wouldn't Reinhart have a record of it in his account book?"

"And you think Reinhart is going to let you have a look at his accounts?" Conrad asked sarcastically. "Reinhart protects that ledger like it's made of pure gold. He never lets it out of his sight. I bet he even sleeps with it."

"We could ask him," I said.

"We?"

"You?"

"No way. Sorry, but Reinhart's not someone you want to annoy, and Flora would kill me if I got on the wrong side of him."

We talked a little more, but I felt impatient and my replies to his conversational statements got shorter and sharper until he finally took the hint and said he better go see what Flora was up to.

I needed to talk to Cordelia about the wine delivery and about what to do next. I felt a little foolish that I wasn't figuring out my own plans for how to proceed, but she'd been really good at coming up with smart ideas so far. Then again, those ideas were to save her own skin, so I guess she had a bit of motivation to keep them coming.

I picked up the popcorn boxes, then caught sight of the flyer. It had unfolded when I set it down. Scrawled across the rough surface were words written in bold black letters. The handwriting was impossible to judge, but it looked either like someone was trying to appear stupid or they'd written the note with their non-dominant hand.

My caravan was stuffy and hot, but the words, although clumsily written, sent chills along my dorsal spines.

Stop asking kwestions. The Mop won't be the only 1 to suffer if U don't but out.

I gathered up the boxes of popcorn to drop off to Cordelia, but I also snatched the note in my claws. There was someone who needed to see it.

CHAPTER 29
THE IMPRINTING MYTH, AGAIN

Now, I know I had a lot on my mind, I know I was generating zero ideas of how to solve the various problems before me, and I know I'd just received a worrying (and misspelled) threat. Still, I couldn't help but laugh when I caught up to Boris.

"What's so funny?" he asked. He gave the lapel of his coat a confident tug, then flipped up the collar.

"A trench coat, Boris? A trench coat?" I snorted a giggle.

"I am an investigative detector. I must look the part."

"But maybe you should cut it down to size."

Somehow, somewhere, Boris had gotten his perfectly manicured fingers on a trench coat that had been designed, cut, and sewn to fit a human. Not a very large human, I'll grant him that, but even a small human is about twice the size of a brownie. As such, while the upturned collar did give him a certain air of mysterious authority, the two feet of dragging hemline made him look like he was preparing to audition for a part in the Dumble Dwarf clown show.

Boris glanced behind him at the trailing garment, then lifted his eyebrows in defeated agreement.

"Yes, I suppose some alterations would be a wise idea."

Speaking of ideas, did I just say I wasn't having any? Well, strike that sentence, because I just had one. Stop with your mocking applause, Cordelia.

"Boris, do you clean Reinhart's office?"

"Not me personally. I'm the head brownie, after all."

"Yes, okay, but your crew cleans it, right?"

"Once a week. He doesn't like us in there at other times. And he is very tidy, so daily cleaning isn't much needed."

"And when are you due to clean in there?"

"We did it yesterday."

Crash, bang, boom. That was the sound of my idea plummeting to the earth.

Ooh, new idea. Wow, once you get started with these things, they just don't stop, do they?

"But couldn't you say you had Humphrey do the cleaning and you need to go in and check his work? Him being new and all?"

"Why would I do that?"

"Because there might be something in Reinhart's office."

"There are many things in Reinhart's office. All very organized, which is very much appreciated."

My jaw tensed, and I resisted the urge to grab Boris by his oversized lapels. I took one of Flora's calming and cleansing breaths, then said, "I thought you wanted to be a — what did you call it? — investigative detector? That's what they do. They get in and investigate. And detect, I suppose."

"Yes," said Boris, his eyes widening with realization. "Now the name makes sense. Okay, I'll do it. What am I detecting for?"

"His account book. I need to see if he has any record of the barrel of wine Porter received."

"I thought that was a gift from the town."

"Conrad says there aren't any vineyards around here, and the wine likely came from Portland." I looked up to see Reinhart leaving his caravan, a towel slung over his shoulder. He chatted to himself as he went and appeared to be having quite the debate as he emphatically shook the loofah-topped stick he carried. "Look, he's off to the showers. And he doesn't have his book with him. Just remember, if he gets back before you're done, you'll tell him—"

"I know, I know, that I was checking over Humphrey's work. I am not stupid."

"Right, sorry, just—" I then remembered the note. "Oh, and I received this. Not sure how concerned I should be, but maybe it will help with your detecting."

Boris took the note, scanned it, and said, "Very interesting. I believe I must investigate this further, if I may keep it." I told him he could, not wanting the threatening words anywhere near me. He then re-folded the sheet and slipped it into his coat pocket. Of course, the coat was so long on him, he had to bend over and pull up the fabric to reach the pocket.

"Maybe you should leave the coat with me. Just for now." Boris opened his mouth to argue. "I mean, the caravan's just been cleaned, and that coat is going to drag in a lot of dirt."

"Yes, good point." He ducked out of the garment then headed toward Reinhart's caravan, walking with the confidence of someone who no one would question going into another person's lodgings.

While he was investigating — or perhaps detecting, I'm not sure which — I went to tell Cordelia where things stood regarding the source of the wine and what I'd learned about behemoth saliva that morning.

"So the wine didn't come from town," she mused as she nibbled on a few pieces of popcorn. Her face was still stained from the cotton candy, but if she stayed away from the front of the Cells where the light was strongest, she'd be able to hide her sugary indulgence from Flora. "And we still can't be certain when it was poisoned. It might have been tampered with before it got here. Can you imagine if it was meant to be delivered somewhere else and all this was a bad accident?"

"If we hit a dead end, I'll bring that up. But not many people have access to behemoth saliva."

"True. Good thinking, Duncan," she said, and for some silly reason I felt immensely proud at the slight praise.

Cordelia had apparently gotten over her disgust with the cotton candy because as soon as she finished off the popcorn, she dug out another cone from my earlier delivery and began pulling off hunks of yellow fluff, letting them melt on her tongue as she strode back and forth in the Cells.

"I just wonder why, though. I mean, Porter's disapproval wouldn't really stop Zin from selling, would it? This all seems more personal, more direct, more like it was about getting to you."

"Me? How do you mean?"

"Well, it's no secret how much you like to drink."

"I have a healthy appreciation for a good vintage."

"Duncan, you guzzle wine from a bucket. You're not exactly a candidate for Wine Aficionado of the Year."

"Okay, but I haven't had a drop since I started trying to sort out this puzzle." And come to think of it, I hadn't craved any either. Which struck me as completely out of my own character.

"Still, you have a reputation for your 'appreciation'. Someone knew you'd drink that wine. Let's assume they knew how behemoth saliva would affect you, since that does seem an odd choice of poison. Maybe they were hoping to get you drunk, make you too loopy to make sense of things, and lure you away. They would need Porter out of the way to do that, hence a substance that would poison him, but not you." The thought of someone being so calculating left me unable to speak. Cordelia ate the last bit of yellow floss, then muttered, "But that still doesn't explain why they did it. Why would they go to such lengths?"

"I don't know. But I do know that my poking around has gotten under someone's skin."

When I handed Cordelia her popcorn, I'd placed Boris's coat to the side of the Cells. Now, I slipped the note out of the pocket and passed it to her.

"Seems a little over the top, doesn't it?" she said, her left eyebrow arched skeptically. "I mean, you're a dragon, it's not like someone's going to sneak up, knock you out, and drag you away without anyone noticing."

I'm so used to my size and I'm so used to being around smaller creatures that sometimes I forget I'm not as vulnerable as other beings. Cordelia was right. Unless someone did get me drunk enough to lead me away, what did I have to worry about? I mean, I had my issues with the hook, but in most hands that only caused superficial damage to my hide. I didn't like my wings being clipped, but unless they were chopped down too far, they'd grow back. And I had my little fire phobia, but even I knew that was mostly mental scars.

"Hold on." Cordelia stopped and pointed her yellow-stained paper cone at me. "There's the whole imprinting thing you dragons do."

This, as I've mentioned, is an utter myth, in my opinion. The idea is that whoever we first see after our previous handler dies will instantly have a magical hold over us and become our new handler, with us mindlessly falling whim to their every command. And if you missed the sarcasm in that statement, this is me telling you that it is overflowing with disbelieving sarcasm.

The whole idea is offensive, if you ask me. As if we dragons have no mind of our own. As if we can't decide who we want to listen to and who we want to ignore. Believe me, one reason Zin got me at a bargain was because I was very good at not taking the commands of my handlers.

Sorry for interrupting Cordelia's rambling theory, but a dragon can't let these stereotypes pass by without saying something.

"What if whoever poisoned the wine was hoping to be nearby when Porter died? With the imprinting, once he was out of the way, you'd do anything that person wanted."

"That whole imprinting thing is a myth. I figured you of all people would—."

"Sit," she commanded, and without a second thought, my hind quarters dropped to the ground, leaving me sitting like a well-trained beagle.

I immediately stood back up to prove to her I was my own dragon. She watched me with a smug expression on her small face. I stared at her, speechless. My sarcasm had gone, but the disbelief was still there. Not over the imprinting concept, but over who Cordelia Quinn might be.

See, sometimes myths and rumors have some truth behind them. I've told you about the imprinting at birth thing. And while we dragons might question this idea of imprinting upon the death of our handler, there is a smidgen of truth in it.

Now don't start yelling at me, saying I just told you the imprinting-upon-death thing didn't happen.

The deal is, there's a legend, rumor, myth, whatever you want to call it that says certain people are born to be our handlers. I don't know if the fairies have blessed these people, if it's a genetic quirk, or if it's just blind luck — I really haven't paid that much attention to the tale. But I do know they can't just wander in and take control of us. The bond they're destined to have with us only forms if a dragon's free of his old handler. We're loyal like that.

CORDELIA: Loyal? I thought it was because you couldn't concentrate on two commands at once.

DUNCAN: Well, yes, there's that, but loyal sounds better, don't you think?

CORDELIA: You're stepping dangerously close to lying, Duncan.

DUNCAN: You're a bad influence on me. And don't look so proud about that, it wasn't a compliment.

Anyway, I tried to tell myself that my butt plopping to the ground had nothing to do with this myth-rumor-whathaveyou. I tried to tell myself that Cordelia was just some ordinary handler who understood the dragon training protocol. After all, 'Sit' is one of the first commands we learn. It becomes so ingrained that, even if I overhear the word *sit*, I feel a compulsion to lower my backside to the ground.

"You're not proving anything," I grumbled. "I've had other handlers die, and I was perfectly capable of disobeying my next one."

Again, that's a story for another day.

"So why do you think you keep coming back here and bringing me treats?"

"Because I'm a nice dragon who's feeling empathy for a fellow being."

"Okay, let's pretend it is a myth, but say someone believed that myth, someone who would poison another person just to gain control over you. Do you think they're going to be your best friend, treating you with loving

231

kindness? You're big, but you're not above being beaten into submission with a hook, or chained so heavily you can't move."

My stomach turned, and a crawling sensation trickled over my scales. I'd had bad handlers. I'd experienced exactly what Cordelia had just described. The very thought of ever feeling an un-cushioned hook against my skin again and the memory of the soul-shattering weight of chains and shackles made me want to throw up.

"They didn't plan on me, though," she continued. "They didn't plan on you stumbling out of the Tent and falling asleep with me and Benny nearby." Cordelia laughed despite her grave tone. "Just think, if you had turned the other way, Benny might be your handler right now. How's he doing, by the way?"

I told her of my new diet regimen. "I haven't checked on him since, but I'll go as soon as I leave here. And no, they didn't count on you, but if we don't figure this out soon, they won't have to."

A shiver ran up my ears. If whoever had killed Porter did so because they thought I would imprint on them, would they also kill Cordelia? She was a sitting duck in the Cells. Once I sorted out why a duck would sit and not swim or paddle or just bob about in the water, I would have to see if Conrad could have one of his centaurs guard the Cells.

"You need to pay attention to who stays close to you," said Cordelia, as if she'd just had a similar realization of the danger she might be in. "And let me know what you find out about the wine."

"Any other ideas to check out?"

"No. Which does worry me." She glanced to the sky. The sun was already on its downward trip for the day. We had little time before the jailor came for her. "Keep me informed, alright?"

"Will do, Quinn."

I turned away and started to head back to where I was to meet Boris, when from behind me came the word, "Sit."

My back end dipped, almost touched the ground, but I fought it (barely). I kept walking, flipping the middle claw to Cordelia, whose laughter bounced off the walls of her prison.

CHAPTER 30
BANDIT BREAK IN

"The account book shows no wine barrel having been purchased and no record of one being received," said Boris.

I heard him, I understood the words, but I couldn't take my eyes off the fedora he'd picked up some time between his leaving Reinhart's caravan and joining back up with me.

Unlike the trench coat, the fedora did fit him. It was a child-sized hat, one of the prizes that could be won in Eisenberg's Entertainment Alley if you managed to outsmart the tricky physics of their games. Boris wore it tilted at a rakish angle and pulled low over his left eye. It might have given him a look of mysterious derring-do, if not for the thing being pink with glittering purple sequins sewn across the band.

"Well, that's another dead end. Thanks anyway, Boris," I said, handing him back his oversized trench coat.

"I did not say that was all I found." My ears twitched forward with curiosity. A curiosity that had to wait while Boris wrangled his way back into his coat. "Reinhart writes with dwarfish runes."

"And?" I asked, not seeing his point. Of course, he would use dwarfish runes. He was a dwarf.

"And that means only elf species can read it, including brownies," he added as he tugged proudly on his coat's large lapel. "My detective had a case of fraud once and she told me all accounts are supposed to be kept in English so any species can do an audit on them."

"So you think he was trying to hide something?"

"I don't like to make assumptions. Perhaps Zin has told him to use runes to cover something up. They could then pick and choose what they transcribed into English for the auditors. Also, there was a large withdrawal from petty cash the day we arrived to this spot."

"But that's not unusual. Zin always needs cash to buy supplies when we get into a new location."

"Yes, but Zin normally pays that cash back from the first day of ticket sales. The cash has not been returned. It also didn't have Zin's signature next to it."

The rule was anyone could use petty cash as long as it was repaid within a week. You signed your name next to the withdrawal amount as a promise to repay the sum. It also let Zin know who to send the trolls after if you failed to repay.

"Whose signature was there, then?"

"There was no signature."

Before I could begin to guess what that might mean, Helga hurried up to us on her short, spindly legs.

"Sir, Boris, sir," she said breathlessly.

"Helga, I have told you not to disturb me when I am busy with someone."

"But sir, you also said to start working on Mr. Zinzendorf's caravan. But I don't think I can do it myself."

"Have more confidence in yourself, Helga. You're a very capable brownie and you've shown good leadership skills. I would hate to have to put a bad mark on your performance evaluation."

"Yes sir, I would hate that too, but it's too much for one brownie. There's no way I can do the job in time."

As you've seen, Zin isn't the tidiest of satyrs. In fact, satyrs are slobs as a rule. They are part goat, after all, and that goatish aspect leads to certain cravings such as scraps of paper, tin cans, clothing. Our junk is like chewing gum to them, and the leftovers remain scattered where they fall. But even a satyr mess is rarely a problem for a brownie to tackle.

I went with Helga and Boris to see what she was so worried about. The moment I peered in, I knew she was right. There was no way even the most diligent brownie was going to be able to clean up the chaos in the half hour Boris allotted his crew to do each caravan. Drawers were pulled out of the dresser. Papers had been scattered. The bag of peanuts looked like it had exploded. And most of Zin's costumes and clothes were strewn across the rumpled bed. Although, again, that last bit could have just been the usual state of Zin's living quarters.

"This is not Zin's mess," Boris said. His face had paled at the sight of the disarray. "I know Zin's mess. This is not his."

"Then who did this?" I asked. "Wait, why isn't Zin back yet?"

Zin should have returned by now. The town wasn't far away, and I doubted the items on Gregg's list would have taken long to find. Well, except for the specialty cat food.

"He is back. Returned maybe twenty minutes ago," Boris said, a flash of annoyance sparked through his eyes. "And apparently, my team now has to clean up after kittens. Kittens! Do you know the havoc they can wreak on curtains?"

I said I didn't, although they couldn't be worse than a baby pyrodon who hasn't learned to control his firebox.

"I take it Zin hasn't seen this?" I asked.

"No, he was already in a foul mood when he dropped the kittens off at Gregg's caravan. I don't know where he went from there, but he's going to be fuming when he catches sight of this." Boris let out a heavy sigh, the sound of utter disappointment. "Helga, when's the last time you saw Humphrey?"

Helga turned a bright shade of red. "I, that is, why would I know anything about where he goes and when he goes there?" Boris stared levelly at her. "Fine, I saw him about an hour ago at the Cantina. But he scurried away when he saw me," she added dismally.

"And you only just found this?" Helga nodded. "Ask around. See if anyone has seen Humphrey since he was at the Cantina, then bring him to me if you find him. Meanwhile, I get the miserable task of explaining this to Zin. He is not going to be happy about that," Boris said, pointing to the paperwork that now looked like we could add it to the Dumble Dwarfs' confetti cannon.

Helga left to hunt down Humphrey while Boris and I

went in search of Zin. We checked the Tent, the Cantina (where Pepper was whipping up what smelled like the most delicious cinnamon swirl bread), then — after Boris insisted that, no, we could not stop for a snack — made a circuit through the caravans.

As we went, we asked if anyone had seen Zin. The most recent person who had seen him was Gregg — who was cuddling two kittens, one all-black shorthair and one orange tabby.

"Do you think he went back into town?" Boris asked.

"Maybe. He could be trying to convince the people that the show will be up and running tomorrow. But that doesn't seem like his style. He'd be more likely to send Reinhart to drum up business than go himself."

Helga found us mulling this over. She was dragging a shamefaced Humphrey behind her and seemed to have channeled her unrequited crush into contemptuous fury. A woman scorned is nothing to a brownie scorned, I'll tell you that.

"Found the lousy bogart. You give us a bad name, you know. You and your kind." She looked about ready to kick him in the shin, when Boris signaled me to pull the two apart.

"There'll be none of that, Helga. Now go round up a crew and try to make a dent in the mess of Zin's caravan."

"Fine, but if he's getting punished, let me know. I don't want to miss it."

Helga dashed off and Boris turned a stern glare on Humphrey, who was watching Helga with a definite twinkle in his large eyes.

"I thought you wanted to reform."

"I do, sir." Humphrey craned his neck to look up at me. I gave him a weak smile, but this exposed my one fang that extends a little farther than it should. Humphrey gave a tiny shriek and tucked his head down to stare at his oversized feet. "Don't let them eat me. I were only trying to help."

"Help?" Boris barked. "What are you talking about?"

"I were going to clean up around the Cantina like you tell me needs to be doing every couple hours. On my way I passes Mr. Zin's caravan. I hear noise. Sounds like messy noise and I thinks maybe it's bogarts. I peek in and sees exactly that. Small creatures making a mess of insides. I bang on the wall and they only tear through things fasterer. I bang again, tell them to knock it off, but they no listen to me. I think the banging only make them more furiouser. I try to find you, but you with big lizard, and you said no disturb you when you with people, so I not disturb. Then I sees Helga disturb and she gets you to go see mess, so I thinks to myself I don't need to."

"You didn't recognize who it was?" I asked. "Or what kind of creature exactly?"

"No see exact, just small. Not satyr. Not wood elf. Not human. Not centaur."

"It could be any one of my kind. Brownie, dwarf, bogart, pixie."

"Were they saying anything, Humphrey?" I asked, trying to keep my voice as gentle as possible.

"They, that is, I," he stammered as his scrawny body shook.

"He's not going to eat you," said Boris, clearly exasperated with his new hire. "Just tell him what you heard, if you heard anything."

"They had hats pulled down, face covered so words muffled, but I thinks they say something about finding license. That Mr. Zin is being taken care of."

"Oh well, good, as long as he's being cared for," said Boris.

"No, Boris," I said, "I don't think they mean *taken care of* in a good way. I think they mean to ruin him. Or to kill him."

At this, Humphrey trembled even more, and I wondered how his limbs didn't rattle right off his frame.

"Oh yes," said Boris, "I suppose that could be one way of interpreting it. But what is this license, do you think? His operating license?"

"It could be. If the license were stolen, and someone came by to check, they could close down the circus until Zin was able to prove he's allowed to operate shows in the region. A few days of closure could push him over the brink if he's in as much financial trouble as he's implied."

There was also another possibility for a license, and I hated to think of the consequences if someone got their hands on it.

A copy of all licenses to operate is kept in the main records hall in Portland, so losing one would be a hassle but only a temporary one. However, licenses for acts and performers are generally only held by the owner. If someone stole Zin's license registering his ownership of me, that someone would essentially have every legal right

HOARD IT ALL BEFORE

to me. Sure, if you had a good lawyer, you could fight it, but Zin might not be able to afford a good lawyer.

Someone wanted me, and while that would normally give your ego a little boost, this was not the kind of wanting I wanted to be a part of. Especially since this someone was proving how far they would go to get me.

CHAPTER 31
HYPNOTIC MEMORIES

Boris told Humphrey to go help Helga, and that if she gave him any trouble, to make it clear who sent him. Once the skinny creature trotted off on his gangly legs, I told Boris my theory. He agreed the dragon license was far more likely what they were after than the operating license. Which was disappointing since I'd really been hoping he'd tell me my idea was laughably off course.

Despite the distraction of the kittens, Gregg and his team had the power back up and running by half-past five. A few people trickled in and I did a handful of simple acts with Molly. Problem was, Zin still hadn't returned, and as I've mentioned, it's not as impressive to see a dragon balancing on a small object without someone cracking a whip and yelling, "*Hup-hup*" at him.

So, sometime after my third lackluster act—

MOLLY: The audience was lackluster; Duncan and I were superb.

—-we decided against any further performances for the day. A good choice because the grounds were nearly empty before the sun had even set.

After agreeing with Molly when to practice the next day, I went back to Cordelia to deliver news and treats. When I saw Flora was already at the Cells, I hurriedly tossed the caramel corn I'd brought with me into the nearest trash bin.

"Duncan," the centaur said in greeting, "I was just seeing if the oat grass blend had done anything to calm Cordelia's aura."

"And has it?" I said, biting back a smirk.

"Wait, are you speaking in front of the—" She flicked her eyes toward Cordelia.

I nodded. "I have a feeling she might be trustworthy."

"Oh, you see that too? That tiny hint of aquamarine at the edge of her aura?" Not having any clue of what an aura looked like or what part of the body it might be attached to, I shrugged vaguely in response. "Unfortunately, despite the cucumber and mint in the oat blend I gave her, the rest of the aura remains very fiery."

"Yeah, well," said Cordelia, "that might have more to do with being locked in a cage against my will than your healing skills."

"That's very kind of you." Flora beamed a smile that I'd bet was full of healthy aura-ness. She then said to me, "I've been meaning to tell you how much I enjoyed that stunt with Molly. The headdress tickling your nose was such a wonderful touch."

"That headdress almost caused me to kill Molly."

"Dear me, yes, Conrad did make that point. I thought he was only teasing me. He does like to play on my sensitive nature at times."

"What headdress is this?" Cordelia asked, so I explained to her the act, the sneeze, and the blue floof someone sent as a gift to Molly. "And you didn't ask her who sent it? You didn't ask if there was a note with it?"

"I—"

"That's right," Flora said, saving me from digging up an excuse for my own ineptitude. "Conrad tells me you've been sleuthing. What a wonderfully noble use of your time, Duncan."

"*Trying* to sleuth is a better way to put it. Everything just comes up a dead end. Sorry, bad choice of words."

"But you were right there with Porter that night. You don't recall anything?" Flora stepped back, tilted her head and looked into the distance. "Ah yes, I see now. Your aura is a little wobbly from that particular time."

"Wobbly? And wait, where exactly are you seeing my aura?" I turned and squinted my eyes in the direction Flora had been gazing, but could see nothing except the tops of caravans and the Tent in the distance.

"No, not like that. To see an aura, it's best to view it with your peripheral vision. And by wobbly, I mean, your aura shakes, wobbles, doesn't seem to be able to hold itself steady. Were you drinking that night, Duncan?"

Cordelia barely held back a snorting laugh.

"I drink every night, Flora. And please don't lecture me on that. I have cut back lately."

"I would never lecture you. Lecturing is patronizing. I would want you to work with me so we can delve into which plants, which scents would assist you in reducing your dependence on such things. But is that why you say you saw nothing? Perhaps you did, but you just can't remember."

"There are a few holes in that night's timeline, yes."

"May I try to help you see?" I was picturing her making me gaze dreamily off in the distance and was about to decline, when she added, "It could be the solution to the problem."

"Yeah, come on, Duncan. I'm running out of time here."

"Fine, but I doubt you'll discover anything."

"Mindset, Duncan. Just as I advised you when I had you set up your vision board: If you believe it won't work, it won't work."

So, I told myself it would work. For Porter. For Cordelia. But I don't think my "self" was buying it. Also, Cordelia was now doing her laugh-snort thing over the mention of my vision board.

"Close your eyes," said Flora, her voice wispier than ever. "Go back to that night. You've just had a good day. You're happy. Porter is happy."

"No, he was upset. About Gladys. And about an argument with Zin. Not sure which bothered him more."

"Good, but we don't need to see inside Porter's mind. We need to see inside yours. I want you to count with me, and when we reach the number nineteen, you will see Porter again for the last time. You will remember that night."

So I counted. By fifteen, I still thought it was utterly ridiculous. More of Flora's fluffy nonsense. Sixteen. I mean, the vision board was one thing. Seventeen. Like I said, it covered up that water stain. But this? Eighteen.

The next thing I knew, I was shaking my head, and Flora and Cordelia were staring at me.

"See, like I said. I don't think this will work."

"It did work," said Cordelia. "You snored a little, but it really did work."

"No, it— Wait, how long was I out?"

"Mere moments," said Flora. "And I can't say it was entirely fruitful, but it does prove Cordelia didn't kill Porter."

"I could have told you that," muttered Cordelia.

"Unfortunately, hypnotic statements are never allowed during a trial. But I hope it can help you with your sleuthing."

"Why? What did I say?"

"You said when you staggered away from Porter, you saw two small creatures watching. You said they looked like they were hiding, spying on you, but from your angle you could only see the tops of their hats."

"What type of creatures were they? Did I say?"

"No, only that they were small. I do hope it isn't the brownies. They are such good little workers. But I also can't think of it being the Dumbles. How could people who bring such laughter to children be murderers?"

Given that many dwarves are involved in some shady dealings, it wasn't too much of a stretch to imagine our clowns involved in a revenge plot against another dwarf family. But I didn't want to upset Flora by bringing this up.

"Did I say they were human-shaped?" I asked, thinking of the mini-taurs.

"You seemed certain they were. You recalled they smelled like breakfast, but you might have been crossing that with an earlier memory from the day. It does happen."

This was so vague as to be almost pointless. First, Flora just admitted I could be mixing a different memory into that night. What if I was merely recalling a memory of Boris and Helga from a month ago? Second, from my vantage point, most any creature appears tiny, so my describing someone as "small" isn't exactly the best identifier. Unless it was another dragon, Benny, or a rogue leviathan, this "small" creature could be any species. And just because two beings might have watched me and Porter, that didn't exactly make them killers.

"So what makes you think these two could be the culprits?" I asked. "How could what I saw keep Cordelia out of trouble?"

"You recalled hearing one of them ask if the stuff had worked yet and what to do with Porter's body once he died."

"Okay, yeah," I admitted, "that's a pretty good indication they were the bad guys."

"But it still doesn't get us anywhere if you can't sort out who they were," said Cordelia. "Or what they were."

"It does help, though." I told them about the creatures Humphrey said he overheard in Zin's caravan.

"Could it be the same pair?" Cordelia asked. "Or could it just be Humphrey making things up to cover his own mistake? I mean, can he really have switched from bogart back to brownie that quickly?"

"Oh, now, we shouldn't go around accusing people," said Flora.

I didn't like the thought either. I generally try to think the best of my fellow creatures, but Cordelia had a point. A point she was still making.

"Think about it. All this started when Humphrey showed up. He's a bogart. Do you think he suddenly reformed just because Boris took him under his wing? What if he had an accomplice, but that accomplice got away? Duncan, you say Ratcher is after Zin's circus. Humphrey came from Ratcher's. What if that whole 'I was too scared to stay' thing was a ruse so we'd take him in?"

"It's possible," Flora said reluctantly. "I hate to agree with you, though. That little guy does have the most charming aura. But perhaps we should advise Boris to search Humphrey's belongings for a hat or a cap, then see if it rings any bells for you, Duncan."

Something about a cap was ringing a bell, but it was ringing with a dull *thunk* like it had been hit with a muffled hammer on a rainy day. I shook the thought from my mind. It probably only seemed familiar because Humphrey had mentioned caps earlier. And would Humphrey have really pointed out that the marauders were wearing caps if he was hiding one in his belongings? This was all turning into a jumble. I needed to speak to someone with some experience in these things.

"I'm going to go talk to Boris," I said. "I'll see you later."

"Don't forget to check about that headdress of Molly's," Cordelia called after me. "And try to remember that I don't have a lot of *later* left, so if you could pick up the pace of this sleuthing, I'd be really grateful."

I waved behind me to let her know I'd heard, then made my way through the rows of caravans, wondering what sort of green concoction Flora was going to subject Cordelia to next. I reminded myself to bring a hot dog when I next checked up on her.

So many thoughts were running around in my head it was like one of our clown acts where the lead dwarf starts chasing after another dwarf, then a third dwarf starts running after the lead dwarf, and on and on it builds until there's a whole ring of dwarves and no one knows who's chasing who.

The cap tried to poke its way into the front of my mind, but something more worrisome shoved it aside: Molly's headdress and the timing of its arrival.

She said she'd just received the blue floof. The floof had made me sneeze. If I had dropped Molly, if I had hurt her in any way, I would once again have the official label of Dangerous Dragon slapped on me and would be dragged off to the work camps for re-education. My old scars burned at the memory of the last time I'd been thrown into one of those damn places.

Molly said someone had given her that headdress and hoped she'd wear it. Was it just an innocent gift, or had the gift giver hoped I'd hurt Molly and have to be sent away?

I stopped dead in my tracks as another thought barreled right in and parked itself over all the others.

What if it wasn't Cordelia someone was trying to frame for Porter's death? What if it was me? Perhaps this

249

someone expected me to pass out from the wine. If they knew Porter would be killed by the poison and I wouldn't, how would it look if I was found next to my handler's dead body? Even if it only looked like I had crushed him, an accidental death, especially the death of a human, still meant an immediate sentencing of yours truly to the camps.

Someone was after me. Ruthlessly after me.

But why?

CORDELIA: Yeah, don't they know what a pain you are?

DUNCAN: Shut up, I'm trying to add an air of mystery, of fear, of tension.

CORDELIA: Sorry, Master Scribe, I'll let you get back to it.

Chapter 32
Molly's Gift

By the time I left Cordelia and Flora, thick clouds had rolled in. They did nothing to cool the evening air and instead brought with them a mugginess that weighed on my scales. Since Molly's caravan was on the way to Boris's, I decided to stop off at her place before asking Boris about inspecting (or was it detecting?) Humphrey's belongings.

I knocked on Molly's door, then peered in the window and said, "It's just me. Don't worry about doing your makeup."

She trotted over to the window. Blue eye shadow and those spider things that I think were meant to look like eyelashes already decorated her face.

"Don't be silly. I'm always dressed for visitors. Oatmeal?" she offered.

"No, thanks. I was just wondering where you got that blue floof you wore the other night. Did you ever figure out who sent it?"

"Nope, all I know is they're an admirer. I do hope they saw the show that night. I'm sure it would just give them the biggest thrill to see their gift being put to use."

"No card? No wrapping?"

"Nope, darlin', but there was a note. Like I told you, the admirer hoped I'd wear it for my next act."

"A signed note?"

"No, silly, how many times I gotta tell you? It just said, *From an admirer*. I still have it if you want to see it." She turned toward her vanity table. "Is this to do with Porter?" she asked over her shoulder.

"Maybe. I'm not sure."

Molly pulled the note from where she'd stuck it in the frame around her vanity mirror. I examined it. The writing was familiar. Sort of. It was far tidier on this little gift tag than it had been on the threatening letter someone had slipped through my mail slot, but the M of *Molly* on this note and the M of *Mops* on my letter were an exact match.

My stomach went queasy, but I also felt a little bit of pride. I was proving to be quite the sleuth.

CORDELIA: Sorry, who exactly is quite the sleuth?

DUNCAN: You were just the idea man — or idea woman — at this point. I was the one having to go around asking all the questions.

CORDELIA: But you wouldn't have known what questions to ask without me.

DUNCAN: I might have come up with a few.

CORDELIA: Yeah, like "Where's my omelet?" "Hmm, what's in this omelet?" "When will Pepper make me another omelet?"

DUNCAN: Those are all very important questions, I'll have you know.

I thanked Molly. The note really was a great clue, but unless we forced everyone in the circus to hand over a writing sample, it wasn't going to help at that exact moment. I went to Boris, who had neatly folded the trench coat and placed it on his bed with the pink fedora centered on the garment. I told him about the memory Flora had helped me excavate from my own brain, as well as my suspicions of Humphrey's role in all this. And my doubts.

"We can check, but Humphrey's proven himself a good worker. Plus, although the *Handbook* does allow such things in certain situations, I don't like the idea of snooping around in my crew's things."

"Just this once."

He agreed reluctantly, and — since Humphrey was still helping Helga clean up Zin's caravan — began searching the small area around a cot Humphrey now called his own.

I felt like an idiot. Humphrey had nothing. Boris had thrown out the rags Humphrey had been wearing when he showed up, and the only clothes he now owned were two shirts, a few underthings, and a pair of trousers Boris had given him. His only other belongings were a small sack with nothing but a teaspoon and a tin of soup inside, along with a blanket that Boris told me had been issued to him at the same time he gave him his dukie book.

"The dukie books," I said, mostly to myself.

"Duncan, I know this means a lot to you, but I can't go rifling through—"

"No, our dukie books. They should have handwriting in them."

I pulled out mine. We're all supposed to keep them with us because they're basically like cash in the circus. If someone took your book, they could charge up meals and other expenses without dipping into their own pay. I flipped mine to the first page where the issuer would have written his name.

And written across the top was *Ely Zinzendorf*. No M's of course, but the handwriting was completely unlike anything on Molly's gift tag or my note. I cursed and slipped the book back into my pocket.

CORDELIA: Pocket? You're a dragon. You run around naked.

DUNCAN: Yeah, but I have these little flaps of skin at my sides. See? They're very handy.

CORDELIA: Huh. Do all dragons have them?

DUNCAN: You know, I haven't made a habit of feeling up my fellow dragons to find out. What kind of weird stuff do you humans get up to when we're not looking?

CORDELIA: I don't think you want to know.

"Let me see yours," I said, holding out my hand for Boris's dukie book.

"Duncan, this is going too far."

I eyed Boris. An odd feeling clawed its way along my arms.

Why had he so readily volunteered to lead this investigation? Could I really trust he was making inquiries and diligently delving into this problem? Because other than trying to dress the part, it didn't seem like he was doing much detective work. Boris had access to everyone's caravan, including Flora's, from where the behemoth saliva had gone missing...

I cursed my suspicious mind. I really needed to find out who was behind Porter's murder and all the rest of this mess before I started accusing myself.

"Just let me see who issued it. I need to check if there's handwriting in there that matches the two notes."

Boris heaved a great sigh, then pulled out his book, a red one like mine. He flipped it to the front page and held it out to me.

His also bore Zin's signature.

The floor of the caravan rumbled as I growled my frustration.

"You were expecting something different?" Boris said. "We all have books signed by Zin."

"I know. I know," I said impatiently. "Zin went wild autographing a crateful of them."

"Yes," Boris said, an indulgent smile on his normally stiff lips, "you should have seen his caravan then. Spick and span with everything alphabetized. Zin was so eager to have everything in order. He didn't want to waste time when new recruits came, wanted a tight ship, so he thought he'd sign the lot in a whir of efficiency."

"Zin was orderly? Efficient?"

"Was. It didn't take long for the efficiency to break

down. That's why I took my own stack of the signed books. I wanted to get my recruits up and cleaning as soon as they were hired. Inefficiency has no place in my business. *The Handbook* advises all new hires be provided with meaningful work within an hour of their employment. My aim is to get that down to half an hour."

I dropped down to my haunches, annoyed and disheartened by it all.

"How did your detective do this? How did he—"

"She."

"She?" Boris nodded. "Okay, she. How did she handle all this running around, asking stupid questions, and bashing into dead ends, and still manage to keep plodding on to solve the case?"

"Well, she is in the regional mental hospital now."

"You're not serious."

Again, Boris nodded. "Couldn't deal with not being able to solve her last case, so they said. But the other cases, I think she just kept going out of sheer stubbornness. That, and she didn't get paid until the case was solved. But you've got more motive than that, don't you?"

"You mean avenging Porter?"

"And clearing Cordelia's name. You won't be able to live with yourself if you let her go to the Pits, will you?"

CORDELIA: Wait, I wasn't your first concern?

DUNCAN: Um...hold on, maybe I've written this out of order. Yes, yes, there it is in my notes. I most definitely was primarily concerned with saving Cordelia Quinn.

CORDELIA: Great chimera balls, you really are the worst liar.

DUNCAN: Well, yeah, we already established that.

CORDELIA: Oh, right.

I went back to my caravan. I needed to think. I needed to let my mind wander. I needed a drink. Yeah, so much for my sober sleuthing, but this had proved to be a frustrating and confounding day.

From the kitchen area of my caravan — which was little more than a small icebox and a shelf with snacks and drinks on it — I pulled a jug of whiskey. I normally stick to wine and beer during a performance run, but as I said, the day had been an awful one. Plus, it was uncomfortably hot and humid, and the whisky should be refreshingly cold from being kept near the icebox.

I popped the cork off the jug and tipped myself a mouthful. Or tried to. Apparently, I'd already consumed this stash, so what dribbled out wouldn't even have filled a human-sized shot glass.

Still, what I did manage to get out burned like an alcohol-filled chili pepper. I checked the label. It was one of the jugs of chili pepper whiskey I'd picked up when we toured down south over the winter.

South, I pondered gloomily and glanced over to the corner above my bed where I'd placed a brightly colored sombrero Porter had given me. The thing was far too small for me, but we thought it could serve as comic relief for a show one day.

A tear trickled down my cheek. Stupid Porter going

and getting dead. I tipped the jug back just in case there might be a couple more drops of booze hiding in there somewhere. There wasn't. I flopped onto my back and stared up at my vision board.

I still thought the thing little more than decorative, but drifting my eyes over the board's meandering path to my supposed Full Potential Circle unleashed my mind, allowing it to wander freely from sombreros to the hat-wearing creatures that had made a mess of Zin's office, to my suspecting Humphrey, to his sad tin of soup where I hit a dead end.

With a heavy sigh, I started back at the sombrero again, my thoughts clicking along in my head as they roamed around to Cordelia and how she might look in the sombrero, to the colors clashing with her features, to how long it might take Zin's goat side to take over and eat the hat, to Cordelia begging Zin for a job handling me, to her altered photo of me and Porter that had slipped out of her dukie book, to—

I jerked up. Despite only having a tiny amount of whiskey, the motion sent my head spinning. Cordelia's dukie book. It had been a different color. It hadn't been one of the original bunch Zin had signed.

Signatures. Signatures. Something about signatures. Something was clicking into place about the signature on the paperwork. No, not the signature, the paperwork itself.

I lay back down. Who knows, maybe the vision board was working.

Click click click, my mind went, but no new insights

poked through. My eyelids grew heavy. I snorted awake, wiped away a dribble of drool, then rolled over to check the jug once more. Still empty. I caught the scent of something frying. Who was cooking at this hour?

My eyes drooped shut. The clicking continued. Was my skull made of metal? No, it had to be coming from outside. It had to be—

I drifted into sleep.

CHAPTER 33
IT'S A BIT TOASTY OUT

I jerked awake, feeling beyond certain that something was wrong.

The instant I stepped out into the muggy darkness, I darted a glance around. I could have sworn I saw movement, but perhaps it was only my own shadow.

My nose twitched. Fully alert now, I realized I hadn't smelled someone frying up something to eat, I'd merely caught the thick scent of old cooking oil. Pepper saves the stuff for the gremlins to convert into fuel for various engines and mechanical doodads around the circus. Until they come to collect it, she stores it in barrels kept behind the Cantina.

Just as I wondered if someone had knocked over one of the barrels, my ears perked up. Literally perked. Their normally floppy tips stood up straight while the rest of the ear swiveled in the direction of the metallic clicking. They picked up a hissing sound that reminded me of Fergus lighting his latest cigarette. With the strange sense of being watched, I moved toward the noise. Maybe that's all it was: Fergus returning from a day of seeking out a new lap, his hooves clicking on the hard ground as he chain-smoked his health away.

I didn't move stealthily toward the sounds. After all, I'm a dragon, I don't have a lot of ninja instincts and even if I did, they'd be pointless with the size of me. Besides, no one was raising a fuss. In fact, it was eerily quiet, so I had no reason to think anything was amiss. Still, something in the air felt dangerous.

The hissing sound — accompanied now by an occasional popping noise — led me in the opposite direction of the Cantina, through the rows of caravans, and toward the Cells.

I was still a couple rows of caravans away from the Cells when something deep within me cringed, freezing me in place. The very second I wondered what was wrong with me, there came a rushing *whoosh* and a burst of orange glowed through the gap between the caravans. Someone screamed. Several people shouted. So much for that eerie silence.

The scream pierced through the night again, and this time I recognized it as Cordelia's. I charged forward, my feet acting before my brain could tell them not to. But the instant I saw the flames licking up the front bars of the Cells, I cowered back. I couldn't do it. I knew if I had to, I could smash the side of the cage and make an opening for Cordelia to escape through. But I couldn't. I couldn't go anywhere near those fiery tongues. I didn't even want to be in the same town as them.

My legs shook. My shortened wings flapped as if they could actually lift me off the ground to somewhere safe.

"Stop it, Duncan. Stop your damn wings." It was Fergus, speaking around the cigarette in his mouth. "You're fanning the flames, you overgrown gecko."

I pinched my wings to my sides, then someone shoved a hose into my hands.

"Hold it steady," said Conrad. "From your height, you can douse the entire thing."

Without warning, water pulsed and gushed through the hose at full force. A smaller creature might have been knocked back into last week with the power of it, but my weight kept me in place.

I couldn't look at the flames. I hated the heat of them on my face. I wanted to throw down the hose. I wanted to run. I wanted to fly. Dear Smaug, how I wanted to fly. I forced my wings to remain squeezed tight against my back as I held the hose in place with shaking hands. I hated myself for the fear coursing through me.

I really wish I could tell you it was fear for Cordelia, but I honestly couldn't make room in my head for her, for anyone, with my own phobia crowding out everything else.

I was just about to drop the hose and flee when the water stopped flowing and the hose went limp. Conrad was shouting at people to get the Cells open. I stood, shaking uncontrollably, clutching to the hose. It was all I could do as activity flurried all around me.

"You all right there, man?" Fergus asked.

"Is it out?" My voice trembled.

"Yeah, open your eyes, you daft thing."

I did. Slowly. The flames were out. The Cells were a blackened heap. The phobia moved aside, and fear for

Cordelia finally flooded in. Was she okay? Had she become the next victim? If so, and if the stupid imprinting myth was true, did that mean Fergus was now my handler since he was the first creature I was seeing after she died? Talk about a thought that would keep me up at night.

"There she is," Fergus said, a hint of true relief in his voice. I glanced down at him, an arch expression on my face. "What? I was worried there for a second. I mean, it'd be a shame to see a lap like that burnt to a crisp."

Conrad and a couple other centaurs pulled Cordelia from what was left of the Cells. She was coughing and she looked like a drowned pixie, but she was standing on her own two non-crispy feet. Flora galloped up and wrapped a blanket around Cordelia's shoulders, then tried to give her a sip of something that looked like it had been scooped straight out of Benny's wallow. Cordelia held up a hand of refusal until Molly handed her a beer. Cordelia gulped it down, only coming up for air to cough a few more times.

I turned away. The sky rumbled with thunder, the wind picked up, then the temperature dropped. Before you could say, "Strange weather we're having," came a gush of rain that would have put out the fire if the inferno had started only a few minutes later than it had.

See, I told you there'd be a dark and stormy night in here somewhere.

Fergus called after me, but I ignored him. A few people congratulated me on what I'd done, but I hadn't done anything. I'd stood and held a hose with my eyes clamped shut. I could have acted faster, I could have rushed in and pulled Cordelia out straight away, but I'd let the old fear take over.

With the unshakable sense of everyone watching me, I kept my eyes to the ground and went to the Cantina's pantry before heading back to my place. I'd have Pepper note what I took in my dukie book later.

Once back to my caravan — and even there I couldn't shake the feeling of judgmental eyes on me — I guzzled three jugs of Pepper's fortified wine, one after the other. Or maybe it was four. Either way, I passed out and didn't wake until morning.

CHAPTER 34
I'VE SEEN THIS BEFORE

With the Cells being rather more open-air charcoal sculpture than lock-em-up prison, Cordelia later told me she spent that night at Flora and Conrad's caravan under the watchful guard of the centaur couple. Or rather, the pampering treatment of Flora and the indulgent, gossip-seeking kindness of Conrad.

Fergus showed up at my caravan the next morning. Rather too early in the morning, if you ask me.

Fergus doesn't exactly knock. For one thing, he has neither hands to pound with, nor knuckles to rap against a door frame. Also, he likes to make his presence known. Instead of a gentle *thump*, Fergus was kicking my door with sharp, quick strikes of his rear hooves. Over and over and with increasing force until I finally fumbled out of bed, staggered over some empty jugs (I was wrong, there were five), and yanked the door open.

To my pleasure, Fergus was in mid-kick when I did this. His intended blow hit nothing but air and he lurched for balance as the cigarette nearly dropped from his lips.

"You even going to bother to see her taken away?"

Fergus asked critically as I squinted against the bright morning sunlight. The rainstorm's intense, but short-lived downpour made it feel as if the circus grounds had been given a thorough wash. Although the dark clouds had departed, they'd left behind a gusty wind that now whipped around the tents and caravans.

Speaking of thorough washes, I needed to get to Benny. He'd likely spent the night enjoying the extra muck of a sopping wet wallow and would be a filthy mess again.

"I mean," Fergus continued with feigned disinterest, "I'm only going so I can get one last glimpse of that lap, but she came to Zin's for you, man. You should be there."

"They've come for her already? The jailor was supposed to be gone until tomorrow."

"He's not here yet. Conrad heard the guy's yogurt retreat was cut short. Is that right? Yogurt?" I shrugged. Who knew with humans? "At any rate, he's on his way. And he's not in a good mood. Guess the guy really likes yogurt."

I cursed myself. I felt like I was right on the edge of figuring out how to prove Cordelia's innocence. I then cursed Zin for whatever role he might have played in all this, whether it was the murder itself or the coverup of whoever really did it.

And where the hell was he, anyway? The coward. After he'd brought back Gregg's supplies and kittens, no one had seen him. One of his structures just burnt down. One of his employees was about to be hauled off to a terrible fate. Shouldn't he be here? Or was he off drinking champagne with Ratcher to celebrate their deal?

Fergus waited outside smoking while I splashed water on my face and brushed my fangs. I stepped out of my caravan and grimaced at the sound and feel of mud squelching between my toes. Shaking my legs to clear the gunk from my feet, I told Fergus I wanted to loop around and see the Cells. I don't know why. Morbid curiosity? A weird need to torment myself with a bit more guilt? Either way, Fergus agreed to make the detour. On the way, I noticed there were no lights on in the caravans, no hum of electricity pulsing through the wires strung between tents.

"I thought the gremlins got the power back up," I said.

"They did. Then the storm knocked it out again. Gregg says it'll be a quick fix. I think he's in a hurry to get the work done so he can get back to Mango and Olive."

"New hires?"

"No, the kittens. The supposed mousers," Fergus added sarcastically. "Mango's the orange tabby, Olive's the black one. The way he's spoiling them, they'll be too well-fed to bother with rodents." We rounded the last caravan and stopped in our tracks. "Man," Fergus said, his voice a shocked whisper, "she had a close shave, didn't she?"

It was awful. The roof had burned away entirely, and the bars at the front had warped from the heat. The east side of the structure was blackened and charred, but the flames hadn't quite reached the west side, which is where Cordelia must have taken refuge while I—

While I did more than Zin had, I told myself. But I still felt like quite the reptilian heel over my hesitation and my stupid fear.

267

CORDELIA: Wait, do reptiles have heels?

DUNCAN: Sure we do, see. It's that bit there.

CORDELIA: Huh. And ankles?

DUNCAN: Of course we have ankles. How would we turn and waggle our feet if we didn't? Now, we're getting to a really critical bit, so maybe we should save the dragon anatomy lesson for later.

CORDELIA: Oh right. This is a good bit since I'm in it quite a lot. You know, for being the co-hero, I'm not in the book much.

DUNCAN: I offered you the chance to be the point-of-view character, but you said it'd be better through my perspective.

CORDELIA: Yeah, I suppose me sitting in the Cells reporting on Flora's foul drinks and the garbage fluttering by wouldn't have been very intriguing.

DUNCAN: Neither is this conversation. To the readers, that is.

Sorry for the interruption, but Cordelia has created a perfect segue. The Cells were near where we kept our garbage. It was sort of an added punishment to have to smell rotting food scraps and centaur leavings.

It was also where Helga and Humphrey had dumped the mess from Zin's office. They'd put the few still-intact papers in order, but most of the documents had been shredded and even the best jigsaw puzzle enthusiast wouldn't have been able to piece them back together. So, despite Boris grumbling that the *Handbook* strictly forbade discarding a client's personal belongings, they bagged up the worst of the mess and placed it alongside the garbage for kindling or bedding or confetti making.

And, not expecting the dark and stormy night, nor the sunny and windy morning, they hadn't tied the bags closed. Which was probably also against the *Handbook's* protocol.

A gust of wind ruffled my ears. Tattered bits of paper went zipping by. Fergus cursed and tried to protect his cigarette from burning away in the breeze. As he turned, he lowered his head and one of the scraps skewered itself on his horn.

The sight of it stuck there broke through my foul mood, and a fit of giggles hit me. The giggles turned into a full-on belly laugh when Fergus twisted his head and began scraping his horn on the ground in an attempt to free the stubborn scrap. It wouldn't budge, and I was nearly hyperventilating with amusement.

"It's not that funny. Pegasus's shining balls, I wish I had hands like the centaurs."

Laughing so hard I was shaking, I told Fergus to hold still, that I'd get it off of him. But when he lifted his head, the paper fluttered in the wind and I lost it again.

"Oh, yes, hysterical. I'm so glad you're enjoying my indignity."

"Okay, okay," I snorted a restrained giggle. "I'll get it, just hold still."

Snorting a few more times, I plucked the paper from his horn. I was about to crumple it up when I saw what it was. The contract I'd seen in Zin's office. Well, part of it, at any rate. Had he torn it up, or had the intruder done so? If it was Zin, why now? And if it was the intruder, could it have been one of the troupe who knew about the contract and didn't want Zin to sell? Or had it just gotten shredded in the chaos of someone wanting to make a mess?

Something else caught my eye. Something I'd noticed before but hadn't paid much attention to. Ratcher's logo was at the header of the sheet. It was a new logo, not the one that had been plastered on billboards for the past couple years. That one had been a white square at the center of which was a blocky R made of vertical purple and black stripes to mimic Ratcher's main tent.

This new logo was an R, simple but stylized to be memorable. The white letter stood out against the silhouette of a red circus tent.

"You gonna get rid of that, or what?" Fergus asked.

"The cap," I muttered.

"Cap? Man, what are you on about? You coming with me to see The Lap— Sorry, to see Cordelia, or are you going to stay here cuddling that piece of paper?"

"Reinhart's cap." I turned the sheet to him. "Reinhart was wearing a cap with this logo on it."

"So what? People wear other circuses' gear all the time. We're cheap. We like free handouts."

"But Ratcher rarely gives free handouts. And when he does, it's when he's trying to offload old stuff he can't sell. This logo," I pointed to the sheet, "is new. Anything with this on it would also be new. It wouldn't be given away to just anyone. We need to talk to Reinhart."

"The jailor is going to be here any minute. You really think chatting with a dwarf over his fashion choices is the best use of time right now? Or maybe you're trying to avoid seeing Cordelia being sent away?"

"I'm not trying to avoid anything. I'm trying to keep it from happening. Hear me out. What if Reinhart is working for Ratcher? What if he's trying to sabotage Zin's circus to force him to sell to Ratcher?"

Fergus stared at me. He pulled a long drag on his cigarette before saying, "And why would he do that?"

I tapped my foot impatiently. Irritated with my throbbing brain for not conjuring a dozen brilliant ideas to solve this case. I really should know better than to drink so much fortified wine. That stuff gives the worst hangovers.

"I don't know," I finally admitted.

"Motive, man. You gotta have motive. Otherwise, no one's going to listen to your theories."

"I need to go back to my caravan. I need to check on something."

"Your whisky supply?"

"No," I replied confidently, since I knew that was already gone. "I think I might have remembered something."

"Man, seriously, for a dragon, you are a big chicken."

"Reptiles are closely related to birds, you know."

"Yeah, but you've gone from distant cousin to twin sibling." My nostrils flared and heat kindled in my firebox.

"Come on," Fergus said, speaking more calmly, "How do you think Quinn's going to feel if you aren't there?"

Yeah, that extinguished my firebox more thoroughly than a deluge. My shoulders sagged. I crumpled the paper, stuck it in my pocket, then met Fergus's eye.

"You're right. Let's go get this over with."

Chapter 35
The Jailor Arrives

On our way to the Cantina, the main gathering area from where Fergus told me the jailor would collect Cordelia, we came across Boris and Helga returning from a night's work with bucket, broom, and a bag of garbage. Boris wasn't wearing his trench coat, but did have on the glittery fedora. It suited him, really.

Fergus was right. I had to be there for Cordelia. I couldn't just let her think I'd abandoned her to her fate. But ever since I'd left my caravan, there'd been a question scratching at my brain. Boris was just the brownie I needed.

"One sec, Fergus."

"Man, you are the king of delaying tactics."

I ignored the unicorn and signaled to Boris I wanted to speak with him.

"The case," Boris said dismally, "it's hit a dead end. My detective would be so disappointed in me."

"There's one more clue. I think."

Boris's ears twitched forward with interest. "What is this clue?"

"I don't know," I said, suddenly wondering if Fergus was right. Maybe I was just grasping at straws and avoiding the inevitable. I had failed both Porter and Cordelia, and now Zin would be able to sell me off to save himself the expense of a new handler.

"No, tell me. It might be helpful. It certainly can't hurt."

"I have this weird feeling someone was hanging around my caravan last night. I thought it was just a trick of the light or my own guilt, but what if it wasn't? If Cordelia had died in that fire, my next handler would supposedly be whoever I saw next." According to a rumor I didn't believe in, I wanted to add, but now was not the time to debate that topic. "All the troupe knows about my issues with fire. They would have expected me to stay in, to keep away from the flames. What if someone was waiting for me, assuming Cordelia would be dead when I next stepped out?"

"You think there might be footprints of this someone?"

I hadn't really, but that was a pretty smart idea. Perhaps Boris had learned a thing or two from his detective.

"Maybe. The section my caravan is in isn't highly trafficked. With the rain and the mud, if someone was lurking around, they might have left footprints. Unless, of course, they wiped them away. Or if they took off before the rainstorm. Or unless I'm imagining all this."

"Helga, please take this," Boris said, handing her the cleaning gear, then tilting his fedora into that rakish angle. "I've got some investigative detecting to do."

"No," I said, "take Helga with you. You'll need a witness if there is something."

"Now you're thinking like a detecting dragon," said Boris, a hint of approval in his voice.

"Yeah, yeah," said Fergus impatiently. "Now can Duncan the Detecting Dragon get a move on before Cordelia the Condemned is carted off?"

"You're very good at alliteration, Fergus," I said as we continued toward the Cantina.

"My poetry has merited me multitudes of moments in many marvelous laps."

At the Cantina, Pepper caught my eye and held up her omelet pan. I shook my head. I was in no mood to eat. Pepper's eye went wide with surprise, then her brow furrowed into a scowl. What? Did she think I was cheating on her and getting ten-egg omelets from some other chef? I'd have to make amends later, but for now, Cordelia was being led toward the Cantina by Conrad and Flora.

Well, I say *led*, but she was really just walking alongside them with Flora clutching at Cordelia's hand for support, and Conrad walking a pace in the lead as if ready to defend his charge if needed.

Mere moments later, the jailor stepped through the gates. He was a big man with almost no neck. His bald head gleamed in the sunlight and his body, while huge, showed no jiggling sign of fat under his thin, sleeveless shirt. Maybe there's something to that yogurt he seemed to like so much.

"I could take him," said Fergus, narrowing his eyes and

aiming his horn at the monstrous man.

Hurrying alongside the jailor was Reinhart, who, since the gates were still locked at such an early hour, would have had to escort the mound of muscle through the barrier. They stopped at the edge of the crowd that had gathered. The jailor unfolded a document he'd pulled from his trousers pocket. He then extracted a pair of minuscule, wire-framed glasses and perched them on the end of his bulbous nose.

"I have come," he began in a deep, but nasally voice, "to collect Cordelia Quinn, who is to be sent to the dragon waste pits for her role in the murder of Porter Kohl."

Maybe I've read too many dime-store detective novels, but I kept expecting someone to charge forward and, in a fit of guilt, confess they were the villain who did the horrible deed. Or if not that, then perhaps someone performing a dramatic finger-pointing flourish to reveal who really did it. Or, fantasy of all fantasies, to trot out the real Porter Kohl, say it was all a belated April Fools' Day joke and, boy oh boy, what a great prank they'd just played on all of us.

No one did any of these things.

Reinhart indicated to the jailor who he was there to collect. Conrad, a hesitation in his gait, stepped aside, but Flora squeezed Cordelia in a fiercely tight hug. She hadn't let go when the jailor grabbed Cordelia's arm. He pulled the two apart and Flora's eyes fixed on him, blazing with a hatred I didn't think her aura was capable of. Cordelia looked back once, meeting my eye and giving a sharp nod of her head as if to say goodbye.

DUNCAN: *You were saying goodbye, weren't you? Not just flicking a hair out of your eyes.*

CORDELIA: *Yes, Duncan. It was a goodbye.*

DUNCAN: *I suppose we've given away a lot with us chattering back and forth throughout this book, haven't we?*

CORDELIA: *Not really. You could have met with your end moments after I was taken away. I mean, who's to say you're not writing this from beyond the grave.*

DUNCAN: *That would make a clever twist.*

CORDELIA: *Too bad it's not that kind of story.*

No, it's not that kind of story, and the jailor pushed Cordelia into the caged cart he'd left outside the gates.

A fiery sensation ripped through my gut. I wanted to roast him, I wanted him to get his hands off her, but I couldn't get past the barrier. Not with Zin's magic on it, and not with my wings clipped. I could do nothing. I was the biggest, supposedly baddest, dragon in the region and I could do nothing but watch my handler being carted away.

CHAPTER 36
WHAT THE BROWNIES FOUND

As I stood drowning in self-loathing, someone tapped on my toe. I looked down to see Helga staring up at me, practically tipping over backward to glance up so far. She crooked her finger, and I crouched down to listen to her.

"Boris found something," she whispered.

"Then where is he? Why didn't he get over here and say something? Cordelia just got carted off. It's a little late for evidence now." I punctuated all this with a deep growl and bared my fangs. It's no excuse, but I was frustrated with the world, mad at myself, and really hungover. Helga shuddered, but didn't back away. "So what useless evidence did he find? Never mind, I'll go see for myself."

I knew I was being unfair. I was shooting the massager, or something like that. I stopped and took one of Flora's cleansing breaths. It didn't douse all the anger, but it took the edge off. "Sorry for that." I held out my front paw for Helga. "Give you a lift?"

She seemed quick to forgive and climbed up to the bend of my elbow, then onto my shoulder as I headed back to my caravan.

"What did you find?" I asked Boris as Helga slid back down to the ground. Quite nimbly, too. If I ever performed at Zin's again, I'd have to see if she wanted to be part of an act.

Boris stepped aside from where, in an attempt to appear casual, he'd been leaning against my caravan.

"Anyone follow you?" he asked, tugging the brim of his fedora even lower over his eyes.

"We did," said Conrad. Alongside him was Flora, wiping away tears. Boris narrowed his eyes at them.

"They can be trusted," I told him. "What did you find?"

Boris pointed to the ground.

There, in the dirt near the front wheel of my caravan, was a pair of footprints. One had been partially smudged, either from the person turning or from them deliberately trying to cover it up, but the other print looked like it had been freshly stamped into the soil.

A squarish foot, wide by human standards. With four splayed toes.

"Do not leave that print," I said with fire in my voice.

"Duncan, you can't do anything," said Conrad.

"Are you kidding? Reinhart's foot made that. This proves everything."

"This proves nothing," Conrad insisted. "That could be the print of any dwarf in the circus. And even if it is Reinhart's, he has as much right to walk around here as you do."

"But Reinhart also has a hat from Ratcher. Ratcher who wants to buy out Zin's circus to acquire me. You know about that stupid imprinting rumor. If Cordelia had died last night and Reinhart was the first person I saw, he would have believed he'd become my handler. He'd have believed he could command me to go anywhere with him. Even to Ratcher's. He waited here. Even in the rain, he waited here, thinking I'd have been bound to him."

"But why?" asked Conrad. "What would be the point? If Ratcher really wants you, he'll just keep upping his offers until Zin can't refuse."

That was a good point, I suppose. But I still wanted to question Reinhart. And Zin. Even if Reinhart didn't have much stake in this, Zin did. Who's to say they weren't in on all this together? Zin might have needed someone — some dwarf, to be exact — to help him with his plan to get rid of Porter so they could sell me to Ratcher.

Zin may have disappeared, but I knew where to find Reinhart. I turned away from my friends, ready to storm off toward Reinhart's caravan.

"Duncan, where are you going?" asked Flora, stopping me on the spot. "Violence is never the answer." Apparently I had that kill-the-Reinhart swagger in my step.

Before I could continue on my Reinhart rampage, Humphrey rounded the corner, coming up short when he caught sight of what I'm sure looked like a strange collection of creatures, all of whom were oozing tension.

In his hand was a bucket. Its contents smelled like old cooking oil. Cooking oil. The smell from the night before. That's why the Cells went up in flames so readily.

For an instant, my heart flared with fury at the little creature. He was the one who had spread the oil. He had lit the fire. He was working with Reinhart. But Boris interrupted my accusations.

"What are you doing with that, Humphrey? I told you on your first day that Pepper keeps her used oil behind the Cantina, away from the sleeping areas."

"Is not *from* Pepper. I was taking it *to* them."

"Them?"

"Pepper."

"You mean *her*," Helga said in a tone of charmed amusement at his mistake, "the singular pronoun."

"I no know singular. I know *them*."

"Humphrey," I asked, recalling what he'd witnessed the day before, "how many creatures did you see in Zin's caravan when the mess was made?"

"One." He held up a single skinny finger. "I tell you I see them. You no remember?"

"Yeah, I remember." If it had only been one small creature...

"But you said *they* had been speaking," said Boris.

"To self. Strange creature."

Boris and I exchanged glances. Reinhart talked to himself on a regular basis. He told us it was the only way to have a witty conversation.

"Duncan," Flora asked slowly, as if the idea behind her question was still forming, "do you ever see double when you—" She mimed someone taking a drink. "You said you saw a pair of creatures the night of Porter's death. Could it have been only one?"

"I, that is—" I stumbled over the words. "I might occasionally have a little visual trouble when I drink too much."

"I take oil now?" Humphrey asked, breaking the mulling silence.

"Where did it come from?" I asked, curiosity prickling along the tips of my ears.

"From Mr. Reinhart caravan. I go there. Morning clean job, my first alone," he added with pride. "Them's whole place stink of it. I finded this, more than this, under bed. I leaved windows open while I take it to—"

I didn't listen to the rest. I was already marching toward the main gate. Scanning the area for humans, my eyes landed on exactly the unicorn I was after.

"Fergus, over here!"

Fergus came galloping from the Cantina. "What're you doing, man? You're scaring the mini-taurs, that's what you're doing. Their laps aren't the best, but—"

"Not now. You can get out through the gate, right?"

"You can't keep a good unicorn down," he said cheekily.

"Go, try to stop the jailor. Tell him there's new evidence. We need the judge."

"Where's the judge?"

"We'll figure that out later. Just go. They can't be far. Don't let him take Cordelia to the Pits."

"Sweet lap baby, I'm coming for you," called Fergus, as he charged out of the gate.

"Duncan, what's going on?" Conrad asked as he trotted up to my side. Flora was right behind him. She had carried Boris's hat in one hand, and cradled Boris himself under her other arm like a football. He didn't look pleased about it either.

"Reinhart, he set fire to the Cells then waited outside my caravan for me. The oil, that stinky oil. I smelled it the night Porter died. The wine barrel stunk of it. And I smelled it again last night when the Cells caught fire. Reinhart also has access to the petty cash. There was a withdrawal that would have been enough to buy a barrel of wine."

"Circumstantial," said Boris as he re-adjusted his fedora. "Good evidence, but all circumstantial. Won't stand up in a trial. We need something more concrete."

I thought about the dwarfish writing Boris had found in the account books, about how it could be used to cover up outgoing money. Maybe Zin wasn't doing so terribly after all. Maybe Reinhart—

"Zin!" said Conrad.

I spun around. Which, when you've got a big old dragon tail trailing behind you, is a little tricky to do without causing extensive property damage. Thankfully, nothing ended up battered to bits (this time) as Zin entered the circus grounds.

He wasn't alone.

CHAPTER 37
WHERE HAVE YOU BEEN?

It had only been half a day since I'd last seen Zin, but it felt like month or more. With him was Judge Judge Javert, looking more annoyed than a centaur suffering a plague of biting flies. Then, following behind Zin and Javert, emerged a creature, her head held high as she strode through the gates on long, elegant legs.

Had Fergus been around, he would have abandoned his obsession with human laps forever. Or for a little while, at least.

"The Kailin," whispered Flora, who I noticed surreptitiously glancing toward her husband as if worried he might be contemplating running off with the beautiful unicorn.

With quick, confident steps, Zin strode straight over to me. My body tensed, my jaw tightened like I'd eaten something overly sour. I couldn't help it. I still suspected he had some role in all this. I took a step back from him, but he didn't seem to notice.

"Where's Cordelia?" he asked, looking around as if desperate to see her. With a human so close, I couldn't respond. Luckily, Conrad was there to be my voice.

"The jailor just took her. We've sent Fergus after them. What's going on, Zin?"

"There's been a discrepancy," he whispered.

The judge's brow seemed abnormally sweaty for such a cool morning, but then again, I'm not really up on human physiology, so maybe this was how humans of his breed reacted to windy days.

The Kailin remained standing still, doing little more than observing Javert. There was a cold gleam in her eye I was glad wasn't directed at me.

"Speak, Javert," the Kailin demanded in a melodic, yet evenly stern voice. Everyone watching went silent and focused fully on the pair.

"Um, it has come to my attention—" the judge cleared his throat, but when he spoke again, his voice was just as squeaky. "That is, I was not made aware of certain facts when first presented with the case."

"That's because you didn't ask for any facts," said Conrad. He really was good at voicing my own thoughts.

"Right, that's because the case seemed quite open-and-shut. Had I been apprised of the situation—" The judge's speech halted when the Kailin took one step forward, her horn lowered. "That is to say, I— I was asked not to hear any more evidence than necessary."

"Asked?" the Kailin said pointedly as she took another step forward. Javert was not telling the truth. If he continued with his lies, he'd soon find himself with an extra hole where most creatures really don't want to be having extra holes.

"You might want to get to the *point*, Judge," said Zin, winking just in case we missed his play on words. He was different than he had been since Porter's death. More assured, like a weight had been removed from his shoulders. It eroded some of my lingering suspicion that he and Reinhart had been working together on this. But hadn't I seen him whispering with the judge during Cordelia's rushed hearing? Didn't I see him reaching in and handing Javert something?

"Yes, I am getting around to it. And by *asked*, I suppose I should say some money accompanied that request. However, I must make it clear that this is not normally how I conduct my business. I am a good judge. Fair. Honest. But there was this little row boat I've been saving up for, and—"

A picture of the corpulent man in a "little" row boat flashed into my mind. I'll tell you one thing, I would have been giggling, if not for the Kailin, who was closing in on Javert.

Perhaps realizing how close he was to becoming a kebab, the judge went a shade of green I've only seen on a moldy loaf of bread. He mopped his brow with the fluttering sleeve of his black robes, then hurriedly admitted, "I took a bribe. I ignored— No, sorry, I *didn't ask* for more evidence because I was paid to make a hasty ruling. There," the man said frantically, his jowls trembling, "I told the truth. Now please, step back."

The Kailin remained where she stood, but she did raise her head, lifting the horn to a less threatening position. Well, a little less.

"And who gave you this bribe?" asked the Kailin. I watched Zin, but he betrayed nothing other than curiosity.

"I don't know. I swear it." Javert threw up his hands, palms out, as if his meaty mitts would shield him from the Kailin's deadlier-than-an-elven-blade horn.

The Kailin blinked her penetrating eyes, took a step back, and angled her head away from the judge. He had told the truth. He would live. For now. He let out a heavy sigh.

"Explain," said the Kailin.

"Last week, I received a packet of money with a note saying I could keep it if, when called upon, I ruled against the accused at Zinzendorf's Circus. I didn't know what it meant, but I kept the cash in my breast pocket. Part of me expected someone to stop by and ask for the money back, and another part thought it would be bad luck to spend it before hearing a case that didn't yet exist.

"Then, when this business with Quinn came up, I knew it had to be what the note meant. So, I did as the note said and made my ruling against her as quickly as possible. And I may not have asked the questions I should have, but it did actually seem as if she was guilty. I mean, she had easy access to the poison, and she had a motive, and everything I'd normally see as an—"

"Yes," said Zin, rolling his dark, orange-flecked eyes, "we know. An open-and-shut case." Zin's sarcastic tone earned him a few laughs.

"Well, yes. Precisely."

"Your reasoning is not the best, and your judgment was poor," said the Kailin. "But you have been honest."

287

She shifted so her horn pointed at Javert again. "Mind you stay that way."

"Yes ma'am, um, miss. That is, Your Excellency."

The Kailin turned away from him and sighed heavily at his groveling.

"Do you still have the note?" asked Boris, stepping forward as he adjusted his fedora. The Kailin gave the sparkling, pink hat a quizzical look, then returned her attention to Judge, who paled at the sight of the horn angling in his direction once again.

"Well? Do you?" she asked.

"Me?" Javert yelped. "Yes, that is, I think—"

With a worried expression on his chubby cheeks, Javert dug into his robes' front pocket. His face relaxed as he extracted a folded sheet of paper that was similar to what my threatening note had been written on. He handed it to Boris.

Zin, who had no idea of Boris's new investigative detecting sideline, stared at the fedora-wearing brownie with a look of pure bewilderment. Boris examined the paper, then angled his body to face me. He glanced up without lifting his head from the paper, but his finger was pointing to the M of *Mister Javert* in the heading. Boris's eyes were mostly obscured by the hat, but he didn't miss the small nod I gave him.

Boris turned back to the judge, the Kailin, and Zin.

"Along with other evidence we are ready to present, the handwriting on this note matches some additional clues that have come to light over the past couple days. These words," he said, lifting the paper high and showing it off dramatically, "did not come out of the blue. They were written by Porter Kohl's murderer."

Blue.

A cascade of realization flooded over my brain. I couldn't say anything, not in front of the humans, but my lips were twitching with the effort of holding back what I wanted to tell everyone.

CORDELIA: You don't have lips. You're a reptile.

DUNCAN: I have lips. See, I can purse them and pucker them.

CORDELIA: Please don't ever make that face at me again.

We needed concrete evidence. I don't know why I hadn't seen it before, but I now knew exactly where we would find it. Or at least I hoped so, otherwise I'd look really stupid.

CHAPTER 38
WHAT ZIN KNEW

The Kailin scanned the crowd that had suddenly grown nervous. After all, when you've got a meter-long horn that's attached to a creature who doesn't mind getting stabby with said horn, you tend to shy away even if you've never been guilty of anything more than stealing an extra slice of toast from the Cantina.

"Locate your suspect," the Kailin said. "We will wait here so we can judge this case fairly and wisely. And," she added with emphasis, "without any improper influence."

Judge Javert blubbered out a noise of obsequious agreement and praised the Kailin's wisdom. She shook her head, making no attempt to hide her annoyance with her co-worker.

"You say you have sent someone after the jailor and Miss Quinn?" asked the Kailin.

"Yes," Conrad replied. "Fergus. He's—"

"I know very well who Fergus is," she said, as if she really did know exactly who Fergus was and did not approve. "Perhaps you should send someone, shall we say, a bit more equipped to handle any trouble the jailor might present."

Several centaurs volunteered to prove themselves more than ready to fight for justice. Or maybe just to impress the Kailin. Zin momentarily dropped the barrier, and a trio of horse-men, with Conrad at the lead, charged out of the gates.

Ignoring Javert, Zin told the Kailin she could wait at the Cantina and that she was welcome to anything Pepper might whip up for her. I didn't miss Javert staying as close to the Kailin's side as possible — a position that would make it difficult for her to whip around and stab him. You know, just in case she changed her mind about his honesty.

While everyone seemed to have suddenly developed an appetite and were slipping over to the Cantina to gawk at the Kailin, Boris and Flora signaled me to a spot where we'd be blocked from view by a souvenir stand.

"What is it?" Flora asked. "Your aura looks about to burst."

I whispered to them, "I need to get Cordelia's dukie book. Do you know where her stuff is?"

"What's her dukie book have to do with anything?" Boris asked as a human strode by with a sack of toy dragons made of wood.

"I can't talk here. Can you get the book or not?"

"Should be with her stuff. It's being stored in our supply caravan."

We hurried off, but Zin soon caught up to us. He can be hasty on his hooves when he wants to be.

Before he could say anything, I asked accusingly, "So you didn't do this? Didn't have anything to do with it?"

"No, how could you think that? Porter has been with this show for over ten years. He was my friend, family almost. Did you seriously think I'd kill him?"

"Well, yeah, but I'll tell you about that later. I think we might have figured this out."

"Get on with it, then."

Boris volunteered to go, since he knew right where Cordelia's satchel should be.

I eyed Zin for a moment. He may not have killed Porter, but there still had been that contract. Was he considering selling me to keep his circus afloat? And to Ratcher of all people? I wanted to think he wouldn't, that he realized I was his biggest draw, that maybe we were friends. Still, with the money he might get for me—

"Where did you find the Kailin?" asked Flora, interrupting my thoughts. "What I mean is, what made you go looking for her?"

"Something Pepper said to me the other day. She was having a good laugh over her sister, Nutmeg, who'd just written to tell her she'd seen the Kailin. Nutmeg saying how scared she'd been that the Kailin had come for her because she'd recently substituted walnuts in a dessert where she was supposed to use pecans.

"But what Pepper found even more amusing was that the Kailin had come to their area, saying she'd been requested to rule on a case and wondering why Judge Javert hadn't shown up yet. But no one there had heard anything about a case, no complaints had been filed, and the judge was still here in Sherwood, just as the *Circular* noted on its schedule.

"Pepper thought it was hilarious since the Kailin is supposed to instinctively know who's telling the truth and who's lying, so it was pretty damn ironic she ended up tricked into going on a fool's errand."

"You think she was sent away on purpose?" I asked.

"Exactly. And that got me wondering about Javert's cases. Ours has been his only one over the past week. If whoever sent the Kailin away knew Javert had been bribed, that person would want our venerable judge free to make his ruling without winding up skewered on a unicorn horn."

"Yeah, I hear that's a bit inconvenient for legal work."

Boris returned with Cordelia's satchel.

"It was right where I left it. Hasn't been touched."

"See if her dukie book's inside."

"*The Handbook* says we cannot go through others' belongings unless we obtain written—"

"Just do it, Boris," snapped Zin.

Boris's hand plunged straight into the bag, and after many cringing complaints of the "girl things" inside, he extracted the dukie book.

Just as I'd remembered, Cordelia's book was blue, not the red of the older books Zin had signed by the dozens when he first began managing the family business.

"Open it to the first page, the page where it says who issued it."

Boris again complied, although he was starting to look put out at being made my secretary and errand brownie.

"Reinhart issued it." He held it up for us to see.

As the circus's accountant, Reinhart would have had every right to issue dukie books. In fact, Zin's was the only place I'd worked where people had dukie books signed by the circus owner. A few wondered if they might not be collector's items.

As Zin had done in mine, Reinhart had signed his name on the line for the issuer's name. Cordelia had signed under the paragraph (that was written in illegibly tiny letters) spelling out the conditions of the dukie book.

And under *Job Title* Reinhart had written *Mops/Behemoth Handler*.

"Wait, that looks like—" Boris said. I nodded. The sharp M matched the writing on Molly's gift tag, Javert's bribery note, and the messy scrawl on the threatening letter someone had left me.

The footprints by my caravan could have come from any dwarf, but this made it clear who was behind all the strange and disturbing events of the past week.

I explained everything to Zin. "And there's also some discrepancies in Reinhart's accounts. Did you tell him to write in Dwarfish?"

"Reinhart?" Zin asked in a whisper of disbelief. "No. I mean, I'd seen the marks now and then, but I thought they were just tally marks. This is—"

Zin examined the dukie book, then the notes Boris had been carrying in the inner brim of his hat. As he looked from one item to the next, Zin's brow knitted in stunned confusion. The look soon morphed into an angry scowl.

"Reinhart." He ground the name through his teeth. "Where is he?"

"I don't know when I saw him last," Flora said. I then briefly told Zin about the previous night. About the oil. About the fire. I left out the bit about my paralyzing fear.

"He tried to burn her alive?" Zin fumed. He stormed off in the direction of Reinhart's caravan. "I'll kill him."

Boris followed after Zin to make sure the satyr didn't destroy any evidence in his fury, while Flora and I made a quick tour of the circus grounds. The four of us met up at the main gate.

"No sign of him," I said, huffing for air. I really needed to get in better shape if that little bit of exertion had left me panting.

"Humphrey was right," said Boris. "There's a pretty impressive stash of old cooking oil in the storage space under Reinhart's bed. He must have been collecting it for a while."

"For what purpose?" I asked. "He wouldn't have needed much to burn the Cells."

"He may have been planning to burn more than that if things didn't go according to plan. After you failed to injure Molly, perhaps he intended to make it look like you, a pyrodon, went on a rampage. I think we're lucky that rain storm soaked everything last night. He's also taken several things from his wardrobe and his suitcase is missing," said Boris, who probably had an inventory of the entire circus in his head. "I saw him earlier this morning, so he can't have gotten far."

"Zin, you've got to let me go past the barrier," I said.

"We need to find Reinhart." Realizing Conrad or Fergus should have been back by now, I added, "And we need to make sure Cordelia is okay."

Zin hesitated. Letting a dragon loose, especially a dragon with a reputation like mine, was dangerous. If I caused any damage while out and about, he could lose his license to operate.

"Come on, Zin. I'll behave."

Unless I find Reinhart, that is.

"Fine, but I'm going with you. Someone better tell the Kailin to join us."

"And the judge?" asked Flora.

"If he can keep up."

CHAPTER 39
CAUGHT YA! OR NOT.

Flora returned with the Kailin — the two of them chatting away as if they'd known each other since they were foals. Judge Judge Javert followed after, holding up his robes to keep them from dragging in the dirt. I smirked at the leaping unicorns that decorated his lavender socks, wondering if they might not be a bit of wishful thinking that his co-worker could be so carefree.

After agreeing that Cordelia was our first priority — once a prisoner enters the Pits, it's near impossible to get them back out — Zin performed some magical flourish-y type thing with his hands and something crackled in the air. He gestured me forward to lead the way. I stepped up to the gates then hesitated, wary about crossing the line I was meant to stay behind.

I've never attempted an escape. Not since coming to Zin's, that is. But I did stumble over the barrier once after downing a few buckets of gin as part of one of Benny's drinking games. The sensation as I tripped into the barrier felt as if my skin was being fried from the inside out. And that had only been a brief slip of my foot beyond the barrier. What would walking straight into it do to me?

"Go on, Duncan," Zin said irritably. "The gates are only so wide." I grit my teeth and, with shoulders tensed tighter than the Flynns' high-wire, stepped beyond the gates.

And nothing happened. Well, other than developing a nasty kink in my neck from how fiercely I'd been tensing my shoulder muscles. While Boris and Flora stayed behind in case Reinhart dared to return, Zin trotted alongside me on his hoofed feet, his goat legs giving him a spring in his step that might have been comical in any other circumstance.

Of course, the Kailin had little trouble keeping up with us, but Javert soon lagged behind. I asked (okay, gasped) if we shouldn't wait for him, but the Kailin merely said (and said it without being a bit out of breath) that he'd catch up.

I don't know how far we ran or for how long. It could have been a mile. It felt like ten. I do know we didn't reach the town before we found the cart stopped in the middle of the road.

CORDELIA: Hold on, then you do know how far you ran since the town was only about a mile from the circus grounds.

DUNCAN: I was trying to sound dramatic.

CORDELIA: You sound like you don't know geography.

DUNCAN: Okay, fine. We made it just to the edge of town, which was about a mile away. But it did feel like ten.

CORDELIA: That's because you're out of shape and drink too much.

DUNCAN: Well, I'd jog more, but I might spill my drink.

Although Conrad and the other centaurs were nowhere to be seen, Fergus had caught up with the cart. Unfortunately, he's more lover than fighter and was sprawled on his side on the ground. I didn't see any blood, but also I saw no sign of him breathing.

The jailor had opened the cage's door, but Cordelia wasn't free. Holding her against him so she faced out, the brawny man had a beefy arm around her upper chest, while in his other hand he held a knife's blade to her throat. A ridiculously long blade, too. Seriously, he had to be compensating for something with the size of that weapon.

And standing on top of the cart was Reinhart.

"What did you do to Fergus?" Zin asked.

"A little of this." Reinhart snapped his stubby fingers.

I was so used to the clownish antics of the Dumble Dwarfs, that I forgot all dwarves retain the magic they once used to craft the weapons they'd been renowned for back in the days of sword fights and jousts and all that.

"Let Cordelia go." The words rumbled from my throat. And don't worry, the jailor wasn't human. Now that I was nearer to him and away from the scents of the circus, I detected the distinctive sauerkraut smell of ogre.

"Oh, I don't think so. The minute he kills her, you're mine," the traitorous dwarf replied.

Fire churned in my belly. I'm a pyrodon, so I mean that literally. My fear of fire helped me swallow down the flame, as did the obvious problem that I'd likely scorch

Cordelia to a crisp if I shot a fireball at Reinhart, which at the moment sounded very tempting.

"Reinhart, what's going on? Why are you doing this?" asked Zin.

"I've been made an offer I can't refuse. Kill Duncan's handler, the stupid dragon then falls under my control to do with whatever I choose. And I would choose to deliver him to Ratcher. I'd then get enough money to return to my home region, buy the mine I've had my eye on for a while, and live like a dwarf king. I've tried to build up savings with the little bits I've pilfered from you. They've helped, but there's nothing like a lump sum payment."

I registered Reinhart's speech, but I was more focused on the need to get the jailor to drop his stupid knife. I figured that should be simple enough. The guy didn't know I was afraid of fire, even my own. I lowered my head and fixed a fierce glower on him. This was my fear-inducing look from the act, when I was supposed to pretend I wanted nothing more than to eat my handler. Then, *Hoorah!* the great human conquers the vile beast and I submissively jump through a hoop.

Granted, even just a few years ago, I might well have eaten my handler. But again, we'll leave that story for another day.

I opened my mouth, baring my fangs and letting the sulfurous smell of my firebox flow over him. The menacing glare already had him quivering so much he was having trouble holding the knife steady. That's what happens when you choose a weapon too big for you.

"Duncan," Cordelia warned, her eyes wide as a trickle of blood ran down her neck.

My focus flicked back to the jailor. He may have been shaky, he may have been oozing buckets of sweat, but he wasn't about to release his death grip on the knife that kept nicking Cordelia's pale throat.

I produced a low grumble deep in my belly. The sound of this doesn't come through all that well to most ears, but everyone senses it deep within their guts and deep within that primordial little nubbin in their brains that tells them to flee from imminent danger.

Cordelia told me later that after years of dragon work, she'd grown used to this rumbling sensation, but the jailor had no such experience. The oversized knife slipped from his hand — whether from fear or from his sweaty palms, I didn't care. He darted a glance at Reinhart, then fled, carrying the stink of his fear-filled ogre sweat with him.

The instant the jailor started away, Reinhart hopped off the cart and dashed off. Unlike the jailor, he didn't stick to the road, and instead cut his own path through the tall grass that edged the road. Not far beyond was an expanse of woods. If he got to the thick stand of trees, there wouldn't be room for me to maneuver between the trunks and limbs. The dwarfish bastard would get away. And by the blood of Smaug, I wanted him to die for what he had done. He *would* face the Kailin for judgement.

But I'd been training my brain to come up with ideas over the past several days. And now that training paid off with some quick thinking on my part.

"Barrier!" I shouted to Zin.

CHAPTER 40
LET'S TRY THIS AGAIN

Zin either understood exactly what I meant, or he'd already come up with the same idea himself, because the moment the word passed my lips, he flicked his hands. A brief glow swirled around Reinhart, then faded as the barrier formed, locking him in place.

And yes, he was still running at the time. And yes, I did feel a sadistic satisfaction when Reinhart ran straight into the barrier and squealed when it delivered him a jolting shock.

Fergus soon stirred to life, mumbling something about needing a cigarette. As he staggered to his feet, Cordelia dabbed at her neck, pulling away her hand and grimacing at the sight of her own blood.

"That was a bit too close, Duncan," she said.

"You're welcome," I replied. Judge Javert still hadn't caught up yet, but the sound of his wheezing wasn't far off.

"You idiot," Reinhart scoffed.

He then, easy as you please, stepped out from the barrier and, none the worse for wear from his shock treatment, hightailed it for the trees. As much as dwarves can hightail it, that is.

I cursed myself. I should have remembered Reinhart wasn't bound by Zin's barriers.

"Oh, no you don't," shouted Fergus. We'd all instinctively started chasing after our quarry (from somewhere behind us I heard Javert objecting to so much exertion in one day), but Fergus put on a burst of speed, charging past us and zipping between the trees with more dexterity than I'd ever seen from him.

Zin, Cordelia, the Kailin, and I followed after. Well, I tried to follow. I couldn't squeeze through the narrow gaps between the trees, so I had to loop around to the road, racing to where it intersected the wooded area.

And that's when I found Conrad and his centaurs. He told me later that they hadn't seen one lick of the cart or of Fergus, and had run all the way into town, calling in at every house and business to see if the townspeople had seen anything. When it was clear no one had, he realized they'd been tricked — you just never know what powers dwarves have up their woolen sleeves — and made the call to retrace their steps.

Oh, and when I say *I found them*, I should clarify that they had been charging at full gallop down the road and had already whizzed past me when I shouted, "This way!"

The fleet-of-foot creatures made a sharp turn. Our ears all twitched in the direction of footfalls and snapping twigs coming from the forest. Just as they did during a show, the centaurs whipped around and formed up in a tight semi-circle. An instant later, Reinhart burst through the woods and crashed face first into one of their flanks.

With a few quick, coordinated steps, they blocked Reinhart in. The Kailin halted at the sight of the group, then lowered her horn, training it on the betraying dwarf.

Fergus came careening through a stand of fir trees and nearly plowed into the Kailin. Doing his best not to look out of breath, he stood up straight, his eyes wide as he took in the other unicorn.

"Nearly had him," gasped Fergus. The Kailin gave him a sidelong glance, but said nothing.

"I call a trial," Zin said. His words, spoken through deep breaths, formally brought the Kailin into the matter. Reinhart would be judged.

"I could take care of him now," the Kailin said with chilling calm. "There's no good in his heart."

"I've no doubt of that," said Zin, "but this needs to be done properly."

The Kailin took a step back and Zin reached out to scruff Reinhart. Yes, he scruffed him. By the skin of his neck like a misbehaving kitten. I tried not to laugh, but it did bring a smile to my lips to see the sturdy little dwarf kicking and flailing as Zin held him until Conrad's centaurs could bring the cart over. Zin then tossed Reinhart in. Turns out it's just as amusing to hear dwarves curse as humans.

"Where's the judge?" asked Zin, once he'd snapped the padlock shut.

"On the road a ways back," said Conrad. "He didn't look well, so I told him to stay put."

After much grumbling about not being pack animals,

the centaurs agreed to pull the cart back to where Javert waited — his robes now a dirty mess at the hem and a sweaty mess at the neck. Fergus followed along, too much in awe of the Kailin to speak (and I might be wrong, but I think she risked a couple peeks back at him as she walked between Fergus and Zin).

Me? I lingered behind, walking with Cordelia and staying apart from the others as they escorted Reinhart back to the circus grounds for his trial.

As we walked, I filled her in on all she missed since the Cells had burned down, and shared with her the list of evidence that pointed to Reinhart.

Once back to the circus grounds, Helga went to fetch the account books, and Boris asked Cordelia to assist him while he fussed with my threatening letter, the bribery note, Molly's gift tag, and Cordelia's dukie book, putting each item into its own folder and labeling the folders with evidence numbers to present at the hearing.

When they were done, Cordelia nodded to me, signaling that Boris had filled her in on the full details of the case.

CORDELIA: You know, you're very intuitive for a reptile.

DUNCAN: Actually, Boris told me later that he had — as he put it — "briefed" you on the details. Does that mean he gave you underwear?

CORDELIA: No, Duncan, it most definitely does not.

DUNCAN: They should really change that expression, then.

We gathered once again at the Cantina. Reinhart in his cage, Judge Javert looking somewhat less disheveled as he sipped a glass of strawberry-mint iced tea, and the Kailin stoically observing it all.

Chapter 41
The Trial

"Now, what is the case you'd like to present?" asked Judge Javert.

Zin, looking about ready to slap the man, replied, "You know very well what the case is: the murder of Porter Kohl."

"Oh, we're still doing that, are we? I thought this was something else."

"It is," said Cordelia, Boris standing proudly by her side. "It's now also about stealing money, arranging underhanded deals, killing a dragon handler, then trying to kill another dragon handler."

"Oh, that's quite a lot, isn't it? And I've yet to have any lunch."

"You could miss a meal or two," said the Kailin. Fergus watched her with the dopiest of doe eyes.

"Wait, can she act as prosecutor?" Javert asked, pointing a fleshy finger at Cordelia. "Isn't she a suspect?"

"She is no longer a suspect, and she has agreed to present the case with myself as second counsel," said Boris, who kept a tight hold on his evidence folders as he gestured for Cordelia to continue. She swallowed hard, and my ears picked up Flora saying something about her aura looking wobbly.

"Reinhart has been taking money from Ely Zinzendorf for several months, if not years. He would falsify entries in the main account books to hide his own version of accounts to adjust for the funds and petty cash he was withdrawing from the circus. Money that did not go to business expenses, but was instead used for his own personal gains. The account books Reinhart keeps and the one Zin keeps will show this. Boris can translate the runes, if needed."

"Wait, the account book Zin keeps?" said Reinhart incredulously. "He doesn't keep any books except the ones I hand him."

"Doesn't he?" Boris asked archly.

"Just a small tally of the day's takings and expenditures," Zin said, pulling the tiniest notebook from a pocket in his vest. "When I tried to reconcile my numbers with those you were giving me at the end of the day, I thought I was doing my sums wrong and worried I might be falling into satyr senility."

"Reinhart," Cordelia continued, "was also plotting to gain control of Duncan and sell him to Damian Ratcher, who had already made offers for the dragon and had recently increased his offers to include the whole circus. Yes?" she asked Boris.

"Correct. When Reinhart realized what could be gained from the sale of Duncan, he killed Porter. He likely hoped to be the first creature Duncan saw, but Duncan ended up near where Cordelia worked. She then became his handler."

"How's that?" asked the judge.

"Imprinting," Cordelia answered. "In this case, it means when a handler dies, the next person the dragon sees will become his handler and have full control over him."

I couldn't stop a rumble of disapproval, but since this imprinting bit was necessary for the trial, and since there were humans all over the place, and since it wouldn't look good to object to the person whose side I was on, I didn't point out that imprinting was only a legend. Or was it? Why did I feel such a strong connection to Cordelia Quinn?

"That's why when Reinhart saw the chance, he tried to kill me by burning the Cells. He then placed himself again near where Duncan would be, or where he thought Duncan would be. He failed, both in killing me and in guessing Duncan's whereabouts."

"And you have proof of this?" Javert asked, leaning forward with true interest.

Cordelia's voice had gone dry by this point, so Boris took over.

"My crew found a dwarf's footprint outside of Duncan's caravan. Since it's been dry in this area up until the night of the fire, the print could only have been made then. Circumstantial yes, but we've also discovered in Reinhart's caravan the same oil that was used in the attempt to kill Cordelia Quinn." Now that Boris had the floor, he couldn't hold back his excitement to share what he'd detected. Or investigated. "This oil was also noted on the barrel of poisoned wine that killed Porter Kohl. And in conclusion, we have handwriting matches between some threatening notes, his bribery letter to you, and the dukie book he issued Cordelia."

"It seems to be an open-and-shut case," said Javert.

"You should really stop saying that," the Kailin told him. Fergus sighed at her saucy tone.

"Reinhart, do you have anything to say?" asked the judge. "And do remember, the Kailin is here."

Reinhart shifted on his splayed feet, then crossed his arms over his barrel chest.

"I did it. Yes. Very good. You caught me." He uncrossed his arms and began counting his crimes on his stubby fingers. "I have been taking money from the accounts for years now. I'm saving up to buy the biggest mine in my homeland, but I used a portion of it to buy a barrel of wine which I poisoned with behemoth saliva I stole from Flora's caravan when I pretended to collect some headache medicine.

"I also made a deal to sell Duncan to Ratcher once I had control of him. My first attempt to get Duncan didn't work out, so I then tried to kill Cordelia with oil I'd saved to burn this place down and frame Duncan for the inferno. He'd be taken away to the Pits. And since Ratcher is a shareholder in the Pits, he would have access to this stupid dragon that I can't understand being worth a single penny. Did I miss anything?" He stared defiantly at the Kailin.

Molly stepped forward. I think it was the first time I'd ever seen a scowl on her perpetually smiling face.

"You also gave me a headdress to sabotage our act.

You wanted it to look like Duncan was a dangerous dragon. You could have injured me with that stunt, you flatfooted poop head."

"Yes, yes," Reinhart said with a dismissive flick of his hand. "I did that as well. I also stole cupcakes from Pepper when she wasn't looking, took more than my share of the leftover food from the concession stands, and I like to wipe my nose on all the stuffed animals we give away for prizes."

"Well, that's just uncalled for," said Flora.

We all looked to the Kailin. She wasn't moving toward Reinhart, but neither was she lowering her gaze from him.

Judge Javert cleared his throat. "Kailin— I mean, Your Excellency, is he telling the truth of his crimes?"

"He is," she said, then glanced toward Pepper's kitchen, from which was emanating the smell of fresh-baked oatcakes. "Now, get your ruling and sentencing done with. As you say, we have missed lunch."

"That's it?" Cordelia asked. "Shouldn't you—?" She made a stabbing gesture toward Reinhart.

"He has confessed his crimes. I can only use my form of punishment if someone lies, if they refuse to face up to their deeds."

"Well, that's stupid," Cordelia said.

"Don't insult her," said Fergus, marching up to the Kailin's side.

"I didn't mean *she* was stupid. I meant the rules of the whole stabby thing are stupid."

"Oh, well, yes, that's different." Fergus turned a nervous smile on the Kailin, but she'd already strode off toward a waiting plate of oatcakes and orange marmalade. "She's got no lap, but damn," he said with a disturbing grunt of approval as he flicked his head to drop his spare cigarette into his mouth.

"You haven't got a chance," said Cordelia.

"Don't be jealous. Your lap is nice, but it's far too tiny. It would have never worked between us."

"I'm sure I'll manage my heartbreak somehow."

Javert and the Kailin had no other cases to hear that day, so Zin invited them to stay for the final show in the Tent. With a promise of fresh cream that night, Zin then cajoled the brownies into arranging a couple guest-of-honor seats.

We didn't actually have guest-of-honor seating, but Helga (with Humphrey helping at every step) cordoned off a small section in the front row where she tossed a couple cushions on a sturdy chair for the judge and set up a table with a bowl of toasted oats for the Kailin.

Boris had returned Cordelia's satchel to her. She approached me with it slung over her shoulder and signaled for me to walk with her. Something tugged inside me and I followed after her without hesitation. Seriously, I needed to find another dragon to clarify this whole imprinting thing. Was it just Cordelia, or was the imprinting-upon-death myth true?

I checked the area and spotted no other humans. "Are you leaving?" I asked, trying to sound supportive, but feeling something inside fracturing. "I mean, I wouldn't blame you. Murder accusation, nearly burnt alive, forced to drink Flora's odd green mixtures."

"I kind of got used to them after a while. Although the popcorn and cotton candy helped see me through." She kept walking. "But no, I'm not leaving." She stopped at Benny's enclosure and handed me her bag. "Can you take this back to my caravan? I should get him spruced up before the show."

She then picked up the scrub broom and began to work on Benny.

"No, not like that," I chided, taking the broom from her. "He likes it better this way." Benny rolled over without even being asked and let me get into all his rolly-polly nooks and crannies.

The instant Benny had shifted, Cordelia hustled back and pinched her nose shut — a quickly developed instinct when you work with a behemoth. Then she cautiously lowered her hand and took the most tentative sniff.

"He doesn't stink. I mean, his mud still has a stench to it, but he's far less pungent." She crouched down next to Benny's large brown eyes. "What have you been doing with yourself while I've been away?" She then looked up to me for the answer.

"Just a little change in diet."

Benny was easing himself back onto his belly when Zin marched up to us.

"There you are," he said to Cordelia. "Why aren't you getting ready?"

"I'm getting Benny ready. Or well, Duncan is getting Benny ready."

"No, I'll put someone else on this."

Benny gave a whine.

"He really likes how I do it," I said with a shrug.

"Does he? Then would you mind tending to him for now? Just for a little bit. I, well, I can't afford to bring on anyone new. It's terrible to say, but if it weren't for Porter dying and Gladys leaving, I don't know how I'd pay any of you."

"Reinhart?" I asked.

"Yes, it appears he's made it so the money he took can't be recovered. Spent it, hidden it, down payment on his mine. He won't say."

"He used some of it for the wine. And to bribe Javert. You know, I thought it was you who bribed the judge," I admitted.

"Thanks a lot, Duncan. What exactly made you think that?"

Knowing now was not the time to get into all the other things I had suspected Zin of, I merely said, "I saw you whispering to him before the trial. Your hand was in your pocket and I thought you gave him something."

"Javert's sister is a doctor," Zin said, a flush warmed his already dark cheeks. "I showed him my account book, the little one, and said I couldn't get the math right and that maybe I might need to see a doctor to find out what was wrong with my brain. Senility, dementia, it runs on my mom's side of the family. He gave me his sister's address and seemed pleased to be able to send business her way. But it looks like I don't need to go anymore. You really thought I'd bribe a judge?" I shrugged apologetically. "Kind of makes me not feel so bad about sticking you on behemoth duty."

"I could probably do with a hobby other than drinking, anyway."

"Well, then stop standing around and get to it. We're opening—" Zin stamped a hoof in irritation when the thirty-minute warning bell sounded. "Oh, great monkey balls! I completely forgot I need to put someone on the ticket booth with Reinhart gone. Duncan, hurry up and get Benny ready. You, Quinn, get your things together. The gates open in thirty minutes and I can't have you out here."

"Get ready? For what? Are you firing me?" Cordelia asked, indignant anger mounting with each question.

"I will if you're going to be this thick-headed about things. I'm telling you to get ready for the damn act. I've had that new brownie lay out Porter's show outfit for you. Oh, and you'll need this." He handed Cordelia the object I hadn't noticed he'd kept close by his side.

The tip was still wrapped and padded. As Zin handed it to Cordelia, I could smell the scent of Porter lingering on the leather grip.

"Hope you can handle him," Zin quipped then strode off, barking orders to anyone in his path.

Cordelia stared at the hook. She then looked up at me.

"I'm your handler," Cordelia said, as if she didn't quite believe it.

"Of course you are," I said, knowing somewhere deep inside that she had been since Porter died.

And maybe even before that fateful day.

CHAPTER 42
SHE'S A NO-SHOW

Because it was our final show of this run, the grounds didn't open until after our dinner hour. When the gates did open that evening, it was mostly to happy and excited guests, but also to a few visitors grumbling about whether or not the gates would stay open. Helga, who had volunteered to work the ticket booth, simply beamed a smile at these complainers and assured them Zin's circus would never dare to disappoint.

"After all, it's our final night here. We're not about to leave before you get a chance to see our newest dragon handler work her magic over the deadliest dragon in all the West."

With all the people taking advantage of their free re-entry from the day before, plus the usual crowd we attracted for the grand finale, the circus was packed. As soon as I finished with Benny, I went to Cordelia's caravan. I then told her about the crowds and Helga's promises.

Cordelia groaned like someone who's eaten too many hot dogs. Her nervousness was becoming contagious and even I was beginning to wonder if I might not screw up.

Still, my worst fear as we'd been getting ready that day had been that Molly would wear the blue floof again. So I'd asked Humphrey — who'd been lugging cleaning rags, a broom, and a dustpan — if he could steal the damn thing when he tidied Molly's caravan.

"I are reformed bogart. I cannot do criminal act." I'd been about to bribe him with a pint of milk, when he'd added, "Could make floof tough to be finded, though."

"You'll do fine," I now told Cordelia.

"I won't do fine. Not in these stupid clothes."

As Zin had promised, Cordelia had found Porter's handler outfit waiting in her caravan. That would be Porter Kohl, who had at least eight inches and forty pounds on Cordelia Quinn. She'd done her best to roll up the jacket's sleeves, but the top hat slipped down over her eyes. "People are going to think I'm part of the clown act."

"Go to Molly. She's a whiz with wardrobe."

Cordelia stalked off, fighting with the trousers to keep from tripping over the cuffs.

Eventually, the bell rang to announce to our guests that the final shows would soon begin in the Tent. On my way there, I caught sight of something blue and fluffy sticking out of the top of Molly's caravan. I grinned as it fluttered on the evening breeze.

Molly was already waiting, and she and I practiced on our own for about twenty minutes while the centaurs ushered a vast and eager (and slow-moving) crowd into the Tent.

Cordelia was nowhere to be seen.

"Did you help her with the jacket?"

"Sure, she looked just splendid," said Molly, blinking eyelids on which large glittery lashes had been stuck. I worried Cordelia might not only have been introduced to Molly's wardrobe prowess, but also subjected to her makeup blunderbuss. Could she be losing a battle against a ferocious pair of false eyelashes at that very moment?

As people filed in, there were further complaints about so much space being allotted to Judge Javert and the Kailin. I believe these might have been the same whiners from earlier, but they shut up in quick order when the Kailin shot them a look and aimed her horn in their general direction.

Once everyone had taken their seats — the Tent was filled to capacity that night — Zin made his ringleader announcement and the Flynns began their act to one side of the center ring. The spotlight shone on them until the centaurs started in with their prancing a few minutes later.

With the centaurs trotting and the Flynns flying, Zin kept to his spot in the center ring. It was nearly time to announce the dragon act. Problem was, half the dragon act hadn't shown up yet.

"Where is she?" he hissed as I lingered back where the spotlights wouldn't reveal me until it was time.

I had no idea where Cordelia could be. Had nerves taken hold? Or had she jumped ship after realizing Zin's wasn't the circus she'd hoped for? Maybe she'd thought it over and wanted nothing to do with a place that would accuse her of murder and leave her locked in the Cells for so long. But I couldn't let Zin worry. We were still in the dark as the lights honed in on Conrad and Flora rearing up in unison with the other centaurs.

"She's, um, well," I sputtered. "She had this idea for a grand entry."

"Now is not the time for improv or changing the act. If she wants to do anything new, she needs to run it by me first. She needs to learn that—"

Just then, the ambient lights dimmed and the spotlight snapped onto Zin. Fully in my show size, I crouched back to keep out of the light as Zin whisked off his top hat. Or well, he tried to whisk off his top hat. His left horn got caught up in one of the holes cut into the brim. The audience loved it and hooted with laughter.

Zin exhaled a fuming breath, got the hat fully off, and made a sweeping bow.

"Ladies and gentlemen, welcome to Zinzendorf's Circus of Unusual Creatures. To your left..."

He introduced the Flying Flynns who, in squirrel form, scampered and bounded across the high-wire, then morphed into their human form to swing from the trapeze, flipping around until they were all back on their original perch.

Zin announced the Stupendous Centaurs, and the spotlight swung to the right to reveal Conrad and the others galloping in a tight circle. They then stopped without any sign of command and turned so their hind ends faced inward as they bowed to the audience.

Applause and cheers, then the circus went dark. The crowd hushed.

Where in all of dragondom was Cordelia?

Yes, I knew the act. And yes, Molly could probably perform it in her sleep. But there was just something that made it all the more impressive when a tiny human appeared to have control over my behavior, that the only thing keeping the crowd safe from my ferocity was a person wielding a hooked piece of metal.

"And in the center," Zin said, drawing out the words, buying as much time as possible, "we have a creature that could only have come from the deepest bowels of Hades, a creature that has killed and maimed and fought against being tamed."

And before you think all that was made up for dramatic effect, I'll just say it wasn't. I haven't always been the sleuthing, caring, omelet-eating dragon you see today.

"Ladies and gentlemen, I ask you to be prepared to evacuate at any moment because although his *handler*," Zin added special force to the word as if to warn my handler that she better damn well show up, "is highly skilled and has a way with such beasts, Brutus is a monster who can never fully be tamed." Okay, that part might be a bit of exaggeration.

"Now," Zin continued, "should anything go wrong with Molly — our mini-taur who dares to enter the ring with Brutus — please cover your children's eyes. If you feel that the danger, the potential risk, might be too much for you, please leave the Tent." He paused a moment. No one moved. "Then don't blame me for your nightmares. I present to you now…" Zin lingered over a long pause that verged on awkward in the hopes that Cordelia would appear.

CHAPTER 43
THE FINAL SHOW

An instant before the lights snapped on, a gentle touch slipped across my withers. The spotlight beamed onto me, blinding me for a moment as it always did. You'd think I'd learn to close my eyes, wouldn't you?

"Brutus Fangwrath, Deadliest Dragon in the West," Zin called out in a voice filled with relief.

Jogging around to stand before me with the hook (unwrapped for the show) was Cordelia. Molly had indeed worked some quick tailoring magic. The jacket fit perfectly and the hat balanced on Cordelia's head without slipping over her eyes.

CORDELIA: *That jacket was only being held in place with about a hundred strategically placed safety pins.*

Zin's shoulders relaxed, and he hurried out of the ring as Cordelia began making *hup-hup* sounds and pointing to where she wanted me to stand to begin my final show, the lengthiest of the run. We hadn't exactly had time to practice, but we fell into a quick understanding.

321

I stood at attention. I bowed my head low. I allowed her to peer into my deadly jaws. I balanced on one foot. I rolled over, and she made a great show of tentatively scratching my belly, all the while holding the hook at the ready, even though the belly rub thing is my absolute favorite part of the act. There are just some spots you can't itch yourself.

And yes, over the next hour, she "commanded" me to stand still, to stay calm, and not to eat my friends when Molly cantered out. When I lunged for the mini-taur, a collective gasp issued from the audience.

Molly almost started laughing and Cordelia winked at me when she jumped between my snapping jaws and Molly. A few ladies screamed, and a few men cheered Cordelia on. Cordelia set down the hook, something I'd never seen a handler do, and raised her hands to placate me. I backed off and, trying not to smile, lowered my head submissively.

Then she began the *hup-hup* thing again, and Molly and I performed our grand finale. The crowd — those who hadn't fainted, that is — burst into applause and cheers.

When he came out to thank everyone, Zin wore a broad grin I hadn't seen on his face in ages. Once the Flynns and the centaurs performed their final flourishes, I took my final bow and the audience slowly filed out.

Zin, still grinning, rushed over to me and Cordelia. "That was an amazing show." He grabbed Cordelia's hand and shook it so hard her hat finally toppled off. "People are going to flock to see your act. You are going to remake this circus. We'll be back above water in no time."

Once Zin stopped gushing with uncharacteristic optimism, we took our congratulations from the troupe. Cordelia later told me she ended up with bruises on her back from the number of times it was slapped jovially.

But eventually things got back down to business, and it was time to start clearing up the show. Cordelia and I were just picking up the props for my act when the Kailin stepped up to us on her long, graceful legs, the judge having ducked out of the Tent as soon as the last call for beer at the Cantina was made.

"A fine show," she said. "Ely should see a turnaround if you keep that up. He deserves success."

"Why didn't you skewer Reinhart?" Cordelia asked. "He killed someone. He stole. Isn't that what you do to people like that?"

"I exact my form of justice when the person lies about what they have done, when there is no chance they will confess their actions. I do not 'skewer' people on a whim."

"What will become of him?" I asked, hating the idea of Reinhart getting away with what he'd done. Skewered Dwarf sounded just fine to me.

"He'll receive the same punishment as had been called upon Cordelia for the same crime. He will go to the Pits. It will be a foul existence for one such as him."

She paused, watching the Flynns unhooking the high-wire and swinging down with it between their teeth. Watching them pack up their act was nearly as entertaining as the act itself.

"Still," said the Kailin, "there is something more to Reinhart's actions."

"More than being a greedy, conniving, murdering little twerp?" Cordelia asked.

"He is that, but I can't help but feel there is a deeper reason as to why he wanted to possess you, Duncan. Why he went to such extremes to get you. I cannot fully detect his motives, but there was something more to his actions than meets the eye. Something more about why Damian wishes to obtain you. Reinhart will suffer in the Pits, but you, Duncan, and even you, Cordelia, must watch out. I feel you may not be safe yet."

The Kailin had nothing to add to this. Or if she did, she didn't bother to say it, she simply strode off, Fergus's eyes fixed on her as she parted the flaps with her horn and slipped out of the Tent.

Soon after, Zin entered the center ring and most of the troupe gathered around. He'd taken off his jacket and his top hat.

"Great show, everyone. And happy first performance to Cordelia Quinn. Tonight, let's get packed up as much as possible. We'll take down the majority of the equipment tomorrow. I hope to be on the road to Salem by mid-afternoon, so don't celebrate too much tonight. We've got plenty of work to do and an early start tomorrow. Again, great show. And I look forward to seeing what you can do in the next."

Zin had eyed me when he made the comment about not celebrating too much. It was like he knew I was already picturing a nice bucket of chianti.

But even thoughts of wine couldn't warm my scaly skin. Something nagged at me. Something in what the Kailin had said made me glad we were moving south, that we were moving away from Portland, away from Ratcher's circus, rather than moving closer to it.

ABOUT THE STORY
OR, HOW AN ELEPHANT BECOMES A DRAGON

Where to begin with this tale behind the tale?

The initial spark for this story began life as a historical novel that wasn't going to be the least bit fantastical, mysterious, nor humorous.

Can you believe it?

I'd recently come across a book on Oregon history, and smack dab in the middle (okay, maybe not the exact middle) was a picture of a guy with an elephant. The guy's name was Al Painter.

Holy hell, my great- great-grandfather owned an elephant!!!

Well, not exactly. Turns out there might be no relation ("might be") between me and this Mr. Painter. Still, I had to know more about the elephant, Tusko, next to him.

Tusko, it turns out, had quite the story. He was the biggest elephant in the country, he had a penchant for whiskey, and he had plenty of violent tendencies. He also had a handler named Slim Lewis who wrote a book all about his life with circus elephants.

Slim's story alone is the stuff of novels, and if you can get your hands on a copy of his *I Loved Rogues*, you won't be disappointed (although you may cry a lot over the mistreatment and misunderstanding of circus elephants).

I desperately wanted to write Slim and Tusko's story. Slim (the inspiration for Cordelia) had made move after move to get a chance to work with Tusko (the inspiration for Duncan), and the bond these two eventually formed was amazing.

Not wanting to step on any toes, I tried contacting Slim's family about writing the novel, but got no response. But Slim and Tusko's story was simply burning in me.

So, as authors are known to do, I thought about how I could twist reality into my own tale. Maybe make the circus elephant into a circus dragon? Perhaps with a handler keen to work with him despite his feisty reputation? And why not throw in some centaurs and satyrs for good measure?

This new idea, which would follow similar lines to Slim and Tusko's journey, was for a single stand-alone fantasy novel (still without a lick of mystery or humor). I'd just come off of writing three series and was in no mood to start another.

Notice I said "was".

See, I knew I wanted my circus to have more than just a dragon act. It also needed other mythical and unusual creatures, so I picked up a book on mythological animals from the library to get some ideas of who I wanted to add.

And that's where everything tumbled into place.

As I took notes on some of the creatures that appealed to me, ideas kept sparking. The creatures could become embroiled in murders and mayhem. The dragon and his handler could solve the mysteries. The circus I had imagined would make the perfect setting for a cozy mystery series.

And there it was. My rather serious historical fantasy novel had turned into a humorous mystery. And with so many ideas for story lines, the stand alone would have to become a full series.

Right now, I have about ten story ideas for The Circus of Unusual Creatures, so if you enjoyed Duncan, Boris, Cordelia, and the gang, you've got plenty more antics coming.

—Tammie Painter, February 2022

Let's Stay In Touch!
My Next Book is Coming Soon...

In fact, it might already be here by the time you read this, and there's probably been loads of exciting stuff you've missed out on. You know, like photos of my cats.

Anyway, I love staying in touch with my readers, so if you'd like to...

- Keep up-to-date with my writing news,
- Chat with me about books you love (and maybe those you hate),
- Take part in silly book surveys,
- Receive a free short story or exclusive discount now and then,
- And be among the first to learn about my new releases

...then please do sign up for my monthly newsletter.

As a thank you for signing up, you'll get my short story *Mrs. Morris Meets Death* — a humorously, death-defying tale of time management, mistaken identities, cruise ships.... and romance novels.

Join in on the fun today by scanning this QR code or by heading to *www.subscribepage.com/mrsmorris*

THE PART WHERE I BEG FOR A REVIEW

IF YOU ENJOYED HOARD IT ALL BEFORE….

You may think your opinion doesn't matter, but believe me, it does…at least as far as this book is concerned. I can't guarantee it mattering in any other aspect of your life. Sorry.

See, reviews are vital to help indie authors (like me) get the word out about their books.

Your kind words not only let other readers know this book is worth spending their hard-earned money and valuable reading time on, but are a vital component for me to join in on some pretty influential promotional opportunities.

Basically, you're a superhero who can help launch Duncan and his pals into stardom!

I know! You're feeling pretty powerful, aren't you?

Well, don't waste that power trip. Head over to your favorite book retailer, Goodreads, and/or Bookbub and share a sentence or two (or more, if you're ambitious). Even a star rating would be appreciated.

And if you could tell just one other person about this story, your superhero powers will absolutely skyrocket.

Thanks!!

By the way, if you didn't like this book, please contact me and let me know what didn't work. I'm always looking to improve.

Book Two Preview

Tipping the Scales

When a vivacious veela shows up, jealousies flare and people keep turning up dead. If only there was a dragon who could untangle the mess…

The second mystery from the Circus of Unusual Creatures rolls into town in Spring 2022. Here's a quick sample…

Prologue

Lying flat out on my belly, I stretched my legs, then my wings. Something mooed in the distance. Okay, well, not 'something.' At first guess, I'd say it was a cow.

Or it could have been the human snoring next to me. Which she had been doing all night, mind you.

CORDELIA: I don't snore.

DUNCAN: No, of course not. It's just the gentle murmurings of your slumber.

CORDELIA: Exactly.

DUNCAN: Murmurings that I believe were responsible for a few reports of earthquakes in the vicinity.

Still, despite the noise, it felt amazing to sprawl out as I slept, to have the stars winking at me when I opened my eyes in the middle of an early summer night, and to perform a full-body stretch first thing in the morning.

That's not to say my caravan isn't adequate, but in a

traveling circus there's only so much space you can provide a dragon — even a dragon who can reduce himself to the manageable size of a Clydesdale stallion.

From the direction of the mooing, a man began cursing.

And no, I don't know why all my lovely stories have to start with a human cursing.

"Get off my bleeding strawberries, you great lump of a lizard!"

Mr Furious Farmer didn't actually say *bleeding,* but I'll leave it to you to fill in the angry swear word of your choice.

Cordelia shook herself awake.

"Wuz goin' on?" she mumbled as bits of hay poked out from her short auburn hair.

"You best not have ruined the snarking tomatoes!" shouted Mrs Furious Farmer — again, using something a little saucier than *snarking.*

Cordelia got to her feet, squinting in the direction of the farmhouse. She might not have fully knocked the sleep out of her eyes, but that didn't stop her from yelling back at the couple.

"You know, there was a time people might have been thrilled to find a dragon in their strawberry field."

Which to me sounded like the perfect song lyric for a wandering minstrel to put to a tune. But it had been at least five hundred years since minstrels wandered around singing tales of dragons in strawberry fields. A shame, really.

I thought it might be time to show Mr and Mrs Furious

Farmer exactly which dragon was gracing their strawberry patch. I stretched again, then stood, increasing myself to my full show size and doing my best not to crush any strawberries as I did so.

"Holy corn cobs," muttered Mr Farmer, not loud enough for Cordelia to pick up, but one of the benefits of being a dragon is having a keen sense of hearing. "Is that—?"

At the sight of full-size me — imagine a winged reptile as tall as a giraffe with the bulk of a gorilla — Mrs Farmer's jaw had fallen open. It worked itself a few times, as if not quite sure closing was appropriate in the circumstances.

Finally, she got her gob shut, swallowed hard, then said, "Brutus Fangwrath," in a tone of such awe it brought a delighted smile to my lips and sent tingles along the spines that run the length of my back.

Mrs Farmer might have been in awe, but Mr Farmer was reaching for something stashed behind a rocking chair on the porch.

Knowing how much humans love things that go *Boom!*, I had a sneaking suspicion of what he was reaching for. Unfortunately, as a dragon, I'm not supposed to speak to humans, and shouting "Run!" would have broken the No Speaking Rule of 1274.

Doubly unfortunate? Before her first gallon of coffee, Cordelia's brain isn't exactly lightning quick at grasping the severity of certain situations.

"Um, Cordelia," I said, doing my best not to move my lips, "maybe now's a good time to tell them we aren't here to eat them."

"Oh, right." To Mr Farmer, who had been trying to tell his star-struck wife to get inside, Cordelia shouted, "It's okay. I'm his handler. He's under my control." Out of the side of her mouth she whispered, "Maybe not being the size of an African elephant would help."

"Good point," I replied while maintaining my grin.

"And stop smiling. The sight of your fangs is doing nothing to keep his trigger finger from blasting us into last week."

As I pulled myself back down to my smaller size, Cordelia flourished her hands at me to make it look like she was in charge of the transformation.

"See? Perfectly tame under my power." I groaned at her showman's boast. "Did you want to pet him?"

"Seriously?" I grumbled under my breath. "I'm not part of the petting zoo."

"Shush."

Mrs Farmer started forward, but Mr Farmer snatched her hand and pulled her back. Warily, he said, "We're good. Thanks for showing him to us, but you best move along." With the barrel of his shotgun he indicated the road in the distance.

"Where's Zin setting up the circus?" Mrs Farmer asked eagerly.

"Just a few miles down the main road. If you tell him you're friends of Cordelia Quinn, he'll let you in for free."

"Oh, Zin's just going to love that," I whispered. Cordelia elbowed me.

"Golly, that would be a real treat. Did you hear that, John? Free tickets to Zinzendorf's Circus—"

"Yeah, yeah, of Unusual Creatures. Lord knows I hear you going on enough about that damn show. Suppose I gotta buy you popcorn and you'll want to play..."

Even I didn't catch the rest of Furious Farmer John's griping as he steered his wife back into the house. Before he closed the door, she turned around and waved at us enthusiastically, then called out, "And take as many strawberries as you like."

To which her husband barked that her dragon fancy was going to bankrupt them both.

The door slammed shut. It was time for me and Cordelia to join up with the rest of the troupe.

After a strawberry breakfast, of course.

Find *Tipping the Scales* today at *Books2Read.com/TippingtheScales* or by scanning this code.

Also by Tammie Painter

THE CASSIE BLACK TRILOGY

Work at a funeral home can be mundane. Until you start accidentally bringing the dead to life.

The Undead Mr. Tenpenny

The Uncanny Raven Winston

The Untangled Cassie Black

THE OSTERIA CHRONICLES

Myths and heroes may be reborn, but the whims of the gods never change.

The Trials of Hercules *The Bonds of Osteria*

The Voyage of Heroes *The Battle of Ares*

The Maze of Minos *The Return of Odysseus*

DOMNA

Destiny isn't given. It's made by cunning, endurance, and, at times, bloodshed.

The Sun God's Daughter The Regent's Edict

The Solon's Son The Forgotten Heir

The Centaur's Gamble The Solon's Wife

AND MORE...

To see all my currently available books and short stories, just scan the QR code or visit books.bookfunnel.com/ tammiepainterbooks

338

ABOUT THE AUTHOR
THAT'S ME...TAMMIE PAINTER

Many moons ago I was a scientist in a neuroscience lab where I got to play with brains and illegal drugs. Now, I'm an award-winning author who turns wickedly strong tea into imaginative fiction (so, basically still playing with brains and drugs).

My fascination for myths, history, and how they interweave inspired my flagship series, The Osteria Chronicles.

But that all got a bit too serious for someone with a strange sense of humor and odd way of looking at the world. So, while sitting at my grandmother's funeral, my brain came up with an idea for a contemporary fantasy trilogy that's filled with magic, mystery, snarky humor, and the dead who just won't stay dead. That idea turned into The Cassie Black Trilogy.

When I'm not creating worlds or killing off characters, I can be found gardening, planning my next travel adventure, working as an unpaid servant to four cats and two guinea pigs, or concocting some sort of mess in the kitchen.

You can learn more at *TammiePainter.com*

Handy Dandy QR Codes

To join my mailing list and get a free story...

To check out my complete list of other books and stories, see any current specials, visit my website, Browse my bookstore, or just get some free books...

(or simply visit TammiePainter.com)

Printed in Great Britain
by Amazon

31063474R00193